TESSA FINCH isn't GOOD ENOUGH

RITA HARTE

Copyright © Rita Harte, 2023

First published 2023

Email: ritaharteauthor@gmail.com

All rights reserved. Without limiting the rights under copyright reserved above, no part of this publication may be reproduced, stored in or introduced into a database and retrieval system or transmitted in any form or any means (electronic, mechanical, photocopying, recording or otherwise) without the prior written permission of both the owner of copyright and the above publishers.

Cover by Cover Ever After

ISBN: 9798377968771

Imprint: Independently published

For every reader who's ever thought that they're not good enough.

Tessa Finch Isn't Good Enough

A romantic comedy with anxiety

Rita Harte

1 Tessa

"You know Tessa, you look entirely too confident with that knife. It's rather frightening."

I looked up from the chopping board, a scaly brown onion in one hand and a sharp paring knife in the other. "This knife?" I asked innocently, holding it aloft.

"That knife," Alan confirmed with raised eyebrows. "I'm not sure whether you're preparing my dinner or planning to murder me."

"Oh, I'd never try to murder you with this," I said, giving him a reassuring smile. "The blade's kind of short." I tapped the largest knife in the block. "If I had murder on my mind, I'd definitely go for the chef's knife."

"Tessa is correct. A paring knife would not be suitable." Marcel's bald head appeared in the doorway and was followed by a body clad in a black turtleneck and unnervingly tight jeans. "The chef's knife would be a superior choice. The blade is long enough to reach vital organs in a single movement."

"I'm going to ban you two from watching those true crime documentaries," Alan pointed a finger. "You're a bad influence on each other."

"You're a dictator, Alan." I gave a long-suffering sigh. "I don't know if I can work under these restrictive conditions. I could abandon this pie right now, even if I did find the most delightful Kipflers at the market."

"Pie, you say? Let's not be hasty. What are Kipflers?"

"You've never had a Kipfler potato? You might be the toast of the art world, Alan, but you've clearly lived a sad, sheltered life." I shook my head sadly at the thought of a life without Kipfler potatoes and Alan snorted his amusement.

"Very droll, Tessa," he said. "What's so special about these potatoes?"

"This," I said, reaching into a hessian produce bag, "is a Kipfler potato. They're smaller than regular potatoes and kind of finger-shaped. They've got this fabulous, nutty flavour." Triumphantly, I held up the largest of the Kipfler potatoes, waving it in front of him.

"Finger shaped?" Alan repeated. "I suppose if one has very large fingers."

I looked at the potato again and my cheeks flushed. Nope, definitely not finger-shaped. Instead, it looked like a—

"Penis," Marcel announced in his soft Belgian accent. "It resembles a penis."

"If your penis looks like that, you should see a doctor." A deep voice broke the silence, and I looked over to see—

"Dylan!" Alan turned his wheelchair in a tight circle to greet the man slouched against the doorframe. Dylan was looking at me – I was still holding up the potato – with a quietly amused expression. "Why on earth didn't you tell me you were coming?"

I dropped the potato, and it rolled off the bench to the floor with a thud. I dove for it, mainly so I could hide my flaming cheeks.

"I didn't want you to make a fuss," I heard Dylan say to his father. "You knew I was planning to come home. I booked a flight, so here I am."

"Here you are," Alan echoed. "You look like the result of that Soviet sleep-deprivation experiment. Didn't you get any rest? I thought you were flying first class!"

I looked up from the ground to see Dylan shift uncomfortably, as though he didn't want anyone – like me – to hear he had flown first class. But it was hardly a surprise. Alan had told me all about his fabulously successful son, who had just sold his tech start-up in Silicon Valley for a truly eye-watering price.

Personally, I didn't think Dylan looked like the result of a Soviet sleep-deprivation experiment. He was broad-shouldered and tall, despite his slouched posture. Sure, there were rings under his eyes, his dark hair was plastered to one side of his head, and he clearly had foregone a shave or two, but that was to be expected after a fourteen-hour flight. Even if it had been spent in the luxury of a fully reclining sky bed. The dark rings and stubble only seemed to emphasise his high cheekbones and the depths of his very green eyes.

Besides, I'd always found that haunted look strangely attractive. Not that I had any intention of admitting it. Nor did I have any intention of admitting that, actually, I already knew what Dylan looked like. Between photos unearthed during my interviews with Alan and a little light online stalking, I was very much aware that Dylan was handsome. Already nervous to meet my boss's son, I hadn't imagined I'd be brandishing a potato that, apparently, resembled diseased genitalia when I did.

"It was a long flight," Dylan said, shrugging and taking a seat at the long hardwood dining table with its artfully mismatched chairs. "And I haven't been sleeping well."

"It is good," Marcel placed a hand on Dylan's shoulder and nodded once, "that you are home."

"Thanks, Marcel," Dylan looked up at his...father's partner? I didn't know if he thought of Marcel as his stepfather. "How've you been?"

Marcel frowned. "I have been here. Where else would I have been?"

I couldn't stop the laugh that escaped me, and suddenly three pairs of eyes were fixed on me, still on all fours, crouching in front of the kitchen island like a feral potato gremlin.

"Um," I said, wishing the floor would open a portal to a hellish dimension of eternal suffering so I could jump right in. It had to be better than my current situation. "I was just getting my potato?"

"Dylan, this is Tessa." Alan gestured at me, and I stood up, taking my unfortunately phallic potato with me. "I told you all about her. She's been helping me with my autobiography. And taking care of the housekeeping."

"Hi," I said weakly, one hand half raised in a wave as my stomach twisted sickly. "It's nice to meet you."

"You're Tessa?" Dylan was looking at me like I had both deliberately shocked and seriously disappointed him. "I thought you'd be older."

I supposed that made some kind of sense. The word 'housekeeper' always made me think of Alice from the Brady Bunch, and I was definitely younger than her. "Sorry about that," I said, even though it wasn't in the least my fault. But apologising for things that weren't my fault was just one of my many bad habits.

"It's nice to meet you," Dylan said finally and looked away.

"You need a drink," Alan decided. "Have we got any champagne in the fridge, Tessa?"

I was extremely glad to have a reason to turn away and bury myself in the enormous stainless-steel fridge. I knew there was champagne in there, of course. Memorising the contents of the fridge was vital both to my job as housekeeper and as Alan's ghostwriter. Knowing whether there was sufficient chilled Bombay Sapphire, fresh cucumbers, and tonic water to encourage Alan to keep talking into the recorder when he was in high spirits was critical. Still, hiding in the fridge and pretending to search did wonders for cooling my very red face.

"We do have champagne," I said, when it would have become socially awkward for me to hide in there any longer. "It's a nice one, too; the children's charity sent it over when you donated that signed print for their silent auction."

"None for me," Dylan shook his head. "I just want to sleep. I'll go and put my bags in the studio."

"Uh—" I began, still holding the champagne.

"Tessa's in the studio now," Alan cut in, saving me from having to explain. "Didn't I tell you that? She has to live here; you never know when inspiration for my book will strike! But your old bedroom's set up for you. The cleaning lady changed the sheets."

"Sorry," I said to Dylan, even though that wasn't my fault either. "I didn't mean to take your place."

Dylan looked at me, and he seemed more tired than ever. "You didn't take my place. Just the studio."

Of course I hadn't taken his place. That had been a seriously stupid thing to say. He was Alan's son, and I was just a temporary employee. I could feel my pulse quickening, my hands trembling as mortification set in. I knew I'd be torturing myself about this particular faux pas tonight as I tried to sleep. Not to mention the incident with the Kipfler.

"I guess I'll go up to my room then." Dylan rose from the table.

"It is fortunate," Marcel said, "that we replaced your bed. Now, I do not think you would fit in your Formula One car."

Dylan made a strangled coughing sound. I chanced a look at him, and could see he was embarrassed. I might be a stranger with a penis potato, but he clearly didn't want me to know he had once slept in a racing car bed. Not that I thought that there was anything wrong with that. I had once coveted a red Ferrari-shaped bed with headlights that really lit up, but my mother had vetoed the Ferrari in favour of the French Provincial look.

"Are you sure you don't want something to eat?" I pretended I hadn't noticed his embarrassment. "The pie will take a while, but there's some leftover pasta and maybe some chicken curry—"

"The curry's long gone," Alan interrupted. "But the pasta's not bad. You should eat something, Dylan."

"I'm not hungry," Dylan said. "Really, I just want to sleep."

"You can sleep later," Alan waved a dismissive hand. "We should talk! Now that you're home, you can tell me why you decided to leave San Francisco for our rather provincial life here in Brekkie Beach."

"I told you," Dylan said, rather sullenly. "I needed a break. From—" He paused and sighed. "We're not talking about it. Not right now. Not...in front of everyone."

I cringed at that. Dylan didn't have to say that my presence wasn't welcome; I got the message loud and clear. I wished I could make myself scarce, but I still had eight potatoes to chop and a pie crust blind-baking in the oven.

"Well, suit yourself then," Alan made it sound as though Dylan was intentionally trying to upset him by being tired after his long flight. "Perhaps you'll have time for your father in the morning."

When Dylan's eyes met mine for a moment, I tried to shoot him a look of sympathetic commiseration. It probably came out as a cross-eyed smirk. He looked away quickly and didn't say another word as he sloped out of the room.

He must be jet-lagged, I thought. Or maybe he just wasn't in the mood to explain his life choices to the stranger who had usurped his rightful place in the studio that adjoined the main house and forced him back into his childhood bedroom.

"Well, that's my charming son." Alan stated the abundantly obvious with a raise of his eyebrows. "He's usually more pleasant than that. You'll have to take my word for it."

"He must be tired," I said in a carefully neutral tone. "From his flight."

"It's not just that," Alan said, wheeling himself around the kitchen island. "He's having some sort of quarter-life crisis."

And what the hell was I supposed to say to that?

"Oh," I said, keeping my eyes fixed on my potato as I chopped it into neat pieces. "I thought he was really successful. Didn't you tell me he just sold his app? The one where people can rent parking spaces?"

"Something like that," Alan sighed. "I thought that would be good for him. Sell up, take the cheque, and then on to the next thing. But now he says he doesn't know what to do with himself! Which is preposterous, of course."

"Oh," I said again, wishing passionately that Alan hadn't told me that. It seemed kind of personal, and while I was coming to know everything there was to know about the life and career of Alan Huxley, I was still a stranger to Dylan. I didn't think he'd be delighted to know his dad was telling me about his so-called crisis.

"I told him, Dylan, you're young, you're healthy, you've got plenty of money, you could do anything you want! But all he said was that he didn't feel like doing anything yet. Can you imagine?"

"Um, do you think he'd be okay with you telling me all this? It seems kind of personal," I ventured. I didn't like to disagree with my boss, but there was a limit.

"You're helping me with my autobiography," Alan objected. "No secrets between us, Tessa."

I swallowed. That was kind of true. Except that I wasn't so much helping Alan with his autobiography as I was writing the entire thing. But I wasn't going to argue on that point. Plenty of the celebrity 'authors' I had worked with liked to pretend that my role was simply to facilitate their burgeoning literary genius.

"You're right," I said quickly. "I just thought, that, whatever he's going through, he probably doesn't want me to know about it. I'm a stranger to him."

"Nonsense." Alan was once again dismissive. "You're part of the family. And it's hardly a secret. You young people are so sensitive these days, I think he's making a storm in a teacup."

I bit my lip, deciding it was best not to say anything else about it. "The pie should be ready in an hour," I said, taking the blind-baked pastry from the oven. "I hope it's worth the wait."

"It will be," Marcel said, taking Alan's hand in his, perhaps to distract him from sharing any more of his son's private business. "All of your cooking is masterful, Tessa."

"Thank you," I smiled my gratitude. But as I began to arrange the potato slices in the crust, I couldn't stop my brain from beginning to replay the whole scene with Dylan, complete with highlights of just how ridiculous I'd managed to look holding that potato.

Not ideal. Really not ideal.

• • • ● • ● • • •

Tessa: i met my boss's son tonight. it was bad <upside down smiley face emoji>

Abby: bad how? did anything bad actually happen or are you in one of your anxious self-criticism spirals?

Michelle: why not both?

Tessa: it was legit bad. he came in just as i was showing alan what a kipfler potato was

Abby: your boss didn't know what a kipfler potato was?! i thought he was cultured!

Tessa: he is! he's an amazing artist and knows all about wine pairings. anyway, the potato looked kind of like a

<eggplant emoji> and i was waving it around like a pervert when dylan came in

Michelle: i'm sure he didn't even notice

Abby: it could be a good thing. now he knows you're comfortable handling that kind of equipment <winking emoji>

Tessa: he definitely noticed. him and marcel both commented. i. was. mortified

Michelle: <laughing emoji>

Abby: using <laughing emoji> officially makes you old. people use <skull emoji> now

Michelle: why? that doesn't make any sense

Abby: it means you're laughing so hard you're dead

Michelle: i don't buy it

Abby: which one of us successfully markets her small business on social media? i know this stuff!

Michelle: so you say

Tessa: can we please get back to my utter mortification?

Michelle: it really doesn't sound that bad

Abby: more importantly, is he as hot in person as in those pics you sent?

Tessa: ...yes

Tessa: not that it matters. he's got a lot going on. alan told me he's having a quarter-life crisis after selling his start-up. he doesn't know what to do with his life now, apparently

Michelle: his dad told you all that?

Tessa: it was very awkward. he seems to think that because i'm doing his autobiography, there are no secrets between us

Abby: well that's kind of true. he did tell you all about him and marcel's exciting and rampant sex life

Tessa: i was trying to forget that <vomiting emoji>

Abby: then you shouldn't have told us. i have an excellent memory

Tessa: so, what should i do when i see dylan? pretend i don't know about any of this?

Michelle: you're overthinking it. just smile, say hi, try not to wave any more wang-shaped veggies at him, and you'll be fine

Tessa: of course i'm overthinking it! this is me!

Abby: don't waste your anxiety on this one. you did nothing wrong. plus, you said he was jetlagged. i'm sure he's already forgotten your sexy carrot

Tessa: it was a potato. a kipfler potato. what happened to your excellent memory?

Abby: i only remember important things

Tessa: ...are you saying marcel and alan's sex life is important?

Abby: uh, yes! if i'm ever with the same dude for 20 years, i hope we're banging as much as they are #couplegoals

Tessa: i'll be sure to tell them that <eye roll emoji>

Michelle: how's your kids' book going, anyway? the one with the girl who learns to stand up to the bullies?

Tessa: it's not going anywhere. everything i've written lately is garbage

Abby: how can you tell if you won't even let your own sisters read it?

Tessa: you can read it if i ever get published

Michelle: you know you'd have to send it to an agent for that to happen, right?

Tessa: <sad face emoji> i know

Abby: i know the thought of sharing your work scares the hell out of you. that's why you should see someone about your anxiety

Michelle: yeah, you really should

Tessa: it's no big deal. anyway, i'm busy

Abby: we're all busy. and it is a big deal, you're just avoiding it

Michelle: you said moving to brekkie beach would be a fresh start and you'd get your anxiety sorted

Tessa: ...is it gang up on tessa night? i'm fine!

Abby: you're not. you really should see someone. like a doctor

Tessa: please don't. can we drop this?

Michelle: fine. i gtg anyway. quarterly progress meeting. i need to be brilliant

Tessa: you always are

Abby: #bossbabe

Michelle: pretty sure using #bossbabe makes you officially old <winking emoji>

Abby: <middle finger emoji>

Tessa: i should try to get some sleep

Abby: don't worry about this dylan dude. you didn't do anything wrong and he's not worth your brain space

Tessa: don't worry?! this is me, remember? i always worry!

Abby: <hug emoji>

Abby: and that's why you need to see a doctor!

• • • • • • • • • •

I sighed as I exited the chat, throwing my phone down. My sisters were intelligent women and pretty damn brilliant in their respective fields, but I was sure they were dead wrong when it came to not worrying about how I would act when I next saw Dylan.

I mean, I had embarrassed myself in front of him, and I knew an uncomfortable amount of personal information about the guy. There was no way that I couldn't worry. Frowning, I patted the deliciously expensive moisturiser (a gift from Michelle) into the places where I really hoped fine lines weren't appearing.

Flopping down onto my back, I looked up at the roof of the studio. It was a bright, airy space with huge windows that let in the soft morning light and looked out onto the serene garden that Marcel took such pride in maintaining. The walls were dotted with paintings Alan had deemed unworthy to be hung in the house. And maybe they weren't sufficiently brilliant to hang next to his best work, but they sure beat the vintage film posters I had once thought were so sophisticated in my old flat back in Birmingham. The bathroom was small, and there was an oddly placed mirror that forced you to stare at your own face while sitting on the toilet, but the existence of the heated towel rail made up for that. The studio was seriously luxurious, as far as I was concerned.

A sick twist of guilt. Dylan had thought he'd be staying in here, just as he had when he had visited his dad and Marcel before. Instead, he was in his childhood bedroom – minus the racing car bed. If he was struggling to work out what he wanted to do with his life, I doubted that being surrounded by his teenage taste and schoolboy memories was helping.

What the hell would I say to Dylan when I saw him next? Make a joke about the potato? What if he had forgotten, and I looked like a creep? Apologise about the studio? What if I offended him all over again? And I certainly couldn't bring up what his dad had told me or even let on that I knew.

I closed my eyes briefly, forcing myself to focus on my breath. I could feel my stomach twisting in on itself and my heart thumping in my chest, faster and faster, like a drum and bass track reaching its crescendo.

"I should try to be mindful," I told myself. I had once read that mindfulness exercises were a great way to combat anxiety. What was it again? Focus on your five senses. I could do that.

Sight. I could see my own sock-clad feet on the bed, bright pink and purple stripes against tasteful white linen sheets. Sound. The faint patter of rain against the roof of the studio. When had it started raining again? I couldn't believe how much it had rained since my arrival in Australia. Leaving England for a beachside town in Sydney, I had expected to be drinking in the sunshine every day. In reality, it rained almost as much as back home.

"Shit, I'm supposed to be being mindful!" My body tensed; trying to relax was, it seemed, making me more stressed. What was next? Smell. I could smell the moisturiser, the sweet scent of lilac and the chemicals needed to prevent the thirteen signs of aging. Touch. My fingers brushed the sheets, rubbing the cloth between my fingertips. Taste. All I could taste was my own mouth. Maybe if I really focused, I could detect the faint remnant of my toothpaste.

"Right," I said out loud. "I've been mindful. So now I should be able to sleep. That's how this works."

I closed my eyes, snuggling down into the crisp linen sheets. Almost immediately, Dylan's face swam into my mind, those green eyes tired but bright.

"Well, I'm going to try to sleep, anyway," I murmured, turning to my other side and punching the pillow as though that would reset my ever-buzzing brain.

It didn't.

2 Dylan

After two hours of tossing, turning, examining my sixteen-year-old self's epically shitty taste in posters, and being forced to listen to the rumble of cheerful conversation – not to mention the wafting smell of freshly baked pastry – from downstairs, I admitted defeat.

I ensured I made plenty of noise on the stairs, so they'd know I was coming down. That way, my dad and Marcel could at least pretend they hadn't been talking about me when I entered the room.

"He emerges!" My father raised his eyebrows as I returned to the kitchen, taking my old place at the table. "I thought you'd be out cold until tomorrow."

"It didn't work out that way," I said, scraping my chair against the tiled floor in a way that I knew annoyed him. Maybe it was the jetlag, but I was feeling petty. Looking around, I could see that Tessa had gone. Well, that was a relief.

It wasn't like my dad hadn't told me about Tessa. He had described, at length, how she was helping him put together his autobiography in response to 'overwhelming public pressure'. I would have said my father was being conceited, but the truth was, there probably *was* decent public demand for an autobiography of Alan Huxley. He was possibly the greatest living artist in Australia. Top five, for sure. It wasn't like I had been unaware of Tessa's existence. It was just that I had assumed that a ghostwriter – especially one willing to be a housekeeper too – would be middle-aged, motherly, and likely have a penchant for bright cardigans and quirky earrings.

Instead, I had been confronted by a young woman with sparkling blue eyes, dark hair tossed into a messy bun, and full lips curved into a bright smile. And she had been holding up a potato that looked like a budding sculptor's first attempt at recreating the male anatomy. Despite the phallic potato, Tessa had looked somehow...wholesome. Standing there in the kitchen, an apron tied over her striped Breton top, her cheeks pink from the oven, she had been chatting merrily to my dad and Marcel. Like she was part of the family. And then I had rocked up looking like I had spent the last month visiting every bar within walking distance of my San Francisco apartment to distract myself from my utter lack of direction.

Which, of course, I had.

"Well, I'm glad you're up," Alan said. "Because I wanted to talk to you. Marcel, could you get another glass? This is an excellent drop, Dylan. A 2017 Cherry Tree Hill Cabernet Merlot. The grapes were transcendental that year. You won't say no to a glass?"

I didn't say no. Instead, I thanked Marcel as he filled up a glass and placed it in front of me. On some level, I knew that the last thing my body needed was more alcohol, but I took a gulp anyway, barely tasting the transcendental grapes.

"It's fine." I shrugged, and my father gave me a disgusted look. "How are you, anyway? Seems like everything's going well here."

"Oh, I'm surviving," Alan said. "I have better days and worse days. I was out of the chair for a bit last week. That was a nice change."

I felt more than a twinge of guilt at that. I knew how much it bothered my father to rely on his wheelchair, even if he did seem to enjoy zooming around at potentially lethal speeds. On my last visit, there had been at least one near miss with Cyndi, Marcel's mercurial hairless cat.

Speaking of...

A loud meow came from under the table, and I felt Cyndi's head press into my legs. "Yes, I'm back," I said, looking down at the cat. "You like me today, do you?"

"Cyndi always likes you," Marcel insisted as I pulled her up into my lap, where she began to purr loudly, pressing her body into my sweatshirt.

I decided not to argue, though Cyndi had swiped me with her claws on more than one occasion and had been known to vomit on my pillow. I was sure it was deliberate. I patted her gingerly – there was something very odd about patting a hairless cat. Without any fur, it was like stroking a wrinkled chicken carcass.

"So, you've come home," my father said, looking at me over the rim of his wine glass. "Because you couldn't work out what to do with yourself in San Francisco."

"Well, it's not exactly like that," I took another gulp of wine. Cyndi headbutted me, clearly displeased at the interruption in pats. "I wanted to come home and see everyone, I guess."

"And then?" Alan pressed. "What are you going to do now?"

"I don't know," I admitted, looking down at Cyndi. Marcel had told me that she was named after Cyndi Lauper. Which was strange, given that Marcel had only ever listened to crooning jazz and modern classical music in the years I'd known him. "After I sold Space2Spare, I thought I'd know. I was working so much, and I thought it would be a relief when it was finally sold. But...I guess I'm still not sure."

"Too much change," Marcel cut in, nodding sagely. Sitting there in his ubiquitous black turtleneck with a glass of red wine, he looked like a caricature of a pretentious art critic. I had never seen him without the turtleneck, even in the height of summer. Did he have special, ultra-lightweight options for hot weather, or did he suffer for his aesthetic? Perhaps, I thought, his shaved head released all his body heat.

"Maybe," I said after realising I had been staring too long at my stepfather's shiny bald head instead of answering. "So, I thought I'd come home while I work out what to do next."

"And we're happy to have you home. But why Brekkie Beach? You could go anywhere, do anything. Why not Paris? Why not New York? Why not Prague? Or Singapore?"

I shifted uncomfortably, causing Cyndi to open one eye to glare at me. I hastily resumed the patting. "I wanted to see you. And Tad. And the baby, of course. I mean, he is my godson."

But that wasn't the whole truth, and I knew it. The fact was that going anywhere other than the beachside town I had grown up in seemed like...too much. Too much change, too much effort. Just too much. I knew Brekkie Beach. Every shortcut down to the water, every pothole in the road, every palm tree lining the promenade. It was familiar and comforting. I needed all the familiarity and comfort I could get.

"And," I went on cautiously. "I worked my arse off for years, barely did anything else. So I thought it would be nice to be with you guys, while I rest up a bit."

"Rest up?" Alan scoffed. "You've not been ill, Dylan. Just working hard."

"I know," I said testily. "It will just be for a little while, I promise." I paused. "I can rent an Air BnB or something. If you'd rather I didn't stay here."

"Don't be ridiculous." My father shook his head. "Of course I want you to stay here. It just seems so odd that you don't have any plans for what to do with yourself next. You've always had plans, ever since you were a boy."

"When you were twelve," Marcel remembered, "you wanted to become a diplomat. So you could travel the world and park your car wherever you liked because of diplomatic immunity."

"I had almost forgotten that." Alan chuckled. "And you tried to learn three languages at once, do you remember?"

"All I remember is enough to pronounce the dishes properly when I'm ordering Tapas or Yum Cha," I said. "I would have been a shitty diplomat."

"Oh, I don't know," my father mused. "You're very charming when you make an effort. You were a bit short with Tessa, but I suppose you're jetlagged."

"Was I?" I thought of Tessa's very pink cheeks as she looked at me with wide blue eyes, brandishing that ridiculous potato. "I guess I thought she was older. Not so young."

"Young and pretty." Alan gave me an annoyingly knowing look like he had suddenly understood something. "I thought that might be it."

"Is she?" I feigned nonchalance. "I suppose she's—"

"Oh, don't pretend you didn't notice!" Alan wagged a finger. "Just because I haven't touched a woman since that extraordinary night with your mother—"

"Please don't talk about that." I curled my lip, unwilling to imagine my mother and father having any sort of night together, extraordinary or otherwise.

"Oh, but it was extraordinary." My dad was clearly enjoying himself. "I'm an excellent judge of beauty, and Tessa's a very pretty girl. And I know you noticed. But," he pointed at me. "Don't get any ideas. She's got a job to do."

"I know that," I said, feeling irritated. "What, you think I came back here just to flirt with your ghostwriter?"

"She's not my ghostwriter!" Alan was aghast. "She's simply helping me tell the story of my life. I'm the author, she's just helping me find the right words."

"How many words have you actually written?" I couldn't resist the jab.

"You can't expect me to do the typing! But it's all me. My career, my life, my story!"

"If you say so," I said, willing to let the matter drop. "Look, I don't have any designs on your...assistant. I can't believe you'd think I would."

"Well, under other circumstances, she'd be just your type. Looks a bit like—" He paused, thinking. "Marcel, who was that actress in those silly vampire films Dylan used to like so much?"

"Kate Beckinsale," Marcel said promptly. I wouldn't have thought Marcel van Wooters, occasional art historian, would have the faintest idea who Kate Beckinsale was. Maybe her tight leather trousers had serious artistic merit. My fifteen-year-old self would definitely have agreed.

"Tessa doesn't look like Kate Beckinsale," I objected, even though it was a reasonably accurate comparison.

"Well, she's been a wonderful help with my book, and she's the best housekeeper we've ever had, so don't go being too charming with her. If you interfere with her and she leaves before my book is finished—"

"Dad!" I spoke loudly enough to send Cyndi yowling off my lap with a swipe of claws that I felt through my jeans. Bloody chicken carcass of a cat. "She's not a nineteenth-century servant maiden and I'm not the lord of the manor chasing after her virtue. I'm not interested in dating anyone. I just want to rest, catch up with people, and...work out what I'm doing next."

"Well, I'm glad to hear it." Alan had finished his wine and was waving the empty glass at Marcel. That annoyed me. Wheelchair or not, my father was perfectly capable of filling his own glass, or at least asking politely for more.

I took the glass from him before Marcel could, stalking over to the wine fridge. "Can I open this?" I picked out a bottle at random.

"No! That's a dinner party wine. Go for one of the tempranillos at the top; there's a good boy."

I selected a tempranillo that didn't seem to be earmarked for better company than myself and brought it back to the table, refilling my own glass too.

Letting out a sigh, I pulled my phone from my pocket, ignored the little numbers next to my email and social media icons – I didn't want to talk to anyone, not really – and flicked open the images folder. While waiting for my flight, I had taken a few photos around the airport. It had seemed like a good idea at the time. The contrast of a bright pink suitcase against a blur of moving bodies in business suits, a scowling bulldog in a crate, and a portrait of a very obliging barista with deep dimples and white teeth. But now that I looked at the photos, I could see they were...

"Pretty shit," I muttered under my breath.

"What's that?"

"Nothing," I said, tucking my phone back into my pocket. "Just looking at my phone."

"You young people are always on your phones," Alan scolded. "I despair of the next generation of artists, you know. They're always looking down at these tiny little screens and never look up at what's around them. No sense of wonder, no sense of scale. It's a sad fate, really."

"The art world is doomed, then? And with it, life in general?"

"So cynical from one so young." Alan clapped a hand on my shoulder. He looked at me more closely then, squinting slightly behind thick-framed spectacles. "You really do look tired, you know. Marcel, doesn't he look tired?"

"I told you; I haven't been sleeping well," I said. "And I haven't been feeling great. Maybe I've got Lyme Disease or something."

"Perhaps," Marcel said quietly. "You are simply experiencing existential angst. Like Sartre."

"I'm flattered by the comparison."

"Oh, don't be ridiculous. You're just unemployed, that's all. You're young, rich, and handsome. And you're my son! What could you possibly have angst about?"

"Well, with an endorsement like that, I should be feeling better in no time." I took another swallow of tempranillo. It tasted exactly like the supposedly superior cabernet merlot, but I decided not to mention that. Dad was very particular about his wines.

"You have not been truly happy for some time," Marcel frowned slightly. "I hope you will find what it is that you are looking for, Dylan. But we are glad to have you home."

I raised my glass to him. "It's good to be home."

But even as I did, I couldn't help wondering. Was Brekkie Beach really my home? Or was it just comfortingly familiar?

• • • ● • ● ● • • •

Thanks to the assorted wines and a couple of sleeping tablets my dad had given me from his disturbingly large stash, I slept hard.

When I finally woke up, blinking against the bright light assaulting me through the unclosed curtains, it took me a while to remember where I was. New Order poster on the wall. An ancient desktop computer on a reclaimed timber desk. A row of meticulously painted figurines on the windowsill. Yep, I was in my childhood bedroom. Back in Brekkie Beach. San Francisco and my tastefully minimalist condo were thousands of miles away, like something from a dream.

My mouth felt horribly dry, like I had been practising kissing on a vacuum cleaner. Not that I had ever done that, but Tad swore he knew someone who had.

Out of habit, I pulled my phone into bed with me from where it was charging on the bedside table. The bedside table was a beaten-up old metal locker, which I had thought was the height of grunge chic when my younger self had found it on the side of the road. Now, it just made me roll my eyes. Like everything else in the room.

Blinking my equally dry eyes into focus, I swiped my thumb over the screen to find five new messages from Tad.

Tad: has your flight landed? everything okay?

Tad: are you at your dad's yet?

Tad: would it kill you to answer?

Tad: are you dead? did answering actually kill you?

Tad: should i get Benji a three piece suit for your funeral or is a black onesie okay?

A reluctant chuckle escaped me, and I managed a response.

Dylan: not dead. at dad's. flight was okay. how's the spawn?

A moment later, the phone vibrated, and I received a picture of my chubby-cheeked godson with what looked like strawberry pulp all over his face.

Tad: spawn is delightful. spawn has been delightful since 5am. being a dad is great. are you coming over to see him today?

"Today?" I groaned out loud, scrunching up my face. The idea of getting myself into a state where I was presentable enough to greet my tiny godson seemed like more effort than I could possibly exert. But it wasn't like I had a decent excuse. What, was I going to say I was busy?

Dylan: give me an hour to get myself together and i'll be there

Tad: <ANOTHER PICTURE OF THE CHUBBY-CHEEKED BABY, THIS TIME LOOKING STRANGELY EXPECTANT> WE'LL BE WAITING <THUMBS UP EMOJI>

And why had I said an hour? I needed to shower, maybe eat something, and try to find appropriate clothes. If I was going to be there in an hour, I needed to get out of bed...now.

With a grunt that was probably indulgently loud, I heaved myself out of the bed that wasn't a Formula One car and made for the bathroom.

• • • • • • • • • • •

Showered, dressed in clean jeans and a black t-shirt, and feeling slightly closer to human, I made my way downstairs.

"Good morning." The bright face of Tessa greeted me in the kitchen. But her smile was a little forced, and her cheeks were definitely pink. Maybe she was thinking about the potato.

"Morning," I said, glad I was more coherent than on our first meeting. "Just wanted to make some coffee. If I can figure out the machine."

"Ah, that could be a problem," Tessa grimaced, her nose wrinkling. "This one's new." She pointed at something enormous and chrome that looked like it would be at home in a chic café. Or a nuclear power plant. "It's taken me two weeks to get a decent brew out of it. You Aussies are so picky about your coffee."

"And you lot aren't picky about your tea?"

"Fair point," she said. "I mean, there was a reason the Americans decided to stick it to us by dumping all that tea in the harbour. But a decent cup of tea only takes a kettle and a bag. This thing, however…"

I let out a breath between my teeth. "Great. A coffee machine I can't use. Just what I needed."

"Aren't you, like, a tech genius?" A smile played on Tessa's full lips. When she smiled, I could see there was a tiny gap between her two front teeth. There was something oddly charming about that gap. After years spent surrounded by people with teeth so blindingly white and perfectly straight that they could have starred in a toothpaste commercial, it was a pleasant novelty.

"Coding an app absolutely does not compare to whatever the hell this is," I inclined my head at the machine. "Mechanical engineering is not my area."

"Especially not with jetlag," Tessa looked sympathetic. "Look, why don't you sit down, and I'll make you a coffee. I'm doing one for your dad and me anyway. And Marcel, if I can find him."

"You don't have to do that," I said. It wasn't her job to make me coffee. "I can..." I didn't know what I could do, actually.

"I don't mind. I'm already making it; it's no trouble."

I watched as she poured fresh beans into a glass funnel and flicked a switch, resulting in a loud and hideous grinding. The sound it produced was what I imagined would result if you forced a pig into an industrial woodchipper. Which, of course, I hadn't imagined before. I'm not that morbid.

"Thanks," I said loudly over the grinding noise. I took a seat at the table, mostly so I wasn't hovering over Tessa's shoulder.

She looked disconcertingly wholesome again this morning, dark eyebrows contracting slightly as she concentrated on the machine. Today, she wore a loose wool dress over thick tights and ankle boots, a heavy cardigan covering the ensemble. She must be feeling the cold, which was surprising. Weren't the English always making fun of Australians for shivering in coats and hats whenever the sky showed the slightest tinge of grey?

"So," Tessa said, looking up at me when the grinding noise ceased. "What are you up to today? You must have lots of friends to visit here."

"Uh, yeah." I rubbed my fingers over my no longer stubbled chin. Did Tad count as lots? I supposed he probably did if you included Benji and Alice, Tad's wife, in the equation. "I'm going to see my godson, Benji. He's nine months old."

"Oh, that will be lovely," Tessa said. "I mean, if you like babies. I don't have a whole lot of experience with them. If anyone hands me a baby, I'm always convinced I'm going to either drop them or say something that will scar them for life."

"I know what you mean," I confided. "I haven't exactly been the best godfather so far. Haven't even met the little fella yet, so I've been making up for it by sending expensive presents. You know, buying his affection."

Tessa's eyes met mine, and she smiled again. "That's good of you. It shows you're thinking of him."

"I guess," I shrugged. "I learned from the best, anyway. My mother didn't visit much, but she always sent the latest gadgets for birthdays and Christmas. I suppose it showed she was thinking of me."

"Oh, right." I didn't have to explain about my mother. If Tessa was writing my dad's autobiography – or 'helping bring his story to life', according to my dad's take on it – then she must know all about her. "I guess it was tricky, her living in America and all."

"Well, I got citizenship out of the deal," I said, not wanting Tessa to feel sorry for me. "That helped when I needed to move Space2Spare to Silicon Valley."

"And you must have seen her a lot more when you were living there," Tessa said, pouring milk into a stainless steel jug.

"Not really."

"Oh," Tessa bit her lip, looking like she wished she hadn't said it. But it wasn't like she was intentionally trying to remind me that my mother had never been interested in spending time with me, even when we lived hours and not an ocean apart. "Um, do you take regular milk?" She indicated the jug. "We don't have any non-dairy milk, but I can put it on the list if you—"

"I'm fine with the cow udder kind," I said. "I tried the whole keto thing, but I can't deal with coconut oil in my coffee. Call me crazy, but I'd rather die young that drink oily coffee."

"I don't think I could do it," she said, setting the milk to foam. She bit her lip. "I kind of get it, you know. Having your mum not around much. My parents were always travelling, so we mostly lived with my Nana."

"Oh," I said, wondering what to make of that. "Sorry to hear that."

"Don't be," Tessa said, expertly positioning a cup where delicious drips of dark black liquid would soon burst forth. "Nana was amazing. She taught me how to crochet and always had time for a chat about anything. She wasn't like a regular old lady, though. Her big passion was dirty romance books."

"What, like, those ones with a shirtless fireman and a strategically placed big hose on the cover?"

"Big hoses were her favourite."

I couldn't help chuckling. "She sounds pretty cool."

"She was," Tessa agreed. "I moved in with her after I finished uni when it got tough for her to do things around the house. I didn't want her to go to one of those old people's homes. She would have hated it."

"Wow," I said. "That's one hell of a sacrifice." And it made me feel like an arsehole because I had spent years living overseas when my father was spending more and more of his days in a wheelchair.

"It wasn't a sacrifice," Tessa insisted, shaking her head and making her bun flop from side to side. "I loved her. I wanted to do it."

"Still," I said. "You must have had your own dreams and plans. I mean, you moved out here, right?"

"I did," Tessa said. "Eventually. Even after she was gone, I..." She shook her head again. "Abby was the one who convinced me to move here. She lives in Brekkie Beach too, and she heard about your dad looking for someone to work on his autobiography and help with the housekeeping. She kept going on about how perfect it was, and how I needed some adventure in my life, and it would do me good. So I..." She looked down at the coffee. "Well, I'm here now, anyway."

"It makes sense why you're so good with my dad," I said, unsure how to respond to the rest of what Tessa had just told me. "I mean, if you looked after your Nana."

"I do my best," Tessa said modestly. "I think he likes my cooking and he seems happy with how the book's coming together."

"He thinks you're great," I told her. "Best housekeeper he's ever had; he said it last night." I had no intention of telling her the context in which he had said it. Tessa didn't need to know that my dad had explicitly told me not to 'interfere' with her like I was some kind of creepy pervert with a van. I didn't have a car in Sydney, let alone a van. I definitely didn't fulfil the creepy van guy criteria.

"That's very nice of him." Tessa shook off the compliment like she didn't quite believe me.

I was trying to think of something else to say when my father rolled into the kitchen on his wheels of fury. "Tessa, how long is that coffee going to take? My evolution into mixed media isn't going to write itself!"

"Sorry," Tessa quirked her mouth. "But the machine takes a while to heat up, and I know how you'd feel if I served you lukewarm coffee."

My father chuckled and looked at Tessa with warm affection. "That's probably true," he admitted. "I do have certain standards when it comes to my coffee." Then he spotted me. "So, you're up!"

"I am."

"You still look tired."

"Thanks, that does wonders for my self-confidence."

"Oh, don't be so sensitive," Alan scoffed. "I would have thought you'd look a bit more perky after all those hours spent slugging in bed."

"I wasn't slugging," I objected, although my habit of rolling myself up in my duvet probably made me resemble a slug more than I wanted to admit in front of Tessa. Not that it mattered what she thought of me. If she had been talking to my dad, slug might be an improvement.

"I've got your coffee here, Alan," Tessa placed a cup carefully on the kitchen island. "I'll bring it through to your office when I finish up mine and Dylan's."

"You don't need to make him coffee! He's a grown man; he can make his own!"

"You did say he looked tired." I was surprised that she was actually disagreeing with my father. Most people avoided that. "And Alan, I can't fault your taste in kitchen equipment, but this machine is a beast. You can't expect your jetlagged son to work it out without a little caffeine in his system to get his brain firing."

"Well, so long as you don't get used to it," Alan nudged me from his wheelchair. "Tessa's not here to wait on you hand and foot."

"I know that," I said, more irritably than I intended. I really hoped Tessa didn't think I expected that from her. "I'm off to see Tad this morning. And Benji."

"Oh yes," Alan said, nodding approvingly. "I hope you've got him a nice gift."

"Uh..." I absolutely hadn't thought to buy Benji something in the time between booking my flight and arriving in Brekkie Beach.

"Hopeless," my father pronounced. "You'll have to up your game if you want to make a good impression."

"I'm pretty sure babies are happy with a cardboard box," Tessa said blithely. "They don't need anything fancy."

"I've sent him plenty of nice presents," I added, wanting to defend myself at least a little. One of the lawyers who had worked on the sale of Space2Spare had been the proud mother of a little bundle of joy with fierce eyebrows and perpetual scowl. Whenever she had mentioned buying something for tiny Groucho, I had simply purchased the same for Benji.

"And that's yours, Dylan," Tessa set another cup on top of the machine and picked up the one she had made for my dad. "Shall we get started in your study this morning? You said you wanted to pull out some of the reviews of your 2003 exhibition, plus that feature article from the Herald."

"Yes, let's get started." Alan rubbed his hands together. "I'm feeling creative today."

As Tessa followed my father from the kitchen, a cup held steadily in each hand, she turned to me. "Good luck with the baby today. Just don't drop him or any f-bombs, and you'll be fine."

"Thanks for the advice." I picked up my coffee and took a long sip.

And damn, it really was excellent coffee. How she had coaxed that machine into producing such a divine elixir, I didn't know. But when I looked up to thank her, Tessa had already disappeared.

3 Tessa

I JOINED ALAN IN the room he called his study, though it could be better described as an archive devoted to Australia's greatest living artist (confirmed by at least six independent sources, not just the man himself). Flipping open my laptop, I took a long sip of coffee, steeling myself for a monologue.

"Now, before we get started," Alan began, steepling his fingers together. "I wanted to have a word with you."

At those words, my heart started to thud in my chest, too loud and too fast, and I had the urge to shove my fingernails into my mouth and chew them into tiny pieces. I had only been able to break the habit by having my natural nails covered in thick acrylics that my teeth simply couldn't chomp through. My body was gearing up to flee from an irate mammoth, and I wished, not for the first time, that a simple sentence didn't set off my flight or fight or even freeze response.

"Right," I said, doing my best to pretend I wasn't drowning in a cauldron of anxiety. "Is this about that Thai Green Curry that made your eyes water? I know it was too much fresh chilli. I won't make it again, I promise. Unless you need your sinuses cleared out."

Alan huffed out a small breath of laughter. "It's not about the curry. Although I prefer my meals to be less aggressive, on the whole."

"Right," I said again, twisting my hands behind my laptop and ineffectually begging my heart to stop racing. "Um, what is it then?"

"It's about Dylan." Alan raised his eyebrows. "I'm sure you know what I mean."

I really didn't.

"Oh." As a professional writer, I can be amazingly articulate like that. "What about him?"

"My son can be very charming when he chooses," Alan sounded like he thought I was being intentionally obtuse. "And I wouldn't want to see you get drawn into anything."

And that made me choke on my mouthful of coffee, splattering it all over my laptop as I tried to breathe. Marcel came running in, looking first at Alan and then at me. He thumped me hard on the back, clearly thinking that would be helpful. It wasn't.

"Are you quite well?" Marcel asked when I stopped coughing.

"Fine," I croaked, mopping up the coffee with the sleeve of my cardigan.

"I was just telling Tessa not to let herself be drawn into anything with Dylan," Alan said because, of course, he needed to repeat that in front of Marcel to ensure my humiliation was complete. "Because he's in no fit state for a relationship of any kind."

"I'm not going to get drawn into anything," I said, looking up. "I mean, he's your son. I wouldn't." My cheeks were flushed, and my mind was racing. My brain began to come up with a horrifying list of possibilities.

1. Had I done or said anything to make Alan think I was interested in his son?
2. Did Dylan think I was interested in him? Had I inadvertently flirted in our brief interaction?
3. Had Dylan asked his father to have this talk with me, just so I didn't get any ideas?
4. Did Alan think I was so desperate I'd throw myself at Dylan just because he was the nearest warm-blooded heterosexual man?

"I'm glad to hear it," Alan said smoothly, but he was still staring at me strangely. "But I know these things can happen, and he's a handsome boy."

"I'm here to work." I tried to remind myself that I had spent barely any time with Dylan and couldn't have done anything too horribly embarrassing. Unless Alan thought that incident with the potato had been an attempt at seduction. "I'm not looking for any kind of relationship."

I had said the same to Abby and Michelle, and they had refused to believe it too. My sisters were convinced that once I arrived in Brekkie Beach, I'd be shagging as many muscular, tanned surfers as I could find. I wasn't strictly opposed to tanned and muscular, but casual flings had never worked for me. It was best to just focus on my job. And getting involved with my boss's son would be the opposite of a good idea.

"I was not looking for a relationship when I met Alan. I was quite convinced I would spend my life alone. But," Marcel smiled at Alan, "love has a way of surprising you."

"That's different. You two are obviously meant to be. You're the great love story running through the whole book." I tapped the laptop. "But seriously, you don't have to worry about me. I'm not going to get involved with anyone."

"Oh, please don't think I'm telling you not to have any fun! I'm all for sowing your wild oats while you're young." Alan shot me a wink.

"And," Marcel added, "the studio is quite soundproof."

My ears grew hot, and my stomach performed a somersault that would have impressed a competitive cheerleading squad. Were they really encouraging me to bring home one-night stands? "Uh, thanks for letting me know."

"But do be careful. I hope you're better at using birth control than I was – after all, that's how I ended up with Dylan!" Alan smirked as though my embarrassment amused him. It probably did.

"I'm a very careful person," I said, wishing passionately he'd stop talking about this. "Um, did you want me to look for that feature article? The one that called you a visionary?"

"Oh yes," Alan looked around as though expecting the article to magically appear from the stacks of papers piled high on every surface. "I suppose we'd better get started, or I'll never finish this book."

"Which would be a tragedy. The public is waiting, you know."

"Cheeky," Alan gave me an indulgent smile as he gulped down the last of his coffee. "Try looking under that pile." He pointed to what might once have been an armchair but was currently too laden with stacks of papers, magazines, journals, and an unfinished masterpiece to be sure.

"I will leave you to your business." Marcel swept from the room, looking like an elegant spider with his long limbs all clad in black.

"See you later." I resigned myself to a morning of shuffling papers while receiving unhelpful and often contradictory directions from my boss.

My boss, who thought I might sleep with his son if he didn't specifically warn me not to. Which I absolutely wasn't going to do. Sure, Dylan was handsome. And I was curious about why someone as smart as him couldn't decide what to do with his life. But nothing was going to happen. Absolutely nothing.

• • • • ● • ● • • •

When Alan announced he was done for the day, I was more than ready for a break. The study, with its dusty piles of papers and sauna-like heating, always made me want to curl up into a ball and hibernate until Spring, swiping a claw at anyone who dared disturb my slumber.

But Alan had been deeply wounded on the one occasion I had dared yawn in his presence, and so I had increased my caffeine consumption to potentially toxic levels. Which I doubted helped with my insomnia.

Perhaps I should have used the time off to work on my personal work-in-progress, *Bully Banisher*, but I needed a good walk. The sky looked clear, but I knew better than to trust Sydney weather, so I grabbed the umbrella I purchased in my first week in Brekkie Beach. I hadn't brought one with me from England. That was a mistake. Big mistake. Australia was nowhere near as sunny as movies made you believe.

Still, the air smelled fresh and clean, with a delicious hint of salt that hit your nostrils as soon as you stepped out the door. It might not be sunny, but Brekkie Beach was a definite improvement on Birmingham. For a start, I thought as I made my way down the street, none of the houses touched each other. My parents' house – and my Nana's – had been terraces, and I was used to hearing my neighbours as clearly as I could hear my own family. But here, the houses sat aloof, protected from their neighbours by leafy gardens and wooden fences. Also, I was pretty sure I had never seen a palm tree in Birmingham. Unless you counted the fake ones in the windows of shops selling optimistically tiny bikinis.

Birmingham did have one significant advantage over Brekkie Beach, however. I knew my way around Birmingham. Or at least around the part of it that I had called home since I was a child. Not so in Brekkie Beach. I had intended to take a shortcut down to the coffee shop but found myself in charming but totally unfamiliar winding back streets. I was sure I had looped back around this block at least once. That pale blue weatherboard cottage on the corner seemed oddly familiar, mocking my lack of spatial awareness with its mottled white shutters. Stupid vindictive cottage.

I was about to admit defeat and let my phone's GPS save my sorry arse once more when I heard my name. Turning, I saw...

"Tessa?"

It was Dylan. Besides, it wasn't like any other tall, slouching, broodingly handsome men in Brekkie Beach knew my name. I was pretty sure his friend Tad was with him, too. The baby strapped to his chest was a dead giveaway.

"Hi!" I said, hoping it wasn't abundantly clear I was lost. "I was just out for a walk."

"Not the most picturesque part of Brekkie Beach."

"Oh, you know," I shrugged, pretending to be nonchalant and casual. "It's good to let yourself wander sometimes. You never know what you might find."

"Well, you found us," the man who must be Tad interrupted. "I'm Tad, and this is Benji. You must be Tessa. Dylan told me about you."

"Did he?" I let out a squeak of horrified laughter. I really hoped he hadn't mentioned the potato. "Um, it's nice to meet you. Hello, Benji!" I stooped slightly to wave at the baby. I didn't know if that was appropriate, but the baby – with his very chubby cheeks – gurgled and reached out towards me, giving me a toothless smile.

"Oh, he likes you!" Tad was jubilant. "Don't you, buddy? You like Dylan's friend Tessa."

Dylan's friend? Hardly. Passing acquaintance at best. But how did you describe the person writing your father's autobiography?

"He's adorable," I said, perfectly honestly. I wasn't experienced with babies, but Benji seemed like a fine example of one, with his fat little hands still reaching for me and a woolly hat with a pompom covering most of his dark hair. "Nine months old?"

"He is," Tad said proudly. "Dylan was just taking some photos of us. I don't know why you never pursued photography, mate. You were so keen when we were in school."

"School doesn't count for much." Dylan shifted his weight from one foot to the other. "You were a great long jumper, but it's not like you went to the Olympics."

"I had almost forgotten that! No one expected the short Asian kid to be any good at long jump, but I showed them!" Tad paused. "And remember how you told everyone you were great at shotput?"

"I didn't tell everyone I was great at it," Dylan's mouth twitched.

"No, but you did tell Katy Hawkins and her friends all about how you were a natural because of your muscle mass." Tad was clearly enjoying himself now. "With your biceps and all."

"I didn't have biceps; I was fourteen!"

"As they found out when the time came for you to throw the shotput, and you dropped it on your foot. You were on crutches for a week," Tad finished. "Katy wasn't impressed, in case you were wondering, Tessa."

I wasn't sure if I should laugh. Was this a funny childhood memory or a traumatic one? Sometimes, it was hard to tell.

"But you were good at photography," Tad continued. "And you still are. You should do something with that, you know. Now that you've finished with that parking space thing."

"I sold my start-up. That doesn't mean my career is over. I could build another app."

"Do you want to?"

Dylan opened his mouth and then abruptly shut it again, once again looking annoyed.

I wished, at that moment, that I could disappear. This was clearly the kind of conversation between old friends that you didn't want your dad's employee to be privy to. At that moment, a fat drop of rain fell from the sky, right onto my nose.

"It's raining!" I pointed out the obvious.

"Shit, it is!" Tad jumped, sheltering his baby with both hands. Benji, for his part, seemed unconcerned with this development. "I'd better get back inside; Alice will kill me if I have him out in a storm."

"It's hardly a storm," Dylan rolled his eyes, even as the drops began to come down harder, faster. "But what do I know about parenting?"

"Nothing," Tad told him. "Look, I'll see you soon, okay?" He was already making his way back down the street, hunched over to protect little Benji from the rain. "Take care of yourself. Don't do anything stupid."

"I appreciate the vote of confidence!"

I popped up my umbrella, congratulating myself smugly on remembering to bring it, and stood on my tiptoes to cover Dylan too.

"I can't believe it's raining. Ever since I got here, it's rained almost every day. I didn't leave England for this!"

"I'm sorry my homeland is so disappointing. I'll have a word with the weather people, see what they can do."

I let out a breath of amusement. "I should probably get back. Um, you can share my umbrella, if you like." And why did that sound like a euphonism for something sordid, possibly involving whipped cream and blindfolds?

"I don't mind the rain." Dylan stepped out from under the umbrella. Maybe he didn't want to be seen under something so aggressively girly. I just had to go for the one with polka dots, didn't I? "But I'll walk you back. You're lost, aren't you?"

"Was it really that obvious?" There was no point pretending I wasn't. "How far are we from your dad's place?"

"Not very," Dylan's mouth quirked as though he wanted to laugh but was trying to be polite. "It's this way. Come on."

I almost had to jog to keep up with his long-legged strides, which was embarrassing because I prided myself on being a fast walker. After a moment, I tried to make conversation. "So, photography, huh? You never considered it as a career?"

There was silence, and when I looked at Dylan's drawn face, I instantly wished I had asked him something else.

"It was just a hobby," Dylan said finally. "Dad was always very keen on me pursuing it, though."

"That makes sense," I said, not seeing his point. "He would have loved to see you do something creative like that."

"He did. But like I said, it was just a hobby."

"Right." I wished I hadn't brought it up. Hell, it would have been better to mention my penis-shaped potato again.

"I always liked messing around with computers, so coding seemed like a good idea," Dylan said after an uncomfortably long silence. "Dad can barely work out how to check the time on his iPhone, so he doesn't really get what I do."

"Yeah, I guess that tech is about as far away as you can get from art." I wondered if that was why Dylan had chosen it. "It was pretty brave of you to do something like that. Most people would have been happy to use their parent's fame to get a leg up. I mean, it worked for Miley Cyrus."

"*Party in the USA* is a masterpiece. I'm sure she would have been successful even without Billy Ray."

"I'm glad to know you've got good taste in music, at least."

"Why did you decide to become a ghostwriter?" Dylan asked suddenly, looking like he was genuinely interested in my answer.

"I don't know if 'decide' is the right word," I admitted. "Fell into, maybe? I was studying English and History at uni and for one of my assignments I interviewed a local veteran and wrote up his story. His family really liked it, and it turned out his daughter-in-law worked in publishing. She offered to give me a trial, ghostwriting for this celebrity chef none of her regular writers could stand working with, and I guess...the rest is history."

Dylan made a soft sound. "You really did fall into it, then." He paused. "Is that what you always wanted to do?"

"Not exactly. I mean, I didn't spend my childhood thinking, 'Oh, if only I could see my words published with someone else's name on them.' But I like it, and it pays pretty well."

"What did you want to do when you were a kid?"

"You mean apart from becoming a princess or running away to the circus to be an acrobat?"

"I wanted to be a lion tamer." Dylan gave me another of those faint smiles. There was a little more warmth in those still-tired green eyes, like he was genuinely enjoying our conversation. And that made my stomach clench uncomfortably in a way that I didn't want to examine too closely. "It wouldn't have worked out; I can't even get Cyndi to stop clawing me."

"I always wanted to write kids' books," I said. "Later I found out that was called middle-grade fiction, for eight- to twelve-year-olds. And I do, in my spare time. Just not anything worth publishing."

"I would have thought it would be easy for you to get your books published," Dylan frowned. "I mean, you're already a professional writer. Didn't your publisher help you get it to the right people?"

"Oh no," I shook my head. "I've never shared my stuff with anyone. No way."

"Seriously?"

"Deadly," I said. "Maybe, if I had got that Master's in Creative Writing, I'd feel more like I could—" I cut myself off, not wanting to explain that anxiety had made me pull out of the course before it had even started. "I've already got a career. I didn't need that kind of challenge."

"If you can cope with my dad on a daily basis, I think you're definitely up for a challenge."

"Your dad's great!" I said because I knew that while you could insult your own parents, most people would be highly offended if anyone agreed with the criticism. "I mean, he's a true living legend."

"And he'll never let you forget it, either." Dylan stopped walking abruptly, looking at me.

"What?" I felt my stomach tighten, my heart rate quickening again. Why was he looking at me like that?

"It's stopped raining." Dylan carefully took my umbrella from my (admittedly slightly shaking) hands. "You don't need this."

"Oh," I said stupidly. "Thanks."

"No problem," Dylan said, closing it up and handing it back to me. "It's still not sunny, but you deserve to enjoy the best Sydney in September has to offer."

I let out a breath, and my stomach clenched again, more urgently this time. It was like a rebellious robot had wrapped its mechanical fingers right around my insides and was squeezing, just for the fun of torturing its human overlord. A thin ray of sunshine burst through the still rain-heavy clouds, illuminating Dylan's face as he looked at me.

Oh shit. I was in trouble. Dylan was so tall, had such perfect cheekbones, so much intensity in his green eyes. And I could have ignored his being ridiculously hot, but then he had gone and taken an interest in me. And made me laugh.

But I hadn't forgotten who he was. My boss's son. And even without Alan's highly embarrassing warning that morning, I would never let anything happen between us. Even if Dylan wanted it to, which seemed unlikely. He was a tech millionaire with a flawless jawline; he probably had a parade of models banging on his door back in San Francisco. I was just the woman who made pie for his dad and had an overly active brain. Maybe, I thought desperately, we could be friends.

Being friends was the best I could possibly hope for. Now all I had to do was make sure that Dylan didn't realise I liked him more than I should. And worrying about that was going to keep me up all night.

At least I'd have an exciting new reason for my inability to sleep.

4 Dylan

It was getting late enough in the morning that it was embarrassing to still be in bed. I wasn't even asleep, just lying there, listening to the occasional bursts of muffled chatter or the grinding of the coffee machine below me. It felt like far too much energy to actually get out of bed. I had been lying there for more than nine hours, but my watch claimed I had actually slept for less than six. That seemed unfair.

I raised a hand to pull my duvet off and then abandoned the mission, closing my eyes again for a moment. Tad's face swam up in my mind, his eyes crinkled in concern, and I groaned loudly. Catching up with my oldest friend had been great, but he had told me he was worried about me and had been almost...gentle? Gentleness wasn't exactly a feature of our friendship. I wanted to blame it on Tad's status as a new father. Maybe he just wanted to nurture everyone and everything. Even his thirty-one-year-old best friend, who absolutely did not require cuddles, burping, and a secure attachment to his primary caregiver.

"I think you should see someone, you know. About your career crisis," Tad had said, and I told him he was obviously too sleep-deprived to see that I was merely taking a break. Thinking about my future, mulling over my options. Even if I couldn't name what those options might be.

"What would he know about it, anyway?" I muttered, snaking a hand out from under the duvet to grab my phone from my still-rusty bedside table. Flicking my thumb over the screen, I asked aloud in a voice heavy with sarcasm. "Siri, what should I do with my life?"

"I'm sorry, I don't understand the question. Did you ask, 'what should I do with my wife?' For marital counselling near you—"

"Shut up!" I jabbed my thumb at the screen and threw my phone at the ground, where it bounced mockingly. "Just shut up."

"—marital counselling can be beneficial—" Siri went on, her voice muffled by the carpet. I was convinced she was doing this just to annoy me.

"Piss off," I grunted, pushing myself out of bed. I rifled through one of my suitcases, pulling on shorts and a hoodie and stepping into my sneakers. "I don't have a wife!"

"Popular dating apps include Tinder, Bumble, Happn—" Letting out a grunt, I picked up the phone and shut Siri off.

"I'm not looking for a wife," I told my phone. "Seriously. Try that shit again, and I'll disable you."

Siri didn't answer, and for a brief moment, I felt like I'd won. Then I realised I was arguing with an AI system, and the sweetness of victory faded.

Clomping down the stairs loudly, I braced myself for my dad's inevitable judgement on both my appearance and timing.

"Oh, so you're alive after all!" Alan wheeled his chair around to face me. "I was beginning to wonder."

"Sorry to disappoint you," I said, making my way toward the coffee machine. The day before, Tessa had (very kindly and without making me feel patronised) talked me through how to make it work.

"We do not want you to be dead," Marcel looked up from the German language magazine he was perusing. Judging from the cover, it was either an intellectually demanding global affairs journal, or an Avant-Garde furniture catalogue. Knowing Marcel, either was possible.

"Who's not dead?" Tessa came in, fresh-faced and laden with straw market bags full of what must be organic farmer's market produce. "Oh, good morning, Dylan. How'd you sleep? Getting over that jetlag?"

"Getting there," I said, busying myself with the coffee machine. "Anyone want a coffee?"

"I'll wait for Tessa to make me one."

"Thanks for the vote of confidence." I resisted the urge to stick my tongue out at my father.

"Coffee sounds great," Tessa smiled at me in a way I knew she intended to be encouraging. "If you don't mind."

"I don't mind," I said, trying not to watch too obviously as she began to unpack a leafy bunch of spinach, four heads of broccoli, a large salami, a bag of mandarins, and what seemed like a ridiculous quantity of ricotta. "You've been shopping?"

"Yeah, the pop-up farmer's market was fantastic," Tessa said, arranging the vegetables in the crisper as though doing so gave her great satisfaction.

"Must be. I don't think we've ever had this many vegetables in the house," I said. "Is my dad really eating all this?"

"Tessa makes vegetables far more palatable than I ever could," Alan said. "Or Marcel, for that matter. Sorry, darling."

"I am not offended." Marcel looked up from his journal. "Improving the palatability of vegetables is not an area of special interest to me."

"I've always liked to cook," Tessa said with a shrug.

"Did your Nana teach you?" I asked, remembering what she had said about living with her grandmother.

"No, bless her," Tessa shook her head. "Nana belonged to the traditional British school of cooking. A vegetable was not fit for human consumption until it was boiled beyond all recognition. Nana was great, but I don't think she'll be remembered for her culinary prowess."

"Neither will I," I poured the frothed milk into Tessa's cup. "Nor for my barista skills. I just hope this is okay." I slid the cup over to her, wondering why I cared so much about her reaction.

"Thank you so much," Tessa said earnestly. She'd probably tell me it was perfect even if it was undrinkable slop. She'd give me one of those smiles too. When Tessa smiled, the corners of her eyes crinkled, and I could see that little gap between her teeth. That gap seemed to be occupying an unreasonable amount of space in my brain.

I took a sip of my own coffee and blanched. "This is horrible." I said, immediately tipping it down the sink. "I'll get one at the gym."

I reached for Tessa's cup, but her hand caught mine. "Let me try it."

"I can't let you. For your own safety."

"That bad?" She still hadn't let go of my hand. Her skin was warm, and I didn't truly want her to let go, even though this interaction was playing out in full view of my dad and Marcel.

"Definitely that bad. Seriously, Dad will be mega pissed if I poison you."

"Indeed I would," my father piped up from the table. "Let him get rid of it, Tessa. And you can make me a decent cup."

Scrunching up her face, Tessa released my hand. "I'm sure you'll get it right next time."

"I doubt it," I said, picking up my gym bag and heading for the door.

"Have fun at the gym!" Tessa called to me. When I turned, she gave me a double thumbs up that was so ridiculously cheesy that it circled right back around to...adorable?

"See you later," I said, giving a half-wave to the room at large as I slipped out the door. I would leave them to their morning routine in peace. Maybe this was my childhood home, but I couldn't help feeling like I was intruding.

• • • • ● • ● • • •

"Why," I asked Tad, "did I receive this email declaring that you wanted to get sweaty with me?" I pushed the screen of my phone into Tad's face. He scanned it for a moment and then burst out laughing.

"I was trying to share a free trial for the gym with you!" He gasped for breath, and Benji, strapped to his chest, was giving me a toothless grin as though he, too, was in on the joke. "I didn't know they'd word it like that."

"'Thaddeus Nguyen wants to get sweaty with you'," I repeated. "That's borderline sexual harassment."

"Someone in their marketing department clearly thought they were very funny and edgy."

"Someone in their marketing department's a twat," I muttered. "I'm glad you're not warm for my form, Thaddeus."

"Can we not use my full name?"

"Why not, Thaddeus?" I couldn't resist goading him. "I'm surprised you didn't name the little guy Thaddeus Junior."

"That's right, make fun of my immigrant parents who were behind on the times when it came to choosing Anglo names for their kid," Tad prodded me. "Kind of racist, dude."

I held up my hands. "Fine, you win." I paused. "Besides, Benji suits him. He looks like a Benji."

Benji gave me another toothless grin as though delighted to hear his own name.

"He's going to the creche," Tad said, leading me through the sliding doors of the gym and towards a brightly lit room full of aesthetically pleasing wooden toys and pastel colours. "So we can work out in peace."

"They offer childcare?"

"I wouldn't come if they didn't," Tad told me, signing his name and handing a gurgling Benji off to a smiling woman in a Muscle Land polo shirt with what looked suspiciously like baby vomit covering the logo. "Alice says she's never worked out as much as she does now that he's old enough for the free childcare."

"Makes sense." I followed him to the front desk. Tad held up his phone, and a man in a skimpy singlet scanned a QR code.

"Have a great workout, Thaddeus!" The man offered him a high five, which Tad reluctantly accepted. "Pump that iron, my brother!"

"Thanks," Tad's mouth was a thin line. "And my friend here's got a trial membership. Dylan Huxley."

The man in the skimpy singlet squinted at his computer for a moment. "Oh yeah, I can see it here. Welcome to the Muscle Land family! Hope you have an awesome sweaty sesh!"

"Uh, thanks," I said and followed Tad past the desk and towards the gym floor. "Does he do that every time you come?"

"Yep," Tad rolled his eyes. "I think they think it's more personal, greeting us by name. We're all part of the Muscle Land family."

"I'm trying to escape my family. I don't need more."

"What, you're already sick of your dad and Marcel? It's only been a few days."

"I'm not sick of them." I watched as Tad loaded plates onto either side of the barbell. "But I know my dad's judging me. For being home, and not having a plan."

"He said that?"

"He didn't have to," I said as Tad lay down, flexing his shoulders impressively before gripping the bar. "I'm spotting you, am I?"

"Since you're here. I've got to get some use out of you."

"Oh, so I'm useless now? Thanks, that makes me feel much better about my life." It wouldn't have stung if I didn't genuinely feel useless. And that wasn't Tad's fault, but...

"See, this is why you need to see someone. Because you do feel useless, and you're stressing about it," Tad said, pushing the bar upwards with what I thought was a totally unnecessary groan.

"I'm not stressing," I said automatically. "I just don't know what to do next. I'm taking a break."

"You say that," Tad grunted, his biceps straining as he pushed the bar up once more. "But you're not yourself."

"How am I not myself? Maybe this is what I'm like."

"Nope," Tad gasped, releasing the bar back onto its support and sitting up to take a gulp of water. "I've known you since you were eight, dude. This isn't you. I mean, I hate to agree with your dad, but it isn't like you not to have a plan. You're always doing something, working towards some goal."

"Am I not allowed a break? I worked my arse off for years on Space2Spare. Can't I just take some time off?"

"That's not what I'm saying," Tad stood up to load another plate onto each side of the bar. "I'm all for you taking a sabbatical. If you were happy doing that. But you aren't. Come on, dude."

"I'm just tired," I insisted, even though I didn't especially know why I was denying it. We both knew I wasn't happy. There was no pretending when it came to someone who had known you for more than twenty years.

Tad scoffed, arranging himself under the bar once more. "Tell you what. If you can bench more than me, I'll shut up. If I can bench more than you, you'll make an appointment with a careers advisor."

"I'm a foot taller than you. Of course I can bench more than you."

"Fine, not the bench press, then," Tad looked thoughtful. "Squats?"

I didn't practice squats much, truth be told. I had always preferred machines to free weights. With a machine, you could zone out. But with free weights, you always had to be fiddling with plates, checking your form, and adjusting your lifting gloves. Too much effort. Still, I wasn't going to admit that.

"Fine, squats," I said, moving behind Tad to spot him. "I hope you're looking forward to shutting up about this."

"I hope you're looking forward to seeing a career—" Tad's words turned into a grunt, the veins of his neck popping as he pushed the bar up.

"Hi there!"

I looked up to see a woman in a low-cut sports bra with so many criss-crossing straps that it looked like her breasts had been stuffed into a string bag.

"Er, hi?" I said, wondering if she had been addressing Tad.

"I'm Sophie," she said. "I was going to work on my bench press today too and I was thinking you could spot me next." She was standing with one leg jutting out in front of her, turning her foot so that her thigh caught the light as it moved back and forth.

"Kind of busy today," I said, looking back down at Tad's grimly determined face.

"Oh," Sophie didn't even pretend not to look disappointed. "Some other time, maybe?"

"I usually just work out by myself." I didn't care if I was being rude. It wasn't my job to spot strangers at the gym.

"I see." Sophie slunk away and didn't look back over her shoulder.

"What the hell was that?" Tad demanded, re-racking the bar and scrubbing at his sweaty face with a towel.

"What was what?" I knew exactly what he meant, but there was no way I was going to help him.

"Turning down that woman. She was cute enough, and you're single. A tumble with a gym babe might cheer you up a bit."

"I'm not interested." And I wasn't. The thought of having to be charming and make polite small talk just so I could go home with some woman I wasn't especially attracted to for formulaic and unexciting sex seemed like way more effort than it was worth.

"Oh, I see," Tad suddenly looked smug. "Saving yourself for Tessa, huh?"

I snorted, rolled my eyes, and shook my head because one gesture of derision was clearly insufficient. "Hardly," I added, just to make my point clear. "I'm not in the habit of hitting on my dad's employees, even if I was interested in her. Which I'm not."

"Oh, come on, it's not like he's some billionaire CEO and she's the lowly secretary," Tad scoffed. "She's a contractor. Barely an employee."

"That's not the point! I'm not interested in her. Not my type. Not at all."

"She's totally your type," Tad disagreed. "Dark hair, blue eyes, curves in all the right places..."

"I'll tell Alice you said that."

"She'd agree with me. We're married, Dylan, not totally blind. And I can tell that Tessa's a pretty girl and definitely your type."

"She's not! Okay, so physically, maybe. But she's not my kind of person. She..." I searched my brain. "She goes to the farmer's market with straw baskets. She looked after her elderly Nana for years. She smiles all the time. I bet she can sew, or knit, or something. She's a nice girl. I'm a tech arsehole. Tech arseholes don't date nice girls."

"You're not a tech arsehole anymore. You could totally date a nice girl."

"I'm not interested," I said again. "I'm not in the right headspace for a relationship, anyway. Or even anything casual. I just want to..." I trailed off because I had absolutely no idea what I just wanted to do. Unless it was going to bed with a bottle of wine until I stopped caring. That sounded pretty appealing.

"See, this is why you need to see someone," Tad said, wiping down the bench and standing up. "You're not yourself."

"I'm fine," I insisted. "Hope you're ready to lose."

But Tad just laughed. "We'll see."

· · · · ● · ● · · · ·

"I don't see why people think squats are so important, anyway," I said moodily, following Tad into the cafe. "They look stupid."

"Says the man who lost," Tad grinned as he turned back to me, baby Benji strapped to his chest once more. "No one likes a sore loser, Dylan."

"Maybe I let you win," I said. "To make you feel better about your dad bod."

"Ooh, those are fighting words! Do you know how much of a workout carrying around this little dude gives me every day? I'm pretty much an athlete."

"Hi there!" Nick, one of the two owners of Nick and Nikki's, greeted us from behind the counter. With his leather apron and a headband pushing back his receding curls, Nick took his role as barista very seriously.

"What can I get for you guys? We've got a delightful cold brew on the go—" He pointed at what looked like an old-fashioned science experiment, a glass vial slowly belching its black contents into a flask. "Or maybe you'd like to try our Superfood Protein Power Balls? Get those gains on after your workout!"

"What's in them?" Tad squatted down to peer at the balls through the glass case. Show off.

"Edamame and acai," Nick said promptly. "With an activated almond-based protein. They're non-GMO, gluten-free, vegan, and totally organic."

"Uh, just a flat white for me, please." My stomach did not appreciate the thought of acai and edamame in combination.

"No problem!" Nick shot me a set of double finger guns. "What kind of milk? We've got lactose-free, almond, soy, macadamia, oat, rice—"

"Just regular milk is fine."

"And an almond milk latte for me," Tad added. "I'll try one of those Power Balls, too."

"Coming right up! You take a seat, and I'll get those right over to you."

Tad sat down at a small table that seemed far too low. On closer inspection, I saw it was an old industrial spool, or at least it was pretending to be. Industrial design had become so popular that you could buy brand new wooden spools made to look old. With copper piping, exposed brick walls, and a concrete floor, I couldn't help thinking Nick and Nikki had committed to the industrial look too heavily for even Marcel's tastes. And my stepfather loved polished concrete almost as much as he loved black turtlenecks. Since when was Brekkie Beach so goddamn trendy?

I sat down gingerly, my thighs already protesting my failed attempt to best Tad in the squats-off. "Since when do you drink almond milk?"

"Since I became a dad. I have to watch out for my health if I'm going to be running around after this little guy." He patted Benji's head affectionately. "Almond milk has half the calories of cow's milk. It was an easy switch."

"It doesn't taste even remotely the same." Living in San Francisco, I had been exposed to every non-dairy milk on the market, and I still didn't like any of them.

"You get used to it after a while," Tad said. "Anyway, stop trying to distract me. You owe me one appointment with a careers advisor."

"Like that creepy guy who used to hang around the library when we were at school? He was always trying to get us to do work experience at his brother-in-law's restaurant. I'm sure he was getting kickbacks for the free labour."

"Career counselling is a legit thing," Tad objected. "Alice saw one when she was made redundant. She said it really helped her."

"But she got another job in real estate."

"A better job," Tad insisted. "And she negotiated a higher salary, all because of that advisor."

"I'm hardly worried about salary. You know I don't technically need a job, right? I could just invest and live off the dividends or whatever."

"Oh no," Tad shook his head disapprovingly. "You'll be a mess if you don't have something to do with yourself. You are not becoming a professional playboy. You don't like clubbing. Or yachts. You'd be shit at it, even if you are disgustingly rich."

"I'm not *disgustingly* rich."

"Dude," Tad rolled his eyes. "When you don't have to work, you're disgustingly rich. Not that it seems to have made you very happy. This is why you need to see a careers advisor."

"If I make the appointment, will you leave me alone?"

"So long as you actually go through with it, yeah."

"Fine." I picked up my phone and search for 'career advisor Sydney book online'. I clicked on the first link, barely glancing at the details. All that mattered was that there were open slots on the online calendar.

"Done." I turned my phone to face Tad so I could show him the confirmation message.

"What?" Tad leaned forward, startling Benji, who made his annoyance known with a loud squawk. "Who is this person?"

I took my phone back. "Julius Persimmon," I read from the screen. "First search result. He must be decent if his SEO skills got him to the top spot."

"You just picked the first search result? I want you to take this seriously."

"I am." And that was a lie; I couldn't really pretend that I had put the slightest bit of thought into the decision. "Look, you wanted me to book in with someone. And I have. And the appointment's next week, so you can't even accuse me of stalling."

"What if he's a total lunatic?" Tad scrunched up his face. "Did you even check the reviews?"

"It was your idea."

"Dude, you're killing me." Tad threw his head back dramatically, but I was saved from further remonstration by the arrival of the coffee and Tad's Power Ball.

"It looks like a testicle." I prodded it with one finger.

"Hands off my ball!" Tad slapped my hand away. "And mate, if your testicles look like that, you need to see a doctor."

• • • ● ● • ● • ● • •

I spent the afternoon with Tad, so my dad couldn't accuse me of lounging about the house all day doing nothing. Now I could tell him I had been bonding with my godson. And I supposed I had been. I had let him pull at my ears with his chubby baby fingers and gurgle into my face. Still, I couldn't help thinking that the bonding would be easier when Benji could talk.

As soon as I opened the door, the smell of something hearty and delicious met my nostrils. I was suddenly acutely aware that all I had eaten were the lightly seasoned rice cakes that Tad insisted were just as satisfying as the potato chips he and Alice had sworn off in the name of healthy living. They weren't.

"Dylan, is that you?"

"Hi," I said, waving as I entered the kitchen. Since when did I wave at my own father?

"Just in time for dinner. I bet you planned it that way, didn't you?"

"No, I just..." I began and then shrugged. "I can make something for myself later."

"Don't be ridiculous," Alan said. "Tessa's made enough for an army."

"A small army." Tessa was making her way to the table with an enormous cast iron pot. "Definitely enough for you. Do you like Dublin Coddle?"

"I have absolutely no idea," I answered honestly. "But so long as it's not got edamame and acai in it, I think there's a good chance I do."

"Edamame and acai?" Tessa wrinkled her nose. "Together? You've been to Nick and Nikki's, haven't you?"

"Yeah, I have. Decent coffee, but bizarre food. Too trendy for me."

"I would have thought you'd be used to that, living in San Francisco," Tessa set the pot onto a heavy marble trivet in the centre of the table. "Dig in," she said encouragingly, lifting the lid on a hearty-looking stew. "I'll just get the bread."

Marcel looked up at that. "Fresh bread?"

"Just soda bread," Tessa said, as though that somehow diminished the achievement. "With Guinness and cheddar."

"Sounds delightful." My father was waiting for Marcel to serve him stew. "Is there any Guinness left over? If we're pretending to be Irish, I want the full experience."

"You'd be better off with whiskey, then," Tessa teased. "But I've got Guinness in the fridge. Does anyone else want one? Marcel? Dylan?"

"Not for me," I shook my head. "When I first moved to San Fran, there was this cheap Irish pub near where I was staying, and..."

"Say no more." Tessa set a can of Guinness in front of my dad. "The pub near my uni had a two-for-one special on Strongbow. Sometimes even the smell of apples still makes me sick."

"You can't let a little thing like overindulgence put you off," Alan chided. "I'd never drink again if I did that."

"Are you supposed to drink with your medication?" I couldn't resist the jab.

My father gave me a hard stare. "I'm an artist. You can't expect me to live like a monk."

"The Westvleteren brewery is run by monks," Marcel said. I wasn't sure whether he was trying to defuse the tension or thought this was a genuinely interesting contribution. "And they make an excellent beer."

"Well, if beer's good enough for monks, this is certainly good enough for me," my father said, taking a sip of Guinness.

"Can I help you with anything?" I was acutely aware that Tessa was still in the kitchen while we were sitting around the table. It made me uncomfortable. She wasn't a servant, and I didn't want her to feel like one.

"No, I'm fine," Tessa insisted, cutting into a loaf of round bread with a serrated knife. "Just cutting this up, and I'll be over."

I shrugged and helped myself to a bowlful of the stew. I could see bacon, sausage, plenty of onions, and potatoes. I thought of the potato Tessa had been holding when I first met her and suppressed a laugh.

Finally, Tessa set the bread down. "Here we go," she said cheerfully. "Sorry for the wait."

Marcel took a piece eagerly, holding it under his long nose. "It smells," he said, "delightful."

"I hope it's okay," Tessa said, and I could see her twirling her fork around in her fingers like she was genuinely worried about it. I wanted to tell her that my dad and Marcel – not to mention me – were lucky to have her cooking for us at all, and she didn't need to worry about her bread being up to Marcel's standards.

But that, I thought, would make my dad give me that look and possibly repeat his sentiments about not 'interfering' with his ghostwriter.

· · · · • · • · · ·

"That was delicious," Alan declared, wiping his mouth and sighing with satisfaction. He put his spoon down in his bowl with a clatter.

"It was," Marcel agreed before I could say the same without seeming like I hadn't thought of it myself. Which was a shame, because it *had* been delicious, and Tessa deserved to know that.

"Shall we start the next episode of that Scandi crime drama you're forcing me to watch?" Alan said, looking at Marcel. "What was it? *The Bridge*?"

"Oh, I've heard that's good," Tessa said mildly as she started clearing the plates.

"Better than anything the Americans can come up with." My father shot me a pointed look as though he expected me to defend the American television industry.

"Probably," I said with a shrug, not wanting an argument. As soon as Marcel and my father had left the room, I stood. "I'll help you clean up."

"You don't need to do that! It's my job."

"Is it, though?" I couldn't help asking. "I know you're doing the housekeeping, but does that mean they never put their own plates in the dishwasher?"

"That was never specifically mentioned in my contract." I could see Tessa was uncomfortable. "I don't mind, anyway. And your dad…"

"Marcel's perfectly able-bodied," I pointed out. "And so am I." I opened the dishwasher and began loading it with plates.

"I don't mind," Tessa said falteringly. "You don't have to do this."

"I don't have anything to do, really. Let me make myself useful. It will be good for my self-esteem." I gave her a grin, which she reluctantly returned.

"Well, if you put it like that..." Tessa acquiesced. "I guess I know what you mean. Keeping busy stops me from overthinking. In theory, anyway."

I groaned. "I know what that's like," I confided. "Maybe that was why I let myself get so caught up with my work for years. I didn't have much time to even think about anything else. And I thought it would be great to finally take a break, but..." I shook my head and pretended to concentrate very hard on wedging a frying pan into the back of the dishwasher.

"Well, this is a huge change. Maybe you just need a chance to get used to having some time for yourself before you go and make any big decisions about what's next."

"That's very kind of you," I said, still wrestling with the pan. "I don't think it's good for me, not having a plan. But I still don't know what I should be planning."

"Maybe you should start a podcast. That's what most men do when they don't know what to do with their lives."

"That is a cruel, unfair and totally accurate stereotype. Actually, I do listen to a lot of podcasts. At the gym, usually."

"Oh, so do I! When I'm out for a walk or doing crochet."

"You crochet?" Of course, she crocheted. Tessa was the epitome of all that was wholesome. Crochet was a given.

"Yep. Nana taught me. It's handy because I feel like I'm doing something productive even when I'm meant to be relaxing. And it stops me from biting my nails."

"You bite your nails?" I looked at her hands then and saw that her fingernails were short, neat, and painted a glossy red. "It doesn't look like it."

"Acrylics." Tessa drummed them on the counter to demonstrate the difference in sound. "I started getting them to break the habit. They're too thick to bite."

"Smart," I said. "So, what do you listen to while you're crocheting?" If I had to hazard a guess, I would have thought something as wholesome as Tessa herself. Maybe *This American Life* or *Stuff You Should Know*.

"True crime, mostly."

I gaped at her, probably looking incredibly stupid with my mouth hanging open. "Seriously?"

"Well, yeah," Tessa frowned. "Is that weird?"

"Coming from you, definitely," I admitted and then wished I hadn't. "I mean, I don't know. You seem like..." I trailed off.

"Like the kind of person who doesn't like true crime?" Tessa's tongue was between her teeth like she was teasing me, which sent a thrill surging through my body that I was going to ignore, thank you very much.

"I guess I was wrong to assume," I said. "I like true crime too. Do you listen to *My Favourite Murder*?"

"Oh yeah, that's a good one. But I'm trying to get more into Australian ones now that I'm here."

"Definitely try *Teacher's Pet*. I mean, it's creepy as hell, but—"

"Trust me," Tessa said, giving me that teasing smile again. "I like creepy as hell." She shut the dishwasher, turned it on, and I suddenly realised I didn't have any reason to linger.

"I should go and..." I hoped she wouldn't ask what I was going to go and do.

"Yeah, me too," Tessa said, nodding. "I'm trying to finish crocheting a beach cover-up for my sister Michelle's birthday. She's promised to take us all somewhere nice to celebrate, but she says that every year. Work always comes up!"

"Well, good luck, I guess? Do you need good luck when you're crocheting?"

"Oh, definitely," Tessa said, looking at me for a long moment. "Have a good night, Dylan."

As she disappeared, I realised I still hadn't complimented her on the Dublin Coddle.

Tessa was... I didn't know what she was. Interesting, I knew that much. Tessa was interesting. She seemed so cheerful, so bright, but there was something brittle and fragile under that gap-toothed smile. Something she was trying to hide. I realised I was disappointed that the dishwasher had taken so little time to load; I hadn't wanted to stop talking to her.

But I decided I wouldn't let myself examine that thought too closely. Instead, I went into the living room to watch the Scandinavian crime drama with my dad and Marcel, and tried not to think too hard about anything. Especially not about Tessa.

5 Tessa

I PLUCKED AT MY bikini bottom, trying to stretch the fabric to cover slightly more of my arse, but it was a losing battle.

"Why am I so pale?" I asked the mirror, which was propped artistically against one wall. "I should have done the whole fake tan thing."

The mirror didn't answer, which was probably for the best. I was more than capable of coming up with everything that was wrong with my body without any suggestions from my reflection.

The bikini had seemed like such a good idea when I had ordered it online. It was red with white polka dots and had adorable ruffles; I was going for a vintage bathing beauty vibe. But now, I saw only a deep-sea creature dredged up from the darkest depths of the Marianna trench and forced into an obnoxiously cheerful swimsuit as some kind of weird joke amusing only to marine biologists.

And while I knew there was technically nothing wrong with my body, the mirror seemed to disagree, even without speaking. If you asked my sisters, they'd tell you my hourglass figure was 'banging', but all I could imagine right now was the impossibly slender, bronzed goddesses who seemed to dominate Australian beaches. Abby would tell you that a bikini body was simply a body that happened to be wearing a bikini, but I wasn't so sure. Everything about me seemed to scream 'pasty British tourist who doesn't belong'.

I seriously considered putting on a thick tracksuit and climbing back into bed when my phone buzzed.

Abby: where are you? I got us a great spot!

Attached was a photo of my sister wearing huge sunglasses and a smile, splayed out on a beach towel. The sand was glistening gold, and the water did look invitingly cool and blue...

I screwed my eyes shut. "Okay, I'm going to do this," I said firmly, even though my body was screaming that the safest option was getting back in bed. But I couldn't disappoint my sister. The thought of doing that was worse than the fear of my pasty body being laughed off the beach. My brain was caught between two warring factions of anxiety, and I could feel my heart thudding painfully, my stomach tight and tense.

Before I lost my nerve, I slipped on a pair of the flip-flops Australians somehow thought it appropriate to call 'thongs', pulled a floaty linen smock over my head, picked up my sunglasses, and forced my feet to carry me out the door.

I didn't go via the main house. I told myself it was because I didn't want Alan to come up with any last-minute jobs for me, even though it was my day off. But really, it was because I didn't want to risk Dylan seeing me in my bikini, even if my brightly patterned smock was currently covering my body.

"Not that it matters what he thinks of me in swimwear," I muttered, but that was a total lie. The clench in my stomach told me in no uncertain terms that I absolutely cared what he thought, and I didn't want to allow him the opportunity to pass any kind of judgement.

When I reached the beach, a little of my tension subsided simply because it was such a stunningly beautiful day. The morning sun was hot in the sky, the ocean smelled impossibly inviting, and it seemed everyone I passed was smiling.

"Finally!" Abby sighed dramatically as I sat down beside her on a towel. "I was beginning to think you were going to bail on me."

"I wouldn't do that."

"I know," Abby gave me a one-armed squeeze. "Because you're a very good sister."

"Maybe not that good," I cautioned. "I was seriously tempted to bail. Me and swimwear? It's a toxic relationship. I think we should break up for good."

"Don't be ridiculous," Abby rolled her eyes. "You're a freaking babe. You should be proud of your body!"

"I'm pasty," I complained. "Why didn't I get the tanning gene? I think that was cruel and discriminatory."

"Take it up with Dad's balls. Or Mum's uterus, I suppose. Maybe it created an environment toxic to sperm carrying the tanning gene."

"Why would you make me think about our parents conceiving me? That's cruel as well. And possibly still discriminatory."

"It's all biology, babe." Abby lowered her sunglasses to look at me critically. "You are wearing sunscreen, though, aren't you? You're a proper English rose, and I don't want to see you cook like a rotisserie chicken."

"Thanks for that comparison. And, yes, I'm wearing sunscreen. Head to toe. Water resistant."

"Then what are we waiting for? Let's get in!" Abby threw off her tie-dyed kaftan to reveal a sleek purple swimsuit that was technically a one-piece but had so many cutouts that it covered less of her than my bikini. Not that she had anything to worry about, she had inherited our dad's olive skin, unlike poor pasty me.

"Now?" I was playing for time. "I need to...acclimatise to the beach. Get used to it. Then maybe I can consider actually getting into the water."

"Tessa, you're not an endangered reptile being released into a new habitat. You don't need to acclimatise." Abby looked over the top of her sunglasses once more. "And besides, it's only going to get busier. More people. So, if we get in now..."

"You make a fair point." I tugged up my smock unwillingly.

Abby let out a loud wolf whistle (I had also missed out on the gene that made one capable of wolf-whistling). "Look at you! Titties for days!"

"Shut up," I said, my head caught in floaty linen. "Stop talking about my breasts."

"Just saying, they look great." Abby helpfully extracted me from the smock.

"I know you're being supportive, but it would help me more if we pretended that I was in a head-to-toe wetsuit. Actually that's a great idea. Do you think they sell those at the surf shop? I could go and buy one right now and—"

Abby yanked me unceremoniously to my feet. "Enough," she said. "You're getting in that water. Ideally, you'll feel like a flawless water nymph and know that these mere mortals are lucky to catch a glimpse of your ethereal beauty. But I'll settle for you just getting in."

The smell of salt water was heavy in the air, and the heat was becoming almost oppressive. A dip in the water sounded incredible, and besides, wasn't that why I had come to Australia? Sunshine, beaches, nothing like Birmingham?

"Fine," I said. "Race you!" I dashed forward, the sand hot and slippery beneath my feet. I heard Abby laughing as she ran after me. Hopefully she didn't realise that my impromptu race was to ensure that my bikini-clad body was visible to the other beachgoers for the shortest possible amount of time.

• • • ● • ● • • •

"That water was much colder than it looked," I said, wrapping myself up in a towel and shivering.

"I have to agree," Abby was drying herself off and arranging her legs to dry in the sun. "But the views are incredible." She inclined her head at a group of men with surfboards making their way down the beach. They looked like a tourism ad for Australia; all sun-kissed skin, lean muscle, and white-toothed smiles.

"So, this is why you love the beach so much. I see it all now."

"One of the reasons," Abby corrected, pulling her phone from her pocket. "Let's call Michelle, make her jealous."

A moment later, Michelle's face appeared on the screen. In her tailored business suit, she looked every inch the sophisticated career woman, but I could see she was tired. "What's up?"

"Look where we are!" Abby crowed and turned the phone to pan over the beach, ensuring that the group of surfers were fully visible to our sister.

Michelle let out a groan. "Are you doing this just to torture me? I'm up to my eyeballs in end-of-quarter reports, and you have to show me sexy surfers without a care in the world! You two must be so relaxed right now."

"Well, it's me. So relaxed isn't really an option."

"Oh, Tess." Michelle scrunched up her nose. "You do make life hard for yourself."

"It's not me! It's my brain. Take it up with her."

"Tessa isn't even interested in the surfer gods. I think she's all hung up on this Dylan guy."

"I am not," I objected. "I haven't even mentioned him!"

"You have, actually," Abby said. "He doesn't like Guinness, his favourite podcast is *Teacher's Pet*, and he has an adorable godson called Benji."

I chewed my lip. "So, I'm not allowed to make a friend now? I mean, we practically live in the same house!"

"You're allowed a friend," Michelle said. "Just sounds like you want him to be way more than that."

"He's my boss's son! And I told you about how Alan specifically told me not to get involved with him?"

"You did," Abby said. "Though he did encourage you to have a good time. What was it, soundproof walls? You could test it out with one of those hotties. What about the one with the curly brown hair?"

I looked over at where the aforementioned curly-haired surfer was paddling out into the deep water, his admittedly impressively muscular back glittering in the sunshine. "Not my type."

"You *must* be hung up on Dylan," Abby declared. "Because, babe, that surfer is everyone's type."

"Not mine," I shook my head. "And I told you, I'm not hung up on Dylan. First off, he's my boss's son. What if something happened, and it got weird, and I lost my job? Potentially ruined my professional reputation and became unemployed? Then there's the fact that he's going through some kind of career crisis and doesn't know what to do with himself. What if something happens, then he decides to move back to San Fran, and I'm all heartbroken?"

I took a quick breath and then continued. "Also, he's totally out of my league. He's a tech millionaire. I'm just a ghostwriter who makes stew for his dad. Even if we did get together, sooner or later, he'd realise he could do much better. Also resulting in my heartbreak. So, nothing will happen with Dylan. Because it's a terrible idea. For the reasons above."

There was silence. Abby and Michelle exchanged a look via the phone.

"I see," Michelle said finally.

"You clearly haven't thought about it much."

"I think about everything a lot," I said, embarrassed that I had shared so many of my worst-case scenarios with my sisters.

"Oh, Tess," Abby wrapped her arm around me. "You're amazing at coming up with disasters. If you get sick of ghostwriting, you could totally go into risk management."

"You could," Michelle agreed, looking as though she were seriously considering it. "But you're a kickass ghostwriter. I read that autobiography you did of that kid's TV presenter. That bit where the little girl in hospital sang her show's theme song made me cry."

"Thanks," I said, shifting on the towel. "But can we talk about something else? Like whether you'd prefer blonde spikey surfer or dreadlock surfer, Abby?"

"Spikey hair, hands down. I can't do white guys with dreadlocks. Not even with a body like that."

"I should go," Michelle sighed. "You two have fun. And try not to worry too much, Tess. Although..."

"What?"

"Did you put on sunscreen? You look kind of pink."

Abby looked at me, taking off her sunglasses. "Oh, Tessa! You're a lobster!"

"I have to go," Michelle said again. "But you should get out of the sun." The call ended, and Abby stared at me.

"Is it really that bad?" I held up my arm, and yep, definitely pink. "How is that fair? I put on a ton of sunscreen." I pulled the bottle from my bag and brandished it at Abby.

"Wait, this is from Boots."

"Yes?"

"As in, from England."

"Why wouldn't it be? I'm from England. So are you, for that matter." I was starting to feel uncomfortably warm.

"You don't use English sunscreen in Australia!" Abby put a hand to my forehead. "That's why you're so burnt. Especially," she looked at the bottle again, "since this expired three years ago."

"How bad is it?"

Abby screwed up her mouth, looking like she was sucking a lemon before taking a shot of tequila. "Let's just say I think our beach day is over."

I let out a wail and pulled my smock over my still wet body. "How long am I going to be bright red? I mean, will Alan and Marcel and...everyone see me like this?"

"Well, think of it like this," Abby said cheerfully, placing a cool hand on my burning shoulder. "You won't have to worry about being pale for a while."

"I take it all back! White is much better than red."

"I don't know if you've got much choice," Abby said, rolling up her towel and stuffing it into her bag. "Come on, let's get going. We can find something at the chemist for you."

"I'm going to get skin cancer," I said, covering my hot face with my hands. "Super skin cancer. I'm going to shrivel up and die like a sad, cancer-ridden raisin."

"I think it takes more than one round of sunburn for that," Abby said levelly, leading me off the sand towards the main street, which was thankfully shaded by towering palm trees, and towards a small pharmacy.

"I just want to go home. And drink a ton of water."

"Chemist," Abby insisted, trying to drag me forcibly down the street, her hand rough on my tender skin.

"No. I'm going home. I want a cold shower and a nap."

"Do you have heat stroke?" Abby pressed a cool hand to my forehead, and I yelped at the contrast.

"No," I insisted, though I did feel ready to faint. "Cold shower, nap. That will be good enough."

· · · ● · ● · ● · · ·

Four hours later, I was more than ready to admit that a cold shower, a nap, and rehydrating were not good enough. Drinking approximately an Olympic swimming pool's worth of icy water and taking a handful of paracetamol had cleared the fog in my brain but my skin still felt like I had taken a dip in an active volcano rather than in the inviting waters of Brekkie Beach.

"It hurts," I said out loud, wrinkling my nose and immediately regretting it, because the tiniest of facial expressions was painful. I looked at myself in the mirror and groaned. I was so very red, and when I pulled at my bikini, I could see the sharp contrast against the white skin that hadn't been touched by the cruel sun.

"I should have listened to Abby," I said mournfully, patting myself with the damp washcloth that provided a minuscule amount of relief. "I blame sunstroke."

Sunstroke or not, it was becoming increasingly clear that I needed to do something about my condition. There was nothing else for it. I had to go into the house and ask Alan, or possibly Marcel, if there was anything in the medicine cabinet that might soothe the skin of one very foolish English ghostwriter. Maybe Alan had some powerful painkillers lurking in a drawer. Painkillers sounded great.

The only problem was...

"Dylan won't be there," I told myself. "It's a beautiful day; he'll be with Tad and Benji, doing something adorable. Or he'll be on a date at the beach with some girl who isn't prone to lobster-like skin conditions. He won't be there. It will be fine."

As I made my way out of the studio, the churning in my stomach told me that I didn't entirely believe myself. I pushed open the glass sliding door to the kitchen and immediately bumped into...

"Tessa?" Dylan looked down at me, concern evident on his far-too handsome face. "Are you okay? You look like—"

"A freaking lobster who's been in the pot for hours?" I supplied. "I'm aware." The only good thing about being this sunburnt was that my blush would be invisible on my already pink face.

"Did you go to the beach?" Dylan looked like he was trying not to laugh.

"Yes," I said. "And before you ask, I did wear sunscreen. But apparently, English sunscreen is no match for the Aussie sun."

Dylan's face contorted in sympathy. "I guess not. Have you put anything on it?"

"Uh, no," I admitted. "Abby wanted me to go to the chemist, but I just came home and had a cold shower."

"I see." His mouth was still tight. "What you need is aloe vera gel."

"Will that help?" I almost didn't care how pathetically plaintive I sounded. "I mean, is there any in the house?"

"Should be some in here," Dylan said, opening a cupboard and sticking his head inside. "Marcel gets burnt easily too."

"Marcel goes to the beach?" I was briefly distracted by that brand new and totally unexpected information. "Really? Does he actually swim?"

"Apparently. But I've never seen it." He paused. "Maybe he's got a black rash vest, too."

"With a turtleneck?" I ventured and was pleased when Dylan let out a small breath of laughter.

"Definitely," he agreed. "Here it is!" Triumphantly, he pulled a bottle with vividly green contents from the cupboard.

"It's not out of date, is it?"

Dylan looked at the bottom. "Nope," he said. "Still good."

I moved to take it from him, but Dylan held on. "I thought...I could help you do your back. It might be hard for you to reach."

My stomach dropped right out of me onto the kitchen floor, oozing my half-digested breakfast over the clean tiles. Okay, so it didn't really, but it felt like it did. Because Dylan had apparently just offered to rub aloe vera gel onto my very sore and extremely red back.

"Unless you're uncomfortable with that, in which case I'll leave you to it." Dylan set down the gel on the counter. "Just wanted to help out. You know how I need to feel useful right now."

Unless I was very much mistaken, he was trying to convince me to let him do this. Not that it meant anything. At least, not anything beyond simply wanting his dad's ghostwriter to become functional and less lobster-like as quickly as possible. I knew that. Even if my brain had already begun whizzing off in all sorts of exciting and terrifying directions. How would his hands feel on my skin?

And was this exactly the sort of charming entanglement that Alan had warned me against?

"I have to admit, I am in no position to reach my own back right now," I admitted. "I can barely lift my arms without intense pain."

"I'm sorry." Dylan looked like he really did feel sorry for me. I guessed I was a pity-worthy sight, bright red and wincing. Was I ever going to stop embarrassing myself in front of Dylan? What was next? He'd suddenly appear in the room the next time I was getting a Pap Smear?

"Uh, maybe if you sat here and leaned on the kitchen island?" Dylan motioned to a stool.

"Sure," I said, wincing as I sat down.

"Uh, you might need to take that off," Dylan nodded at the smock I was still wearing over my bikini. "So I can do your back. I mean, put this on your back." He held up the aloe vera as though warding off any unfortunate double entendré about doing me on my back. Even in my current state of extreme pain, I couldn't help imagining Dylan doing me in just about any position. I really needed to stop thinking about that.

"Oh, that makes sense," I said, not making eye contact as I peeled off my smock gingerly. I rested my cheek on the cool marble of the kitchen island and closed my eyes.

I heard Dylan flick open the cap of the aloe vera, and then came a sound very much like a loud, wet fart as he squirted it into his hand.

"That was the aloe vera. Not me."

"I'd never accuse you of making a sound like that."

"Hasn't Dad told you about my fart joke phase?"

"I thought men never got over the—" I stopped halfway through my sentence to gasp at the sudden feeling of the cool gel between my shoulder blades.

"Is that okay?"

"Really good!" I realised how that might sound. "I mean, it's fine. Just cold."

"Cold is good," Dylan said, slowly and carefully massaging the gel into my super-heated skin. Whether he wanted to avoid hurting me, touching me inappropriately, or inadvertently turning me on, I didn't know. Probably all of the above. He must know that a guy like him offering to rub gel on my back had a certain erotic appeal, even in my lobster-like state. Lobsters were, apparently, more than capable of arousal.

I was suddenly aware of my breathing and how loud it was in the silent kitchen. Was it unnaturally loud? Did it sound like sex breathing? Did Dylan think that? I tried very hard to breathe more quietly and succeeded only in coughing.

Those strong, gentle hands on my back stopped abruptly. "Are you okay?"

"Fine!" I gasped. "Just had something caught in my throat."

"I'm almost done." Dylan's voice was low, and my heart was ready to beat right out of my chest as his hands moved lower, smoothing over my back and brushing over my hips. "You need to be more careful. Your skin's so delicate."

Delicate? Was that a good thing? Probably not. He must mean 'delicate' as in 'incredibly pasty and prone to turn red at the faintest hint of UV', not delicate as in 'deliciously soft and I would very much like to touch said skin under different circumstances.'

"Just a bit more here—" Dylan's fingers were on the nape of my neck, and I couldn't help the shiver than ran through me at his touch. He couldn't know I was so sensitive there. He was leaning close, and I was sure I could feel his breath ghosting over my ear and—

"Get out of it, you bloody cat!" Something pink and swift flashed across my line of vision, and I let out a yelp as paws pressed painfully into my tender skin.

"Ow!" I stood up just in time to see Cyndi, Marcel's hairless cat of uncertain temperament, streaking out of the kitchen, a green handprint on her flank.

"Are you okay?" Dylan looked concerned. "Did she scratch you?"

"No, she just stepped on me. Which is unfortunate, but I'll live."

"She might not. I'll skin her one of these days. Turn her into a set of nice leather gloves."

"Slow down there, Buffalo Bill."

"I should have known you'd be a Lecter fan." Dylan was smiling. "With your true crime obsession."

"*The Silence of the Lambs* is probably my all-time favourite movie," I told him. "And *Red Dragon* was pretty solid. The others, though?"

"Yeah, it got weird. Especially the books."

"The books got very weird," I said, remembering the ending of *Hannibal*. "That's the great thing about ghost-writing autobiographies. I never have to come up with a sequel."

Dylan chuckled, wiping his hands on a tea towel. Suddenly, I was aware that I was wearing only a bikini and my very pink – though now slightly less painful – skin.

"Um, thanks again for doing this," I said, picking up the bottle of gel and not looking at him as I pretended to examine the ingredients list like I had the faintest idea of what they meant. "I can reach the rest myself, I think."

And that was a stupid thing to say. Of course, I could reach the rest of my own body. What, did I think Dylan was going to rub aloe vera all over my thighs, my hips, my stomach—

I was breathing loudly again, wasn't I?

"Uh, probably best not to mention this to my dad. He might think—" Dylan swallowed. "I just wanted to do something helpful, for a change."

"This was very helpful," I said earnestly because it was true. Dylan could have just laughed at me or left me to find the aloe vera by myself.

"This is the only even remotely productive thing I've done today." He raised his eyebrows. "How sad is that? Really, I should be thanking you."

"You're allowed to take a break from work," I said, keeping my tone neutral.

"I know, but—" Dylan shook his head. "It's a lot sometimes. Not knowing what I'm going to do next. Knowing that my dad and Marcel expect so much from me, expect me to have a plan. And I'm just...existing. Sitting around and waiting for some kind of inspiration to strike me." He sighed again. "Sorry, I shouldn't have said all that. It's not your problem."

"But I do get it," I said, turning the bottle around and around in my hands. "Worrying about what you're going to do. I worry pretty much twenty-four seven. Things in the past, things that may or may not happen in the future. It's a wonder I have time for a job."

"Have you ever seen anyone about that?" Dylan asked, looking at me with an intensity that surprised me. "Like a doctor?"

"About worrying?" I screwed up my face. "I've always been this way. It's no big deal."

"It sounds like it could be," Dylan said. "I mean, you do a pretty good job of hiding it. But even then, it's a lot to carry around."

"I'm used to it," I insisted. Why had I told him I worry a lot? Dylan clearly thought I was unwell. And possibly unstable. And that was just what I didn't need my boss's son – who I was pretending I didn't have inappropriate thoughts about – to think of me. "I don't think I need to see anyone. It's not that bad, really."

Dylan chewed his lip. "I'm seeing a careers advisor next week," he offered. "Not by choice, I admit. I kind of lost a bet with Tad."

"That could be a good thing," I said, thrilled we were no longer talking about me. "I mean, having someone to discuss all of this with."

"I doubt it. But I'm a man of my word, and Tad can squat more plates than you'd think."

"You lost a bet at the gym?" I couldn't hide my surprise.

"Don't rub it in. It's been a huge blow to my masculine ego. I'll have to chop some wood or grow a beard to recover."

"I don't think you'd suit a beard. But wood chopping, I could get behind. My Nana used to have a wood-burning fireplace; it smelled amazing."

"I'll have to get myself an axe," Dylan said, miming chopping down a tree. Then he paused again. "You should think about seeing someone. If Tad could get me to do it, you should too."

"Seeing a careers advisor is pretty different from seeing a doctor," I said, my lips curling as I said the word. I didn't like the way it felt in my mouth. "I mean, doctors need to spend their time with people who are actually sick. I'm perfectly fine; my brain's just a little more creative than I'd like it to be. Occupational hazard, maybe."

"If you say so. But you should think about it."

"I'll think about it," I promised, nodding too hard. I probably looked like one of those unfortunate plastic dogs that some drivers felt the need to put on their dashboards. And it was true that I'd think about it. Dylan thought I needed to see a doctor. Well, there it was – a new and exciting way in which I'd embarrassed myself in front of him. I'd be analysing this hot mess for days. "Uh, thanks again for the aloe vera."

"Just promise you'll take care of yourself, okay?" The corners of his eyes crinkled as he smiled. "Or I'll have to get one of those sunscreen sprays and ambush you every time you leave the house."

"It puts the lotion on its skin, or else it gets the hose again?" Since when had quoting fictional serial killers felt so flirtatious?

"Exactly," Dylan said, his eyes still crinkled. "Take care, Tessa."

And then he disappeared out of the kitchen, leaving me holding the bottle of aloe vera and gazing after him.

6 Dylan

Maybe the first red flag was that Julius Persimmon didn't have an office. Despite his website listing a CBD address, I had been instructed to meet him at a coffee shop. At least I didn't think I'd have any trouble recognising the guy. Every email I had received from him included a massive image of his face in the banner, and I didn't think I'd forget those bushy eyebrows – or handlebar moustache – in a hurry.

I spotted him as soon as I made my way into the coffee shop at the appointed time. Julius was seated at a corner table with a laptop open and a hardcover book, also bearing his face, propped up next to it.

"Hello." I offered him my hand out of politeness. "I'm Dylan Huxley."

"Dylan!" Julius stood up and grasped my hand tightly. His handshake was vigorous, but I couldn't help noticing his hand was unpleasantly moist, like he had used an excessive amount of hand cream. I really hoped that was the reason. "How delightful to meet you."

"So, how does this work?" I sat down and inched my chair back slightly because Julius was leaning forward and studying my face with the intensity you'd expect from a dermatologist, not a careers advisor.

Julius stared at me a few moments longer before he answered.

"It can work," he began, sounding very excited, "any way you want it to. It's your life, Dylan! It's not a dress rehearsal; it's opening night! You're the one who chooses your performance, so make it a show to remember!"

"Right." It took a lot of self-control to stop myself from laughing. I considered just getting up and leaving. Despite Julius' sweaty enthusiasm, I was sure I could outrun him. But my wager with Tad had demanded that I got through an entire appointment, and the thought of finding someone else and starting this whole process again was nightmarish enough to keep me in my seat.

"I've done my research on you, Dylan," Julius told me, taking a sip from a tiny cup that probably held a piccolo latte. "Such a talent! Such fire in your blood! You did very well with Space2Spare. An ingenious idea!"

"Uh, I guess it was." There was no point pretending otherwise. "But I'm not sure what I want to do now. That's why I'm here."

"You need to find your true passion for the next chapter of your life!" Julius threw out a dramatic hand. "And I, my friend, can guide you."

"Sounds good." A total lie. The only thing that sounded good was the thought of this meeting being over.

"Now, to begin finding your passion, we just need to go through some questions," Julius fiddled with his laptop. "We need to discover which personality archetype you fall into. But I have a feeling you're going to be a lobster."

"A lobster? I don't remember that one from Myer-Briggs." I couldn't entirely hide my smirk. But at the word 'lobster', I thought of Tessa standing in my dad's kitchen, her face bright pink, biting her lip and deciding that yes, she would let me rub aloe vera onto her back. I felt a clench in my stomach at the memory of her soft skin under my fingertips, and— I decided it was best not to think about Tessa right now.

"No, no," Julius looked offended at the mention of Myer-Briggs. "This is far more accurate, my friend. There are four personality types. The crab works well in a group but can only move from side to side. He can't forge his own path, you see? A seahorse is a hard worker, taking on too much because he wants to be liked. Did you know male seahorses are the ones to carry the babies? Coral is immovable – comfortable where it is and resistant to change. And finally, the lobster. A lobster is a leader; independent, brave, and he'll climb out of a boiling pot to rescue himself!"

"Okay," I said, swallowing the horrified laughter that threatened to bubble up in my throat. Apparently, my careers advisor believed that all people could be defined by their resemblance to sea creatures.

"This is all my original work, of course," Julius continued. He tapped the hardcover book, which I saw was titled *The Ocean in You*. "I don't use commercial tools. None of those standardised questionnaires!"

I managed another forced smile and nodded. I didn't trust myself to speak.

"So, first question. Would you rather be marooned on a desert island or appear naked at your birthday party?"

There was silence, during which I stared at Julius, waiting for him to reveal that the question was a joke. When he didn't, I cleared my throat.

"I thought this was supposed to be about my career?"

"Oh, it is, Dylan." Julius didn't break eye contact. "It is."

• • • • ● • ● • • • •

Dylan: career counsellor was a total waste of time. he's nuts. told me i'm a proud lobster and should consider a career in the performing arts.

Tad: performing arts? has he seen you dance? you're bad even for a white guy

Tad: that's what you get for choosing the first google result

Tad: ...why a lobster?

Dylan: my dancing is flawless

Dylan: i'll tell you the rest when I see you

Tad: <thumbs up emoji> <lobster emoji> <laughing emoji>

I tucked my phone away then, shaking my head and grinning in spite of myself.

At the back of the ferry, I could see a family with two delighted small children peering over the edge and shrieking with joy every time a wave rocked the boat. It made me imagine that maybe, one day, I'd be taking Benji on ferry rides into the city. A dinosaur exhibit, maybe. A pretentious children's art class at the Museum of Modern Art. An obnoxious animated movie and all the ice cream he could eat.

That was, of course, assuming I was still in Sydney as baby Benji turned into boy Benji. And given I had no idea what I was going to do with myself, I could hardly guarantee that.

When the ferry docked, I slowly made my way back to the house, enjoying the walk. Julius Persimmon had been useless – except for supplying a great dinner party story – but the trip had been unexpectedly pleasant. My mood had lifted as the ferry made its way across the sparkling water, away from the city and towards the serenity of Brekkie Beach.

My keys were in my hand to open the door when it flew open to reveal Tessa, now far less lobster-like, and pulling behind her...

"Is that a grocery cart?" It was tartan. Precisely the kind that little old ladies used.

"Yes," Tessa looked down at the cart. "It's much better than lugging all the shopping in bags and cutting off the circulation in my fingers."

"Why don't you take the car?"

"I don't actually have my license." Tessa bit her lip. I noticed, yet again, that little gap between her teeth and how invitingly plump and full that lower lip was. Not inviting, I told myself firmly. Appealing, maybe, but not inviting. I hadn't forgotten my dad's warning, nor did I intend to let myself get drawn into anything. Inviting lower lips be damned. "It's not as weird as it sounds," she added defensively. "Back home, plenty of people don't drive. I lived near the city, so walking or getting the bus was easy."

"I'm not judging." I stood aside to let Tessa and her cart out of the front door. "I didn't have a car in San Fran."

"Ooh, did you get the trolley?" Tessa asked eagerly. "It always looked so fun in movies."

"I'm going to have to disappoint you and say that I got Ubers everywhere."

"Well, that's probably faster but much less aesthetic." Tessa tilted her head as though considering the matter. "I'd better get going; it's a big list today. Marcel found out I've never been to Belgium, and he wants to make dinner tonight. I'm hoping that means waffles."

"It probably doesn't," I hated to disappoint her. I nudged the grocery cart with my foot. "Are you going to be able to fit everything in there?"

"I'll manage."

"I'll come with you," I decided suddenly. "To carry things."

"You don't need to do that! I've always managed before; it won't kill me."

"It's not like I've got anything else to do," I pointed out. "Come on, let me carry some groceries. I can feel all masculine and useful, lifting the heavy stuff."

"It's just grocery shopping," Tessa protested. "It's not exactly an exciting outing. Though I hate to prevent you from displaying your manly strength and vigour." She grinned for a moment and then covered her mouth as though worried she had teased me too much. She hadn't. I liked it. Liked it more than I should.

"That's where you're wrong," I said, taking the cart from her and pulling it towards the footpath. "I barely set foot in a supermarket when I lived in San Fran, and I haven't been to one since I got home either. So this is very exciting."

"Well, in that case, I'll allow it. But do you really want to pull the cart? I mean, it's kind of..."

"Don't tell me you think my masculinity is that fragile? Other men will see me with this bad boy and know it's okay to embrace grandma chic. I'm a trendsetter."

"Oh, I don't doubt it."

As we walked along the path, Tessa looked up at me. "You didn't do any grocery shopping in San Fran? What did you eat?"

"I got meals delivered," I told her. "It was more efficient, and there are hundreds of apps to deliver anything you could possibly want right to your door. You could get groceries delivered here, you know. It would save you the walk."

"I like walking. And I'd never get my groceries delivered. No way would I trust them to choose the best avocados or the milk with the furthest use-by date."

"That's probably true," I mused. "Maybe there's a market for an elite grocery app, where you can be guaranteed they'll pick the best of everything."

"Well, if there is, you'd be the guy to make it happen," Tessa said. "Do you want to do something like that? Another app?"

I opened my mouth to say 'maybe', but then shut it again. Did I want to do that? If I did, I would have been better off staying in San Francisco. But here I was in Brekkie Beach, about as far as you could get from Silicon Valley. "Not really," I said finally, stopping to punch the button at one of Brekkie Beach's three pedestrian crossings.

"I didn't think so. You don't really talk much about tech stuff."

"I guess not," I said, surprised by how perceptive she was. I probably shouldn't have been. After all, she was a ghostwriter; she'd be good at picking up the patterns, the narrative, in what people said about themselves.

"Speaking of." Tessa looked up at me again, her blue eyes clear and bright. "Didn't you have that appointment with the careers advisor? How did it go?"

At that, I let out a groan that was much louder than I meant it to be. It startled a mother pushing a chubby toddler in a stroller, and Tessa laughed.

"That bad?"

"Definitely that bad. He thinks I'm a lobster."

"A lobster?" Tessa wrinkled her nose. "I thought we established that was me, with the sunburn."

"No, he's got this theory that everyone fits into one of four personality types," I began and explained the rest of Julius Persimmon's theory on the short walk to the grocery store that had served Brekkie Beach since before I was born.

When I finished telling the story of my career counselling session, Tessa shot me a sympathetic look. "Yeah, I think that groan was entirely fair," she said, pulling a notebook and pen from her pocket.

"You're very organised," I said, nodding at the notebook.

"I've got to be. Can you imagine your dad's face if I forgot the organic rye sourdough?"

"They sell that here?"

"Oh yeah," Tessa said, pushing her way through the little gates and leading me into the fruit and vegetables. "This place is pretty fancy."

"So I see." I picked up what was apparently a dragon fruit and examined it. "Last time I was here, they only had mandarins, apples, and bananas. Plums, if you were lucky."

"Well, I guess Brekkie Beach is getting kind of fancy," Tessa said. "Especially compared to where I used to live. But it's not too crowded, which is nice. I think the long drive into the city puts people off, but it's only twenty minutes on the ferry. Which you know, of course. Sorry."

"You don't have to apologise." I spotted an array of familiar potatoes. "Hey, are those Kipflers?"

Tessa's face turned as pink as it had at the peak of her sunburn. "I thought you were too jet-lagged to remember that."

"Sorry." I couldn't help grinning. "It was pretty funny."

"Mortifying," Tessa corrected.

"I can pretend I forgot if it makes you feel better," I said as Tessa critically selected red onions, putting them into a hessian produce bag. It made sense that she'd be responsible enough to not use plastic and to actually remember to bring her reusable bags.

"I don't think it would."

"Have you thought any more about what I said?" I asked carefully. "About seeing someone, about your anxiety? Someone more helpful than Julius, ideally."

Tessa shook her head so hard that her bun wobbled from side to side. "No," she said. "Like I told you, I'm honestly fine. Just a bit of a worrywart. And it's not like I let it control me. I mean, I moved here, even though it terrified the crap out of me."

"But there are other things you haven't done that you wanted to because of your anxiety, right?"

Tessa grimaced and bent her head over the asparagus with more attention than I thought asparagus truly warranted. "Maybe. But I can handle it."

"I know you can. I mean, you're clearly handling it. I just..." I let out a sigh. "You've been nice to me. And I appreciate that. A lot, actually. Because I don't know what

I'm doing with myself right now, and it's shit. You hide your anxiety pretty well, but I bet it makes you feel like crap. And you're a nice person. Nice people shouldn't have to suffer unnecessarily."

"I'm not suffering," Tessa said to the asparagus and not to me. "I just..."

"You should at least make an appointment with the doctor. Because if you don't, I'll do it for you."

"You wouldn't do that!" Tessa looked up at me, wide-eyed, her tongue just behind that gap in her teeth.

A jolt in my stomach made me realise that, while I had been joking, I actually would. I would make the appointment for Tessa if she didn't do it herself. Because I cared about her. Which was ridiculous; I didn't even know her that well. I just knew that she was kind, and clever, and funny, and willing to disagree with my dad despite her anxiety and...

Shit. I did care.

"You wouldn't," Tessa said again, shaking her head as though dismissing the thought. "I told you. I'm okay. And I'm so lucky. I mean, I live in Brekkie Beach, and I've got a pretty great job. Do you know how many people would love to get paid for any kind of writing gig? Really, I'm super fortunate, and so—"

"So, you think you're not allowed to get help because you're lucky?" I suggested and examined a basket of chillies that claimed to be imported from Mexico.

"Something like that. I had this plan. If I could do one really big thing that scared me – like moving here – then I'd prove to myself that all of my regular anxiety was stupid, and it would go away."

"How's that worked out?"

"No comment," Tessa said as she pulled the shopping trolley away from the vegetables and towards the meat counter. "Marcel wants a kilo of eel fillets. Do you think he's expecting us to eat them?"

"That's a horrifying thought, but you're totally deflecting," I said, following her. "Look, you're obviously brave, moving here when it scared you—"

"It's not that brave, I had a job lined up, and my sister lives a few streets away—"

"It was brave," I cut her off. "And you're doing a great job. Dad and Marcel think the world of you; I'm pretty sure they like you better than me. And like I said, you've been kind to me, even though I've been a grumpy arsehole—"

"You were jetlagged! And you're working through stuff with your whole career thing."

"Don't make excuses for me," I said. "You're a good person, and you deserve to feel better. And if a doctor can help you do that, then you should make the damn appointment. You deserve it."

Tessa took a tiny breath and looked up at me again with those pale blue eyes. Her mouth was open, but she clearly didn't know what to say.

My hand twitched like it – totally independently of my brain – wanted to reach out to Tessa's, which was grasping the shopping trolley handle very tightly indeed. But before I could do something stupidly inappropriate, a cheerful voice interrupted us.

"What can I get for you, love?"

Tessa started and shook herself slightly before consulting her list. "A kilo of lamb cutlets, five hundred grams of prosciutto, and..." She wrinkled her nose. "A kilo of eel fillets."

The man behind the counter, clad in white, didn't even blink. "Coming right up."

"I'll make a bet with you," I said, my hands behind my back, so I didn't get any more stupid ideas about touching her. "We'll guess the total on the groceries. If I'm closer, you make an appointment with your doctor."

"And if I win?" Tessa raised her chin.

"What do you suggest?"

Tessa looked thoughtful. Then, a mischievous grin came over her face. "If I win, you'll borrow one of Marcel's turtlenecks and wear it until he says something."

"That would be hilarious. I might be tempted to do it anyway."

"Good, because you're going to lose," Tessa told me. "I've been playing guess the total with my sisters since I was a kid, and I'm the reigning champion. Not even Michelle can beat me, and she works in finance."

"And I haven't been to a grocery store in years. It's a challenge, then."

Tessa tilted her head. "I think you could pull off a turtleneck," she said thoughtfully. "But your shoulders are much broader than Marcel's, plus you're taller. It's going to look like a crop top."

"If I get stuck in it, I'm blaming you," I said, enjoying the banter.

"If you get stuck in it, I'm taking photos."

"So confident! What if I win?"

"Oh, I don't think I need to worry about that."

· · · ● ● · ● · · ·

"I don't know how you beat me," Tessa complained. "I haven't lost guess the total in years!"

"I clearly have skills you don't appreciate," I said, unwilling to admit my triumph was mostly the result of luck.

"Clearly." Tessa looked at me. "Are you sure those bags aren't too heavy? I could have come back later for that mineral water."

I flexed one bicep, shifting the bags in my hand. "These are nothing," I told her gallantly. "Not even a warmup weight."

"I see," Tessa said, and I couldn't help noticing she was staring at the way my t-shirt had strained around my bicep. I felt a surge of heat at the thought of Tessa appreciating anything about my body. Logically, I knew plenty of women – and some men – appreciated my body whenever I left the house. But somehow, thinking that Tessa did was very different.

"Maybe I should work on that app," I said, just to make conversation. "You know, for premium grocery selection. There must be plenty of people who are as discerning as you but don't have a useless man around the house to carry everything."

"You're not useless. Just taking a break. And I thought you didn't want to do another tech thing?"

"Not really," I admitted. "But it's what I know. And I'm going to have to do something, eventually, or my dad will have a breakdown. And what else is there?"

"Photography," Tessa said promptly. "What about your photography?"

"That's just a hobby," I said, shaking my head vigorously so she knew I did not consider it a viable option.

"It could be more. I mean, you enjoy it."

"I don't want to do anything like that," I said. "Creative stuff? It's not me."

"Why not? Because of your dad?"

"No," I lied, even though I knew perfectly well that he was the main reason why I had never considered an even vaguely creative career path. "It's just not me."

"What did Julius think about it?" Tessa asked, and I let out a grunt, shifting the grocery bags.

"We didn't discuss it. He was too busy explaining how hard it was to be a lobster in a world full of crabs and coral."

"Maybe he missed his calling as a marine biologist," Tessa suggested, tugging the tartan cart over a bump in the footpath.

"He's definitely missing something," I said, and then paused. "Maybe I won't do anything. I mean, I can live off investing the money I got from selling the app. Not like a Kardashian, but comfortably."

"I don't think you'd be happy doing nothing," Tessa said thoughtfully. "It seems to bother you now, and it's only been a few weeks."

I was saved from having to respond by our arrival back at the house. Tessa tugged the cart over the front step and opened the door for me as I lugged in the bags. If I was honest, the carton of mineral water was starting to make me sweat. Not that I had any intention of admitting it. That might make Tessa less admiring of my biceps, and I baulked at that as much as I didn't like to admit why.

I dumped the bags onto the kitchen island and wondered if I should help Tessa put them away, though I had no idea where anything went.

"Dylan! There you are!" I looked up to see my dad roll into the kitchen.

"Here I am."

"How did it go with that careers advisor? I don't have much faith in the idea, but anything's worth it if it gets you doing something," Alan said, wheeling himself closer to me.

"It was..." I began. "Not great."

Alan scoffed. "I can imagine. Useless thing to do with yourself, advising other people what to do for a living."

"Probably."

"So, if that didn't help, what's next?" My father was circling the kitchen in his chair like a shark intent on its prey. "Are you just going to sit around in your room 'reading' like when you were a teenager? I knew exactly what you were doing, Dylan."

"Dad!" I knew he was goading me, but I wasn't keen on his referencing my teenage explorations in self-love in front of Tessa.

"Oh, it's nothing she hasn't heard before, surely. Tessa, you know what teenage boys do all day in their bedrooms, don't you?"

"The same as teenage girls, I imagine." Tessa's face was impressively impassive, though her eyes were crinkled in amusement. "Hormones are one hell of a drug."

And great, now I was imagining whether Tessa was speaking from personal experience and wondering what she got up to in the studio when she was alone. I shifted awkwardly, willing my body not to react in my tight jeans.

"So they are," Alan chuckled. "Did you get those eels for Marcel?"

"I did," Tessa paused. "Are you a fan of...eels?"

"No," Alan said flatly. "But I don't want to discourage him. I think he gets homesick sometimes. This might make him feel better."

"Isn't Belgium famous for waffles and fries, too?" I asked. "Why can't he cure his homesickness with those?"

"If the menu's not to your liking, you're perfectly welcome to make alternative arrangements."

"Is that what you'd prefer?" I really did want to know. "I can get my own place."

"You're always welcome here, Dylan. You should know that."

"Thanks," I said, not very graciously. "Uh, I might leave you to it. If that's everything?"

"Thanks for helping me," Tessa gave me a smile that I could tell was supposed to make me feel better about my father's deliberate attempts to humiliate me.

"No problem," I said, and our eyes met for a moment.

"I'll make that appointment. Soon."

"What appointment?" Alan asked, frowning. "Are you unwell, Tessa?"

"No, just with immigration, about my visa," Tessa lied surprisingly smoothly. "It should be fine because my dad's Aussie, but I need to sort a few things out."

"Oh, I see." Alan clearly believed her.

I made my way up the stairs, unwilling to risk any more comments from my father. After the extraordinary experience that was Julies Persimmon and the considerably more pleasant experience of grocery shopping with Tessa, I was tired. Even if I hadn't particularly earned the right to be.

Sitting down on my bed, I pulled out the piece of paper Julius had given me, listing the traits of the 'lobster' and the best career matches. The first was astronaut.

I crumpled it up and managed to throw it right into the bin in the corner. I could only hope that Tessa's doctor was more competent than my careers advisor.

7 Tessa

Tessa: i lost a bet with dylan yesterday

Abby: what bet? a sexy bet?

Tessa: not a sexy bet. he thinks i'm anxious and that i should see a doctor.

Michelle: we've been telling you that for years

Abby: years!

Tessa: i know. i just don't think i need one. but i guess i have to now

Abby: wait, so you've known this dylan guy a few weeks, and he suggests it, and now you're actually doing it? why does his opinion matter more than ours?!

Tessa: it doesn't! i lost a bet!

Michelle: what was the bet?

Abby: it doesn't matter what the bet was!

Tessa: we were grocery shopping and played guess the total

Abby: i take that back. you lost at guess the total?

Tessa: i know. i'm mortified

Michelle: maybe you lost on purpose because you know you should see someone about your anxiety

Abby: i repeat, you lost at guess the total!?

Tessa: i'm losing my touch <sad face emoji>

Michelle: so, you two were on a date?

Tessa: grocery shopping is not a date. not under any circumstances. he just came along to help me carry stuff

Abby: he was willing to be seen in public with you and your tartan cart? he must really like you

Michelle: obviously he likes her. he cares enough to want her to see a doctor

Tessa: or maybe he just doesn't want an anxious mess spending so much time with his dad

Abby: nah, he's into you. and you're definitely into him. you barely looked at the hot surfer dudes!

Tessa: it doesn't matter if i am, nothing is going to happen. his dad gave me that talk, remember?

Michelle: ooh, it's totally forbidden love! your boss doesn't approve, but nothing can control your burgeoning passion

Tessa: you read too many romance novels. you know that, right?

Michelle: everyone's allowed a guilty pleasure. don't yuck my yum!

Abby: who cares what his dad thinks? if you like him, just get him alone and take your top off

Michelle: i think that's sexual harassment

Abby: i haven't had any complaints

Tessa: nothing is going to happen between me and dylan. he's trying to work out what he wants to do with his life. i'm not going to get involved with a guy who might take off any minute

Tessa: and let's not forget, he is my boss's son. it's not sexy forbidden love, it would just be awkward as hell

Abby: i hate to admit it, but an unstable guy sounds terrible for you. abort mission remove top

Tessa: i was never going on that mission! and he's not unstable, he's just working through stuff. besides, i'm sure he doesn't think of me that way

Michelle: because men carry groceries for and care about the mental health of girls they don't like <sarcasm emoji>

Abby: we could have worked out you were being sarcastic without the emoji

Michelle: <middle finger emoji>

Tessa: i gtg. i need a walk before i start work

Michelle: good luck with sexy forbidden dylan. don't let his dad stand in the way of your happily ever after

Abby: don't let this unstable dude get under your skin!

• • • ● ● • ● ● • •

I sighed, shoving my phone into my pocket. Then I pulled it out again and stared at the screen. I had promised Dylan I'd make an appointment with my doctor. Who would probably laugh at me for wasting her time.

I let out a groan. "This is ridiculous," I muttered. "I'm fine, and this is totally unnecessary." I wondered if I explained that to Dylan again, he'd let me off the hook.

But then I remembered how he had looked at me when he threatened to make an appointment for me himself. Like he wasn't kidding. It had made my stomach clench and my skin tingle, and not from anxiety. It was because he had sounded like he really meant it. Like I mattered enough to him that he'd do it.

Or not. It was entirely possible that Dylan wanted to fix me because it was easier than fixing his current problem. Forcing me to see a doctor must seem less daunting than working out what he wanted to do with his life.

But even if that was true, I had promised. I flicked my phone screen back to life, sent off a quick prayer of thanks to no god in particular for the existence of online booking forms, and made an appointment with the nice doctor I had seen after catching a horrible bout of gastro on the plane.

"Right," I said out loud. "Well, that's done. For now." I slipped on my sneakers and made my way out of the studio. I needed a clear head; Alan had read a few chapters of my draft, and I knew he'd have copious amounts of feedback.

A glance at the sky made me wonder if I should have brought an umbrella, but it was too late now. My feet pounded the pavement, and I forced myself to breathe in the fresh air that smelled of salt and sand. I reminded myself how fortunate I was and how ridiculous I was being to spend so much time worrying.

A new episode of *My Favourite Murder* managed to drown out the worst of my thoughts, and I was so engrossed by the coroner's description of what they found inside the body that I didn't notice the bulk of a man coming up behind me.

"Tessa?"

I whirled around. "Dylan!" I whipped out my earphones, trying not to ogle his biceps. He had clearly just been to the gym and was wearing a singlet that showed off his bare arms, still damp with sweat. And damn, they were nice arms. I knew I'd be imagining how those arms might feel wrapped around me, holding me close against him, when I was alone. I was only human, after all.

"Out for a walk?" he asked and then smirked. "That was a stupid question."

"I am. And I won't ask if you've been at the gym. Though I might comment on how early it is."

"I know," Dylan grimaced. "Far too early for a gentleman of leisure, but Tad's in the office today, so he wanted to get an early session in."

"Gentleman of leisure? That kind of sounds like an old-timey euphemism for a gigolo."

"Well, there's a career path I hadn't considered," Dylan pretended to look thoughtful, falling into step beside me.

"What would your dad think?"

"I have a horrible feeling he'd be weirdly supportive," Dylan said. "Am I interrupting your podcast time if I walk with you?"

"I'll allow it." I was flattered that he had remembered my penchant for podcasts. "On this occasion. I was going to walk down to the coffee shop."

"Good, I need caffeine. And maybe something nice after my workout. Although Nick and Nikki's treats tend to be a bit too trendy for me."

"Not a fan of the Cardamon and Carob Cronut?"

"Nope. Give me a latte and a Tim-Tam any day, thanks."

"Tim-Tams were definitely my favourite thing about visiting Australia as a kid," I said, glancing at the houses as we passed them. Some were large and set in impressively extensive gardens like Alan's, some were simple weatherboard shacks, and plenty were modern duplexes, two homes squeezed in where just one used to be.

"You visited?" Dylan looked surprised. "I thought this was your first trip."

"Oh no," I said. "My dad's Australian, so we made a few trips to see his family. Mum and Dad would leave us with our grandparents, and we'd mostly just sit in their living room eating Tim-Tams and getting excited about the different shows on TV."

"Seriously? Your parents brought you all the way out here and then just took off?"

I shrugged. "Yeah," I said. "In hindsight, it was kind of weird, but at the time, it was just what we were used to. Mum and Dad always loved to travel, just the two of them. Nana always took care of us back home, so it didn't seem that strange that we hung out with Dad's parents here."

"Do they live locally? Your dad's parents, I mean."

"Not exactly. They're dead now, but they lived in Adelaide. I had never been to Sydney before, so it's still pretty new to me."

"And what's the verdict?" Dylan motioned at the beach on the other side of the main street, at the smell of freshly ground coffee beans, at the group of yoga enthusiasts saluting the sun on a patch of grass.

"Oh, it definitely lives up to expectations. Abby always told me how great it was here – she moved over a few years ago. Sunshine, friendly people, a more relaxed lifestyle."

"So, you came to see for yourself," Dylan said, pushing open the door of Nick and Nikki's.

"Eventually." I tilted my head. "It was hard to leave everything I knew behind. Especially given I'm... Well, you know."

"I do." Dylan looked at me for a moment like he was about to say something important.

"Hi there! What can I get you guys this morning?"

It was Nikki, the female half of the extraordinarily peppy couple who ran the coffee shop. She gave the distinct impression that she sampled her own espresso on the hour, every hour.

"A flat white. With regular milk."

"And a latte for me," Dylan added. "Also with regular milk. And..." He bent down to scan the glass case by the counter. "Does the vegan vanilla slice still have plenty of sugar?"

"Organic coconut sugar. But it will still send your blood sugar skyrocketing."

"Then I'll have one of those, too."

"Coming right up!" Nikki whirled around to the espresso machine in a blur of flashing white teeth.

"So, I guess this is the part where I ask if you made that appointment," Dylan's voice was low, and he had tilted his lips down close to my ear. I could feel his warm breath, and it made my skin tighten.

"I did," I managed to say in what was at least a passable imitation of my normal voice, even as a flash of heat soared between my thighs. "With my doctor. And then she can refer me to...someone else. If it's necessary. Which I don't think it is."

"I'm just glad you made the appointment."

"Well, I made a promise. And I did lose our bet."

"That's not why I'm glad. I think it's a good idea. You deserve to worry less, you know."

I forced a smile, even as my insides writhed and squirmed like the famously deadly snakes I was glad I hadn't yet encountered in Australia. "We'll see."

"Well, while we're making life-changing decisions here," Dylan went on. "Have you thought about sending your books to an agent? Your own books, I mean."

"Absolutely not."

"Oh, I get it. You wrote them solely for your own amusement. They'll never see the light of day and will be destroyed in the event of your death."

I let out a little groan. "No, of course, I'd love to have my books published under my own name. It's just..."

"That your anxiety stops you from doing it?"

"Something like that," I admitted.

"You could let me read them," Dylan suggested like he thought I might actually say yes.

"No chance."

"Why not? I looked over some of the chapters you've done for Dad. You're a great writer."

"You did?" My voice came out a little squeaky. "I... They're meant to be commercial in confidence until publication."

"Well, I was looking for references to me, of course. Glad to see I show up in Chapter Six."

"It's different," I said, trying not to think about Dylan calling me a great writer. What did he know? "Writing as someone else. It's not the same...vulnerability."

Dylan made a soft noise. "Vulnerability," he repeated. "You don't like being vulnerable."

"Does anyone?" I laughed shakily because he was giving me another one of those oddly intense looks.

"I don't. I guess that's why it's been hard, coming back home. Admitting I don't know what to do with myself."

"But you did it."

"I did." Dylan paused. "Anyway, you should let me read your stuff. It would give me something to do."

"You've got plenty to do!"

Dylan gave me a disbelieving look.

"Like going to the gym?"

"I only do that because Tad insists."

"Well, it's something, anyway. And you've been seeing Benji. Spending time with your dad and Marcel. And you did go to the careers advisor, even if it didn't work out."

"That's an understatement."

"Are you going to see a different careers advisor?"

"I doubt it. If I just give myself time, I'll work it out. That sounds reasonable, right?"

"Maybe," I bit my lip. "But it sounds like something I'd tell myself."

"Flat white, latte, vanilla slice!" Nikki called, putting the cups on the counter with a flourish.

"Thanks," I said, picking mine up and taking a long sip despite the piping hot temperature. "That's another plus one for Australia. Best coffee ever."

"So long as I'm not the one making it."

"You're a work in progress," I said, bumping my shoulder against his arm and immediately wishing I hadn't. A surge of hot sparks went through me at the touch and made me want things I knew I couldn't have. "I should get back. Your dad wants to go through the next batch of chapters today."

"Is he making a lot of changes?" Dylan asked as we made our way back down the main street.

"A few. I thought he'd have more, but he seems happy with it so far."

"You see, that's because you're a great writer. Just like I said. If you'd only have a little confidence in yourself."

And I was left wondering, once again, why Dylan seemed to care what I thought of myself. Why he seemed to care about *me*. He must be bored in Brekkie Beach, I thought. That was the only reasonable explanation."

"I'm confident enough in my professional ability," I said after a pause. "But, creative stuff? That's a whole different thing."

"I'm not confident in my professional ability." Dylan took a bite of his slice and chewed it thoughtfully. "Why don't you pick a new career for me?"

"What happened to you working it out yourself, in time?"

"It would be much easier if you just told me what to do."

"I can't do that. I can be your friend, though," I said, the words escaping my mouth before I realised just how earnestly cheesy they sounded. "While you work it out yourself." Yep, cheesy like a Margherita pizza with extra mozzarella and stuffed crust. Cheesy enough to land a lactose intolerant in the bathroom for hours.

But Dylan just gave me a small smile. "I'd like that," he said, and then he frowned. "Stop!"

"What?" I stopped in place. "What's wrong? Is there a snake?!" I looked around wildly, fearful that the time had finally come for me to meet one of Australia's myriad of dangerous inhabitants.

"No, just the light is perfect, and that ivy behind you..." Dylan had raised his phone, and I realised he was about to take a photo of me.

"I'm not wearing makeup!" I said, resisting the urge to cover my face with my hands like an uncooperative tween at a family gathering.

"You don't need it," Dylan told me, squinting at me behind his phone screen. "Look back over your shoulder at me."

I rolled my eyes but did as I was asked.

"Did you know Marcel has turtleneck pyjamas?"

"What?" I laughed incredulously. "That's not a thing!"

"No, it's a total lie. But I needed to make you laugh. And look, it came out perfectly." He held up his phone screen and...

"Huh," I let out a soft breath. Staring back at me was my own face, caught in a half-laugh. Did I really have such creamy skin, such sparkling eyes, such a look of carefree joy on my face? "That might be the best photo anyone's ever taken of me."

"I doubt it; you're very photogenic."

"You need to send that to me," I said, ignoring his compliment. "For my profile picture. And reconsider your stance on not pursuing photography."

"Profile picture?" Dylan frowned. "Are you on dating apps?"

"God no," I shook my head. "Michelle thinks I should be, but Abby's all about the organic connection. They think I should be gearing up for a summer of love, banging as many hot surfers as possible."

There was an uncomfortable silence as Dylan digested this information, and I wished I could rewind time and not have said those words.

"But I'm not into casual stuff," I said, knowing I would probably make it worse. "Or dating. Not right now. So, no apps. Or organic connections."

I could have sworn Dylan looked relieved, but I probably imagined it. "Neither am I," he said finally. "I mean, I don't know what I'm doing with my life, so it would be a terrible idea to invite another person into it."

"That makes sense." I told myself that I was being ridiculous to feel so utterly crushed by that comment. I knew nothing was going to happen with Dylan. Nothing should happen with him. And yet, the thought that he didn't want anyone in his life – and that definitely included me – made me feel like I'd just drunk a glass of unpleasantly icy water instead of a scalding coffee.

"Besides, what kind of woman wants a man who's doing nothing?"

"You're not doing nothing. You're working things out while you catch up with the people you love."

"There you go again, being kind to me," Dylan shook his head and rolled his eyes. "Not sure I deserve it."

"I think you do."

"Then I'm lucky," Dylan said, and he sipped his coffee and looked away at something on the horizon that I couldn't see.

8 Dylan

"It's fucking freezing," I swore as the icy water reached my balls, potentially ruining any possibility of fatherhood. "Why are we doing this?"

"It's good for you!" Tad was shivering despite his determined smile. "Morning exercise, cold water, it's good for longevity. People in Scandinavia do it, and they have amazing lifespans."

"They have world-class universal health care," I told Tad through gritted teeth. "I don't think it's plunging themselves into icy water that does it."

"The water's not even icy," Tad said, duck diving down and coming up laughing, his sleek hair plastered back against his head. "It's just not warm."

"Icy," I repeated before plunging myself in, probably less gracefully than Tad.

"See?" Tad said as I resurfaced, swearing and spluttering salt water. "You feel better now that you're in, don't you?

"I feel like shit," I told him but began to swim after him in slow strokes. After all, now that I was here and absolutely freezing, it made sense to make the most of it.

Half an hour later, we emerged from the ocean, Tad still grinning and me still swearing as I pulled my towel over my shoulders.

"You know, I think I understand how those explorers who died in the South Pole felt. Except they were probably warmer than me."

"So whiney! Let's go and get a smoothie to cheer you up."

"Coffee?" I suggested instead. "Nice, hot coffee to warm my frozen bones?"

"Stop carrying on like an orphan lost in a blizzard," Tad chided, toeing on his flip-flops. "A protein smoothie would be better. You know, catch the muscle-building window you get after a workout."

"I think I liked you more before you were obsessed with this healthy living bullshit," I muttered, following Tad across the sand. I could feel it sticking to my wet feet. Sand was the one thing I hated about Brekkie Beach. No matter how seldom you visited the beach itself, sand was guaranteed to infest your home, crunching underfoot in the kitchen, snaking its way into your bedsheets, and turning up under your sofa cushions. It was insidious.

"I'm just trying to live long enough to see my kid grow up."

"You weren't exactly on your death bed before all this. You went to the gym, but you weren't obsessed."

"Well, I want to be better," Tad said, oddly serious. "I don't want to be one of those dads who can't kick a soccer ball around, can't take their kid camping, can't join them on a fun run."

"My dad couldn't do any of that when he got sick. And he was still a decent dad. No worse than he would have been if he had been able to do fun runs with me. Speaking of which, what exactly is fun about a run?"

"Stopping at the end. Come on, how good does it feel when you finish a hard workout?"

"Almost as good as never starting to begin with," I said, even though I had been an avid gym junkie since I had grown a few feet overnight as a teenager. I had realised it was either muscle building or comparisons to Slender Man for the rest of my life.

"I didn't mean to say that Alan wasn't a good dad," Tad said after a moment. "Sorry, I just..."

"I know what you meant," I said, not wanting my best friend to feel guilty. "You just want to be the best dad you possibly can be. If it helps, I think you're nailing it."

Tad looked at me for a moment, his shoulders tight. "Thanks, man," he said, his voice oddly hoarse. "It's a hell of a thing, being responsible for an entire human life. I just don't want to screw it up."

"You won't," I said, meaning every word. "Like I said, you're nailing it. If I ever find myself with a kid, you'd be the first person I'd ask for advice."

"Well, Tessa does have excellent childbearing hips." Tad tilted his head as though giving the matter serious consideration.

"Tessa will not be bearing my spawn." I followed Tad into the smoothie shop. I squinted at the menu, my eyes adjusting from the bright sun to the artificial light. Neon outlines of strawberries, mangoes, and kale decorated the walls, making me feel like I was in a wellness-themed casino.

"I bet she'd like to," Tad nudged me. "Well, maybe not actually bear your children. At least not yet. But she likes you. And you like her."

"No," I said, trying to focus on the relative merits of Peanut Butter Pow in comparison to Strawberry So Strong. "You know I'm not dating. And she's not either, for the record. She says she's not looking, not even for anything casual. Which is probably for the best. We're just friends."

"Friends," Tad repeated. "It sounds like you're glad she's not looking for anyone else, though."

"It's none of my business," I said, even though I had felt a sick twist of jealousy when I had thought that Tessa might use the photo that I took of her on a dating profile.

Before Tad could reply, a sleepy-looking teenager appeared behind the counter, yawning hugely. "Hi," she said, with none of the energetic enthusiasm one expected from a smoothie store employee. "What can I get you?"

"Maca Maca Man for me, thanks."

"I'll go for the Strawberry So Strong." I looked at Tad. "What is maca, anyway?"

"It's a South American thing. It tastes kind of like caramel. It's good for you. Or so I've read."

"Suit yourself," I said. "And I think Tessa's smart not to be looking to date around here. I mean, have you seen the local guys?" I nodded across the street, and Tad caught my gaze.

A group of local surfers had emerged from the ocean and were now engaged in an impromptu game of hacky sack with a piece of driftwood. The tallest of the group made an impressive dive to catch it, but missed, and the driftwood hit him squarely in the mouth.

"Bro!" I heard one of them say. "Bro, are you okay, bro?"

The surfer sat up, spat out bits of wood, and gave a double thumbs up, which made the others laugh uproariously.

"Okay, they're probably not going to compete in the International Mathematics Olympiad any time soon. But they don't seem to have trouble getting women's attention."

Across the street, a pair of women in jogging gear had stopped to assist the fallen surfer, crooning over him like he was a sad-eyed puppy with a bandaged paw.

"Tessa seems to be a bit more discerning," I said.

"Well, she seems to like you, so I doubt it."

"She doesn't like me," I said automatically and tried not to think about how she had looked at me when I had taken her photo, how she seemed to care about what I was doing with my life – or not doing. How she defended me to my dad, even though he was her boss.

But it didn't mean anything. Tessa was just...nice. No, not nice. Kind. There was a difference. Nice was an undiscerning pleasantness to all those around you whether they deserved it or not. Kindness was more considered. Kindness took action; it wasn't just words. It meant doing what was best for people, even when they didn't like it, because you genuinely cared. Actually, maybe Tessa was just nice. I wasn't sure I deserved kind.

"Maca Maca Man and a Strawberry So Strong," the tired-looking teenager pushed the cups over the counter and yawned so widely that I could see her back teeth.

Tad picked up his cup first and took an eager sip. He had a decent poker face, but I knew him well.

"How's that 'like caramel' going for you?" I asked, taking a sip of my smoothie. It was cool, refreshing, and undoubtedly protein packed but nowhere near as welcome as coffee would have been.

"I think that whoever said that had never tasted caramel." Tad took another sip and didn't bother to hide his wince this time. "This shit better make me live to one hundred and fifty."

"You do that," I said, sipping my smoothie again. Still not coffee, sadly. "Maybe I'll have worked out what to do with myself by then."

"So, I take it you're not going to see Julius again?"

"I could get better career advice from that homeless man who used to take a dump on my building's doorstep every morning."

"Starting to see why you left San Francisco, dude."

"Your wife sent me some links to properties her firm is showing," I said. "I'm thinking about doing the whole investor thing. Buy some apartments to rent out, negative gearing, blah blah blah."

"Yeah?" Tad looked up. "You're interested in that?"

"I might be." It wasn't true. I had never been interested in real estate, and the idea of becoming a landlord wasn't especially appealing. But 'reviewing potential investment opportunities' sounded more like progress than 'sitting on my arse wondering what the hell to do with my life'.

"You should come and babysit."

"Anything to get away from my dad's house." I didn't really intend to object. I owed him some babysitting. "But why?"

"So you can rule out a career as a nanny." Tad nudged me again. "And because I want to take Alice out somewhere nice and eat grown-up food without anyone screaming at us for two hours."

"Do you really think I'd be capable of looking after your precious offspring?"

Tad just looked at me. "I trust you, dude. Maybe you're not a natural with kids, but you wouldn't let me down."

And that? That made me feel pretty damn good. I could almost forget that I was over thirty, sleeping in my childhood bedroom, had no idea what to do with my life, and had an inappropriate attraction to my father's employee. Almost.

• • • ● • ● • • •

When I made my way downstairs after an action-packed day of flicking through emails and deciding to ignore them, rereading an old David Eddings fantasy novel I had found under the bed, and editing some of my least shitty recent photos, it was almost dinner time.

If I hadn't been out for that early swim with Tad, I would have definitely felt more disgusting and useless than I did, so I supposed I'd better be grateful to him.

"The curry's in the slow cooker," I heard Tessa say to Marcel as I came into the kitchen. "And the rice is just in the microwave; a couple of minutes should warm it through. Is that okay?"

"Yes," Marcel nodded solemnly. "But I am surprised you did not ask me to cook. I know you all enjoyed my eels."

Tessa caught my eye then and bit her lip as though trying not to laugh.

"Well, I didn't want to put you to any trouble just because I was going out," Tessa faltered, but then Marcel surprised me by letting out a loud, roaring laugh.

"I am making a joke," he informed us. "I know you did not enjoy the eels. Not one of you. You did not grow up with such food and have no taste for it."

"I'm sure you did an excellent job on them," Tessa said earnestly. "But eels aren't exactly my favourite."

"Nor mine," I said, coming into the room. "Curry smells good though." I lifted the lid of the slow cooker and took in a whiff of turmeric and fresh coriander.

"I hope so. I'm going out tonight, so I won't be around to serve it up."

I looked at Tessa, trying very hard to be casual. "Where are you going tonight?"

"That live music thing down by the beach. Surf n Sounds? Abby's idea, she thinks I need to get more into the Aussie nightlife. And to be fair, it did sound quintessentially Australian."

"Beach parties are iconic for LA, maybe. An iconic Australian party is getting hammered on cask wine in a paddock."

"That's much less picturesque," Tessa said. "But Abby says it will be fun. She knows someone in one of the bands; she did their house a while ago."

"Did their house?"

"She's a professional organiser," Tessa explained. "And yes, it was frustrating to grow up with a sister who snuck into my room not to steal my clothes but to colour code them."

"I didn't know that was a thing."

"It is, apparently," Tessa shrugged. "She's been very successful, especially since Netflix put Marie Kondo on. Anyway, she met this woman Kari, who's the lead singer of a glam folk band called Glitter Gulch. They're playing tonight and Abby thinks it will be good for me to get out and meet people."

I could imagine exactly the sort of people Tessa might meet tonight. Men in ironically loud shirts with beards grooving on the grass and putting their grubby hands all over her body. It was none of my business, but my stomach twisted with jealousy just the same.

"Sounds fun," I said, managing to sound nonchalant.

"It'll be something," Tessa said cautiously. "Anyway, I'd better go and get ready. I don't know what you're supposed to wear to something like this, so it might take a while. At least I won't get sunburnt."

"I don't know, if anyone could get a moon tan, it'd be you."

Tessa paused for a moment and then stuck her tongue out at me. It was such a juvenile gesture that I couldn't help but imagine how many times Tessa had done the same thing, growing up with two sisters.

Before I could retaliate against the tongue offensive, an offensively loud blast of elevator music came from the pocket of Tessa's jeans, and she pulled out her phone.

"What's up?" I heard her ask. "Oh, you've got to be kidding me." A pause. "No, I don't think you're faking it. You do sound sick." Another pause. "Go on my own? Not a chance." Pause, sigh, pause. "I don't care how good it would be for me; I'm not going by myself." Pause. "I do hope you feel better soon." Pause. "Why would I want a photo of what you coughed up, Abby?" A short pause. "Take care, bye."

Tessa let out a sigh, leaning against the kitchen island. "Well, Abby just bailed on me. So, I'll be able to microwave the rice after all."

"A shame." Marcel frowned. "Music by the water is ambient. You should go and enjoy yourself."

"Thanks, Marcel, But honestly, going to a beach party alone sounds like hell on earth. I was kind of looking forward to it, but not without Abby."

"I'll go with you." The words left my mouth before I realised I was saying them.

Tessa looked up at me, her lips parted in surprise, and I tried very hard not to think about how those plump, parted lips would feel under my own.

"Seriously?"

"Seriously," I said because it wasn't like I could take it back. "You said it was quintessentially Australian. I can't let you miss it. The government would revoke my citizenship."

"Is it your sort of thing, though? Music by the beach?"

"It's been a while, but I do know how to have fun." I pretended to be hurt. "Surf n Sounds has been going for years, but I haven't been since I was twenty. It will be fun, rediscovering my roots."

"I think it is a good idea," Marcel inclined his head. "You need fun, Dylan. Music! Dancing! Beer!" He nodded firmly. "I will attend to the rice."

"If you're sure?" Tessa was looking at me through her lashes in a way that I was almost convinced she was doing on purpose. "And we don't have to stay long."

"Is that a challenge? Just for that, I'm going to insist we dance until dawn."

Tessa groaned. "I am not nineteen. If I'm not in bed by midnight, I turn into a pumpkin."

"I don't remember Cinderella that way."

"Cinderella wasn't in her late twenties. Speaking of, I'd better get dressed."

"Do I have to change?" I indicated my own jeans and t-shirt combination.

"Nope. You're fine as you are."

"That doesn't seem fair," I said; we were wearing practically identical outfits. Even if my arse didn't look half as good in my jeans as hers.

"Take it up with the patriarchy," Tessa grinned. "I'll be ten minutes, okay?"

"Fine," I said, taking a seat at the kitchen table.

"It is good," Marcel said as Tessa closed the door, "that you have become a friend to Tessa."

I looked up. "You think so?"

"Clearly, I think so. Or I would not have said it."

"Dad might not be happy. He told me not to 'interfere' with her."

"And are you," Marcel asked, "intending to interfere with her tonight?"

I let out a spluttering cough. "Of course not!" I said, a little too quickly. "Like you said, we're friends. Just friends. I don't..." I shook my head. "I just meant that Dad might get suspicious because we're going to this music thing together."

"Does he have anything to be suspicious of?" Marcel sat down at the table and steepled his long pale fingers under his chin.

"No." And it was only half a lie. Yes, I was attracted to Tessa. And yes, I liked her. It was hard not to. But I had no intention of allowing anything to happen between us. Even if she wanted it to, which I was pretty sure she didn't. Most women tended to prefer gainfully employed men with a direction in life, after all. "We're friends. I'm not looking to get involved with anyone right now. While I'm working out what to do next."

"I see," he said solemnly.

I didn't know what to say to that, so I pulled out my phone and browsed emails I had no intention of replying to. Then I heard the glass door slide open and looked up. Holy shit, Tessa looked...

"Do you think this is okay?" she asked, smoothing her hands over her hips. She wore a little navy sundress, cut low in the neck and finishing just about mid-thigh. I could see the curve of her breasts and I was probably gawking like a twelve-year-old on his first unsupervised search of the internet. I could see her legs, too, toned from long walks up and down the hills of Brekkie Beach, barely covered by the hem of the dress. Her hair was in a messy bun on top of her head, and she had tied a jaunty red scarf around it, a pop of colour against the glossy strands. Her eyes had never looked more enchantingly blue, and I didn't know what she had put on her lips, but it made it hard to keep my eyes off them.

"Looks good," I croaked and cleared my throat. "Um, very appropriate. Beachy."

"That's what I was going for." As she moved, the hem of her dress rose even higher, and I was relieved she wasn't going out to 'meet new people' without me. "Abby approved it earlier today, but..." She shrugged. "You live here; you'd know better."

"You're definitely appropriate," I repeated, even though all sorts of inappropriate thoughts went through my head at the sight of her.

"We should head off, then," Tessa said. "Before it gets too busy. You sure you're okay with the rice, Marcel?"

"Microwave for three minutes." Marcel looked up from his journal article. "And I will not add even one eel."

• • • ● • ● • • •

Surf n Sounds was loud. Extremely loud. So loud, in fact, that I was questioning how the organisers had managed to get council approval to hold the event. When I was fourteen, my dad received a fine because I had blasted music too loudly in my bedroom in the middle of the afternoon. I guess Cradle of Filth wasn't everyone's cup of tea.

Electric lanterns and tiki torches designed to look like they were lit by real flames bathed the park in a soft glow, and a growing crowd was dancing – or at least attempting to dance – in front of the stage. The performer certainly wasn't dropping tracks that were easy to move to.

"Is this typical Australian music?" Tessa wrinkled her nose.

The man on the stage was dressed in a baggy yellow tracksuit and gold sunglasses and had the kind of voice I would have needed a nasty head cold to emulate.

"Definitely not. Australia doesn't need another white hip-hop artist. Especially not one who's clearly in his late thirties."

"I guess he needs to share his struggle. Being a middle-class white guy must be tough." Tessa took a sip of her second Surf n Sounds signature cocktail. It was a dark purple colour, smelled strongly of cheap coconut rum, and tasted like the rocket fuel a teenage Tad used to mix up by taking just a little of everything in his parents' liquor cabinet. Judging by how light-headed and loose-limbed I felt already, it probably had a similar alcohol content.

"If he's rapping about my people, why aren't I feeling connected to the music?"

"Because he's terrible?" Tessa offered me a smile, that little gap in her teeth just visible. "I'm so sorry I dragged you to this. We can go."

"Dragged me?" I scoffed. "I pretty much insisted on coming. And he can't be on for much longer; how many more songs can he possibly have about the mean streets of suburban Sydney?"

"At least let me buy you another drink for your trouble," she said. "I think it's Abby's friend playing next. Glitter Gulch."

"Glam folk, right?" I gave her a quizzical look. "Interesting mix." I allowed her to steer us back to the long line at the bar.

"They can't be worse than that guy," Tessa tilted her head at the stage, where MC White Bread had, disturbingly enough, started throwing gang signs as he beatboxed into the microphone.

"True," I agreed. "Two signatures, please," I said to the exhausted-looking bartender, handing over my card before Tessa could fumble in her bag.

"I was going to get this round!" Tessa poked me. "You're my guest."

"I'm not going to let you waste your hard-earned money. You work for my dad; I know it's hard-earned."

Tessa let out a breath. "I like your dad. But thank you. That's very nice of you," she added as I put another of the murky purple concoctions into her hand.

If I had been a wiser man, I would have insisted we switch to the cheap, foamy beer they had on tap. Cheap beer was like an internal cold shower, and I needed one due to the existence of Tessa and that bloody sundress. God damn it, I should have told her it was customary to wear a bulky sweater and thick dungarees to Surf n Sounds. But she'd probably look good in that too. Like an adorably wholesome farmer, making me have unwholesome and not at all farm-related thoughts.

"You're welcome," I said, trying not to look at her delicate, exposed skin any longer than was strictly necessary. "Is that Abby's friend?" I pointed to the stage, where our hip-hop hopeful had finally departed and had been replaced by a group dressed in a clash of flowing linen, black leather, crochet, and sequins.

"I think so," Tessa squinted. "They look pretty glam folk, right? We should dance. To be supportive."

"I'm not much of a dancer."

"Oh, I'm sure I'm worse." Tessa took a long gulp of her drink. "But it's crowded, so we only need to shuffle. Besides, dancing gives you endorphins. Endorphins are good for anxiety, right?"

"You've got me there." But still, I knew dancing with Tessa was a bad idea. Despite what Tad would tell you, my dancing was no worse than the average white guy. But the thought of Tessa's body moving so close to mine was…

Dangerous. This was dangerous. But it was too late to come up with an excuse. Tessa was already winding her way through the crowd of determined drinkers and towards the crush of the makeshift dancefloor.

Glitter Gulch began to play, and despite my trepidation, their sound wasn't all that bad. Mellow and upbeat with a few electric guitar riffs, the singer's voice rising clear and sweet.

Tessa had squeezed between two groups of teenagers, and I could only follow her. She was swaying her hips, but her arms were at her sides like she was too self-conscious for anything more exuberant.

"They're not bad!" I leaned down so she could hear me over the speaker system.

"Surprisingly good!" She gave me a double thumbs up. And yeah, that cheesy gesture was even more adorable than the first time.

I felt like an idiot, shuffling my feet and trying to blend into the crowd, but at least Tessa didn't seem to expect that we'd dance together like the couple in front of us, who were groping each other rhythmically in time to the music.

Suddenly, the crowd surged, and Tessa fell into me, stumbling. And if I put my arms around her to keep her upright, that was only the gentlemanly thing to do.

"You okay?" I asked, very much aware that I hadn't let go of her. Her skin was soft and warm under my fingers, her chest pressed to mine. I could have sworn I could feel her heartbeat, much faster than the rhythm of the drums.

"Just fine," Tessa sounded breathless as she looked up at me. She began to move her hips again, her body still very much against mine and *shit*. I could feel my lower half taking a definite interest in the proceedings. I tried very hard to convince my body that she was only dancing with me like this because it was so damn crowded, and she understandably wanted to remain standing.

Her body was warm and supple through the thin cotton of her dress, and Tessa was smiling up at me, her mouth open so I could see that little gap between her teeth. It felt...bloody great, actually. Especially with the amount of alcohol in my system. I tried very hard to remember all the reasons why letting anything at all happen with Tessa was such an epically bad idea.

Apparently, I was failing because my hands moved from her arms to her waist. I wanted her closer. I wanted the milling crowd around us – full of men staring at her, I was sure of it – to know that she was off-limits. I knew Tessa wasn't mine, but as she pressed her body against me, electric torchlight reflecting from her eyes and making them sparkle, I forgot why she couldn't be.

Her full lips parted, Tessa was looking up at me like she was expecting something to happen. Like she was just waiting for me to make the first move. Like she wasn't lost in her head, worrying about her past, her future. She was just...there with me.

"Tessa," I knew she couldn't really hear me above the music, but she seemed to have gained the ability to lip-read, along with her many other talents. The music was throbbing, pulsing, the crowd around us a religious ecstasy of rhythm and spilled beer, and I...

Screw it. I leaned down and covered Tessa's too-pretty pink lips with my own, sealing our mouths together like I had meant to do it all along. And maybe I had. The first brush of her lips sent a jolt through me, like being struck by lightning, except less likely to cause my untimely death and far more likely to make me come in my pants. There wasn't a moment of hesitation. As soon as I brought our mouths together, Tessa kissed me back just as fiercely, her arms wrapping around my neck like she couldn't bear to let me go.

We weren't even pretending to dance now, just letting our bodies be jostled by the crowd as we kissed. Clumsy, due to the many cocktails, breathless and desperate, but somehow absolutely perfect. My brain had been starved of dopamine, and the touch of Tessa's lips sent chemicals flooding through me, my nervous system lighting up. Yes, my body screamed. Yes, this is definitely an appropriate reward. Give us more of this.

Tessa was the first to pull back when the song ended, and the crowd stilled. "Shit," she murmured, her fingers going to her lips.

"I really shouldn't have done that." The second that we weren't touching, all of the reasons why I shouldn't have let that happen came flooding back to me, dizzying and fierce. "I'm sorry, I—"

"No, it was my fault." Tessa's eyes were wide and her cheeks flushed. "I was the one who got all grabby. I'm sorry."

"You don't have to apologise," I insisted. I let out a very forced laugh that turned into a cough. "We've both had a few too many Surf n Sounds Specials, right?"

"Yes!" Tessa agreed, latching on to that explanation. "Um, I should go." She dove through the crowd. I followed her, still unwilling to let her out of my sight even though her being in my sight was definitely dangerous.

"Wait!" I caught up with her right at the temporary fence around the park as she powerwalked with surprising speed. She looked up at me in a mixture of horror and embarrassment, probably wondering why I had chased her down.

"I don't want you to walk back alone. Too many creeps about." And was I one of them? I had just kissed my dad's employee, which I had promised I wouldn't do. And yes, she had kissed me back, but...

"Thanks." Tessa didn't look at me. "It's not far."

"No." We lapsed into an uneasy silence as we walked unnaturally quickly. If Tessa got any faster, I would have to break into a jog, which was a) embarrassing and b) unwise, given how unsteady I was on my feet.

When we reached my father's house – my childhood home – Tessa paused for a moment, looking up at me and then away immediately. "I'll, um, go straight round to the studio," she said. "Not through the main house. If Alan and Marcel are up, I don't want to..."

"No, of course not," I said, wishing I could also avoid the potential judgement of my father. "I'm sorry, Tessa."

But Tessa just shook her head. "It's not your fault," she said again. "It just...happened. Alcohol, music, dancing. These things happen. It doesn't mean anything. We can be mature about this, right? Just forget it and be friends."

"Of course," I said. "Best if we just pretend it didn't happen."

"Yeah," Tessa nodded, her arms wrapped tightly around her body in her skimpy dress. Was she comforting herself or protecting herself from me, I wondered? "Goodnight, Dylan. And, um, thanks for coming."

"Goodnight."

• • • ● • ● • • •

I had been tempted to climb up the roof and through the window of my childhood bedroom, worried my face would betray what had just happened if I saw my dad. He'd always been able to read me like a cheap paperback.

Instead, I had sat on the veranda for almost an hour – and peed in the rose bushes – before I had finally felt calm and sober enough to go inside. In the end, Dad had barely glanced up from his Scandi crime drama, and I had been able to grab a bottle of water from the fridge and head to bed without so much as a "Did you have fun?"

But now that I lay in bed, half of the water gulped down to ward off my inevitable hangover, I couldn't sleep.

I couldn't do much except think of how it had felt to hold Tessa against me. To kiss her. The way her lips had opened for mine, how she had whispered my name, wrapped her arms around my neck like she wanted to keep me close. And god, I had wanted her to.

"Forget it," I said firmly to myself in the darkness. "Bad idea. Forget about it."

But forgetting about that kiss didn't seem likely at all.

9 Tessa

I SLID THE DOOR firmly closed behind me as I went inside, and, for good measure, I locked it.

"Shit!" I spat out, throwing down my handbag and collapsing, face-first, onto my bed. Why, why on god's green earth, had I done that?

Why had I been so...

Stupid. I just had to go and suggest dancing, didn't I? And then I had all but thrown myself onto Dylan, and the poor guy had practically had no choice but to kiss me after that. It was only polite.

He clearly regretted it. Even if his lips on mine had felt like the fruition of every daydream and desire I had been nursing in my overactive brain for weeks now. Even if his strong hands on my waist had made me want to swoon into his arms like a waif-like princess from one of

Michelle's books. Even if being with him had been electric, exciting, dangerous, and left me with soaked knickers.

"Shit on a stick!" I rubbed my eyes and rolled over to retrieve my phone from my bag where I had dropped it.

I began to type an SOS to the group chat I shared with my sisters but decided this was way beyond texting. Besides, my fingers were definitely on the finger fumbling side of tipsy.

I pressed the video icon firmly and waited, propping my phone against my pillows. The first thing I saw was my own face, my cheeks flushed, and my mascara now smeared. I looked a mess, which was entirely appropriate.

Michelle answered first, looking calm and professional with her sleek bun and high-necked wool dress.

"What happened to you?" She looked somewhere between amused and worried.

"Urgh," I managed to get out, pushing my hair out of my eyes.

"I see," Michelle hid her mouth for a moment, and then the screen split in half and Abby joined the call.

Poor Abby. She really did look sick, her eyes puffy, and her nose very red. Her usually high ponytail had slid down to one side like something from a low-budget 1980s music video. She let out a barking cough.

"Who disturbs my suffering?" Abby rasped as though she were a dying swamp creature.

"Me," I said. "I did something stupid, and I am freaking out."

"Shit," Abby cleared her throat. "You look rough. What happened? Did you go to Surf n Sounds?"

"I did go," I admitted and had to pause as Abby whooped.

"Yes, girl!" she said, seeming to gain strength as she spoke. "I told you! It's great to go to stuff by yourself! Confidence boosting, am I right?"

"I didn't go by myself," I confessed, my hands over my face again.

Michelle seemed to understand first, and she let out a sound that was entirely too pleased. "Wait, did Dylan go with you?"

"Yes." I groaned as both my sisters crowed their delight. "Don't do that, please. This isn't a good thing."

"Did you drink too much and embarrass yourself in front of him?"

"Not exactly," I sighed. "But yes, kind of."

"Explain," Abby demanded. "Did he try something on you? I'm going to kill him!"

"He didn't try something on me!" I shot back. "No, I...I asked him to dance with me, and then I kind of...threw myself at him. And we kissed. Well, he kissed me."

Michelle let out a shriek of delight, which she muffled with her hand. "Do not say things like that unexpectedly!

Everyone is staring at me through the glass, and I was pretending this was a professional call."

"How am I supposed to prepare you when I need to tell you something like that?" I complained. "Is there a code word?"

"Not the point." Abby waved a hand and blew her nose loudly. "You kissed. He kissed you."

"We kissed. Like I said, I asked him to dance, and I got too close, and then he kissed me. I feel terrible."

"Why?" Abby scrunched up her very red nose. "I mean, it's awkward, sure, because he's your boss's son, but why would you feel terrible?"

"Because he didn't really want to kiss me!" That was obvious, why couldn't Abby see that? "He just felt like he had to because I was dancing too close."

"That's the stupidest thing you've ever said," Abby said. "Except when you claimed that *The Phantom Menace* was better than *A New Hope*."

"I was young! I thought Jar Jar Binks was funny."

"He *was* funny," Michelle agreed. "I don't get the hate for poor Jar Jar. Hesa deserving better, okeyday?"

Abby rubbed her temples delicately with her fingers. "It's times like this I wish I were adopted. I can't be related to you two, I swear. But your terrible opinions aside, you've got to be freaking kidding me if you think you somehow made Dylan kiss you. Michelle, back me up."

"Yeah, Tessa, I don't know how you came up with that one. Unless you've started carrying a revolver, I doubt you could force a guy to kiss you."

"Not force," I admitted. "But I must have made him feel like he had to. And I didn't mean to dance with him like that, but it was crowded, and it just sort of happened, and then he was looking at me, and..." I trailed off, replaying the moment in my mind. Despite my self-loathing spiral, the memory made my stomach flip in a way that wasn't entirely unpleasant. I remembered how Dylan had looked at me. Like the crowd, the band, the ocean wasn't there at all, like it was just him and me, dancing alone.

"It sounds like you two were giving each other major vibes, and he kissed you because he wanted to," Abby said. "What happened after, anyway? Oh my god, did you have sex in a port-a-loo?"

"No, I did not have sex in a portable public toilet."

"Good," Michelle said. "Because I'm fully supportive of you getting some action, but public toilets are a step too far. At least find a nice deserted alleyway."

"We didn't have sex anywhere," I objected. "I pulled away, and Dylan was all, 'I shouldn't have done that'. Then we left. Well, I tried to leave without him, because, you know, awkward. But he came after me because he didn't want me to walk home alone."

"So gentlemanly," Michelle said approvingly.

"So, he kissed you, you were the first one to pull back, and you're still somehow convinced you made him kiss you? Do you have telekinetic powers we should be aware of?" Abby rubbed her chin and dropped a few tablets into a glass of water, where they hissed and fizzed, turning the water a neon orange.

"He clearly regretted it. We agreed that we'd pretend it never happened and focus on being friends. Just a drunk mistake."

"Then what's the problem?" Abby demanded. "It's just a kiss! It's not like you went for his dick in front of his dad. I don't see the big deal."

"Nothing is allowed to happen with him! And his dad – my boss, let's not forget – told me not to let anything happen with him. But it did. And I feel..."

"What do you feel, Tessa?" Michelle asked gently.

"Confused. Guilty. Embarrassed. Worried – no, anxious as fuck. Nervous. Angry with myself," I ticked off the swirl of unpleasant emotions that made me feel like I might throw up. Though, to be fair, that could be the oddly purple cocktails.

"That's a lot," Michelle's voice was still gentle. "But Abby's right. It was only a kiss."

"See!" Abby was triumphant. "It's just a kiss after a few too many. It happens. You just need to stop worrying about it and act normal when you see him next. Easy."

"Stop worrying?" I crumpled up my face. "This is me, remember?"

"True," Abby said with a grimace. "When are you seeing the doctor about your anxiety?"

"Um, tomorrow, actually." I was already dreading it.

"Well, that's good timing," Michelle said. "Look, I've got to go to a meeting, but keep us updated on how it goes, okay?"

"I will," I promised. "Thanks for letting me vent."

"Any time," Michelle said, signing off.

"And I have to go too," Abby said. "Because it's late, and I'm going to drown in my own mucous."

"Do you need anything? I can drop round with some chicken soup, and we can watch movies."

"And you can hide from Dylan," Abby guessed. "Not a chance, babe. And I don't want you getting this; it's disgusting." She sighed. "Drink some water, go to bed, and get some sleep. Don't overthink this."

"I'll try."

But as my screen went black, and I lay on the bed, dizzy and nauseous from alcohol and bad decisions, I knew that the only way I'd get some decent sleep was if someone broke in and chloroformed me.

I almost wished someone would.

When I went into the house the following day, Dylan was (thankfully) nowhere to be seen.

Instead, Marcel wandered into the kitchen as I made coffee, looking unruffled as ever in his turtleneck.

"Did you enjoy yourself last night?" he asked, putting a single piece of organic sourdough rye bread into the toaster, then staring down at it as though he didn't trust the settings.

"Uh, yeah." I was trying very hard to sound nonchalant. "One of the bands was pretty good, but the hip hop guy before them was terrible."

"I do not enjoy hip hop." Marcel was still staring down at his toast reproachfully, as though daring it to become even slightly more golden than he desired.

"I guess not." I wondered what kind of music Marcel did like. Either classical stuff, I thought, or heavy industrial techno. Nothing in between. A brief mental image of Marcel cutting mad shapes in a nightclub, still clad in his turtleneck, flashed into my head.

"Did Dylan enjoy himself?" I had been hoping he wouldn't ask.

"I think so," I said, focusing very hard on pouring the milk into the stainless steel jug to reach the etched line exactly. "It was nice of him to come with me, but we left pretty early."

"It is good that he went out," Marcel said, pressing the 'cancel' button on the toaster and examining the piece of bread before nodding in satisfaction and putting it on his plate. "It is not right for a young man to spend his days at home alone."

"Oh, well, it's not like that's all he does," I said, wanting to defend Dylan. "I mean, he goes to the gym with Tad a lot. And spends time with Benji. And..." And I was out of ideas.

"And walks with you," Marcel finished. "That is good."

"Uh, yeah," I said. "I mean, it's not like we plan it. We just seem to bump into each other sometimes."

"I think," Marcel said, as he mashed avocado into his anaemic toast with more force than seemed necessary, "that it is good you are a friend to him."

"Uh—" I had no idea what to say. Yes, I was Dylan's friend. Well, I was until the kissing incident last night. Now, I had no idea where I stood. But was it a good thing that I was Dylan's friend? Said kissing incident seemed to suggest it probably wasn't.

I heard footsteps on the stairs, and Dylan himself came into the kitchen, his hair tousled and dark circles under his eyes. He was dressed in gym gear, a bag slung over one shoulder.

At the sight of me, he took a step back.

"Hi," I said weakly.

"Uh..." Dylan looked at me and then at Marcel. "I think I forgot my towel. I'll be back."

And then he disappeared up the stairs again.

Shit, I thought, swallowing hard against the tide of anxiety rising inside me. So that was how it was going to be.

I had turned our budding friendship into a total mess, and I only had myself to blame.

• • • • • • • • • •

I spent the morning listening to Alan describe what he wanted the cover of his autobiography to look like. He persisted despite my explaining to him that I had zero authority over this or any knowledge of graphic design.

It was probably good that Alan's monologue hadn't required any concentration because my brain was far away from Alan's stuffy study and firmly lodged in a spiral of anxiety. While Alan droned on, my brain fixated on a number of questions:

1. Had Dylan woken up and decided that the whole kissing thing was my fault?
2. Was he blaming himself and feeling disgusted at his lack of judgement?
3. Would he ever speak to me again? And just how awkward would our interactions need to get for Alan and

Marcel to notice?

4. How did I feel about all this, anyway?

After all, I had wanted to kiss Dylan. Okay, I never would have done it if I hadn't been more than halfway to drunk, but I had definitely wanted to. Because I liked him. Even though I absolutely shouldn't. He was my boss's son. He wasn't looking to get involved with anyone because his life was too unstable. And I wasn't looking for anything either because I was...what, exactly? Too afraid to let myself be that vulnerable was the truth, but I didn't like it. I needed a better reason. Maybe I was focusing on my career, like Michelle. Or perhaps I was guarded, like Abby. But that wasn't true. My job was steady, and my last breakup had been more than two years ago and perfectly amicable.

"And so, I think the title text should be yellow," Alan's voice interrupted my thoughts. "The shade of yellow I featured in my 1996 exhibit. Don't you agree?"

"Uh..." I sat there with my mouth hanging open and swallowed quickly. "Yellow could work?"

Alan nodded with satisfaction. "It will." He rolled his shoulders. "I need some lunch."

I was glad for any reason to get out of the study and distract myself. "I can heat up some soup if you'd like."

"The potato and leak? Yes, I think so."

"I'll put it on," I said, following Alan as he wheeled himself from the room.

Alan reached the kitchen before me, and I could see Dylan searching the fridge.

"Hi, Dad," he said, clearly not seeing me. "Do we have any lemon juice?"

"Ask Tessa. She knows better than me."

Dylan looked past his dad to where I was awkwardly hovering in the doorway.

Our eyes met, and he looked away, unwilling to even offer a greeting.

"Tessa, lemon juice?" Alan pressed when Dylan didn't say a word.

"Uh, we have lemons. In the fruit bowl." I pointed, but Dylan still didn't look at me.

"Right," he said, nodding. "Good to know."

Then he backed out of the kitchen and away from me.

Well, if I had any doubts as to whether he was avoiding me, I didn't now. There was no doubt about it. Dylan couldn't stand to be in the same room as me, even with Marcel and Alan as chaperones. What, did he think I was going to try and jump him?

Humiliation burned through me fiercely, and I buried myself in the fridge. "I'll get that soup on, Alan," I said. "And then I have that appointment this afternoon, so I'll be out."

"Oh yes, that's not a problem." Then he looked at me, frowning. "Tessa?"

"Yes?" Did he know something had happened? I felt my heart begin to race once more.

"Don't heat the soup for so long. It was too hot last time."

"Right," I said, relief flooding through me. "Too hot. Got it."

• • • ● • ● ● • • •

What the hell did you wear to the doctor when there wasn't anything actually wrong with you? Was my striped cotton dress okay, or should I try to look like I was truly ill and go for tracksuit pants and a hoodie?

A part of me – an increasingly large part of me – was tempted to cancel the appointment. After all, it was Dylan who was making me do this, and now he wasn't even speaking to me.

Besides, there was nothing wrong with me. I was wasting a medical professional's precious time for no good reason, and I— I stopped, forcing myself to take a few deep breaths. I was getting that dizzy, sick feeling like I might pass out, which would be counterproductive.

But I couldn't cancel. It was rude to cancel at such short notice, and the thought of phoning up to do so filled me with even more dread than actually seeing the doctor.

My striped dress would have to do. Maybe people would assume I was there to have something horrible and oozing inspected. That would explain both the dress and not looking sick. Having strangers think that the doctor was going to lance a boil in an awkward position was far less embarrassing than having them think I was there to talk about my feelings.

As I made my way past the main house, thinking how much I'd like to turn back and get under the bed covers and never emerge again, I heard my name. I knew, without looking, who was speaking to me.

"Tessa?"

I turned around, biting my lip. "Hi," I said, grinding my teeth together.

"You're going to the doctor, right?" Dylan's hands were forced into the pockets of his jeans, which were really too tight to accommodate them.

"Yes." I was chewing my lip, and abruptly stopped.

"I just wanted to say I hope it goes well," Dylan said, looking somewhere past my left ear as though the fuse box on the side of the house needed his encouragement.

"Thanks," I said, even though seeing him had made my already considerable anxiety about a million times worse.

"Right." Dylan was now looking at his own bare feet. "Well, I'd better let you go."

"See you later," I mumbled, turning before he could say anything else. I had promised I'd do this, so I would. But if Dylan looked at me again, I might lose my nerve.

• • • • ● • ● ● • • •

"So," Dr Tsang swivelled her chair around to look at me. "What can I do for you, Tessa?"

"Um..." I looked down at my balled hands in my lap and considered inventing a disgusting and detailed digestive complaint. "I guess I'm here about..."

Dr Tsang looked at me through her bright red plastic glasses, her eyes warm and full of professional concern.

"My friend said maybe I should see someone about how I worry a lot," I finally blurted out.

"I see." Dr Tsang gave no hint of being even remotely surprised. "You'd like to talk about whether you might have an anxiety disorder and the treatment possibilities?"

"I don't think I have a disorder," I said quickly. "I mean, I've always been a bit of a worrywart. Doesn't everyone worry?" I laughed loudly and falsely, the sound seeming to bounce horribly off the sterile white walls. "But my friend wanted me to come, so..."

I realised, to my horror, that Dr Tsang probably thought I had invented the friend. No! I wanted to tell her. It really was a friend who thought I should be here; I didn't make it up! And yes, it's now very complicated with said friend because of the kissing incident, but I swear he's real!

"If it's affecting how you function," Dr Tsang said kindly, "then it might be a bit more than just worrying. I want to ask you some questions. Would that be okay?"

"Sure," I said, lifting my chin and wanting to show her that I could be a model patient, even though there was nothing wrong with me. "Happy to!"

"I'd like you to think about the last month." Dr Tsang was pulling up something on her computer. "And think about whether these problems have affected you never, rarely, sometimes, often, or always. Do you understand?"

"Sure do!" My voice was still horribly high. To my disgust, I realised I had given her a double thumbs up. I quickly returned my hands to my lap.

"Have you felt nervous, anxious, or on edge?" Dr Tsang asked, looking back at me through her jaunty glasses with an encouraging smile.

"Um..." My mouth was very dry. "Often, I guess?"

"And have you not been able to stop or control your worrying?"

"Often," I said, without having to think about it. The only other truthful option was "always", but that seemed like an attention-seeking answer, so I wanted to avoid it.

"Have you felt you were worrying too much about a lot of different things?"

"Often," I admitted, still looking at my hands. This was going to make me look like I was totally nuts. Why couldn't Dr Tsang ask me a question I could give a different answer to?

"Have you had trouble relaxing?"

"Uh, sometimes," I said and then winced. "Actually, probably often. Sorry."

"That's okay, Tessa," Dr Tsang said. "You can take your time to think about your answers, you know."

Had I been answering too fast? Did that make me seem arrogant? Careless? Like I wasn't taking this seriously?

"And have you had trouble sleeping?"

I forced myself to count to five in my head before I answered. "Always."

Dr Tsang just nodded. "Only two more questions, Tessa. Have you felt easily annoyed or irritable?"

Finally, a question I didn't have to answer with 'often'. "Um, rarely." Annoyed with myself, maybe, but I didn't think I had been irritable with other people. Hadn't Dylan said that I cheered him up? Then again, Dylan had spent all day avoiding me, so perhaps that wasn't a good indicator. Was I irritable, and I didn't even know it? "I don't think so, anyway."

"And finally, have you felt afraid? Like something awful might happen?"

I sat and thought of that heavy, sinking feeling that attacked my chest, settling into my stomach. That feeling of doom, of dread, that I couldn't shake, no matter how hard I tried.

"Sometimes," I admitted weakly. If that feeling was inside me 'always', there's no way I'd be able to get out of bed in the morning.

"And we're done," Dr Tsang swivelled back to me, taking off her glasses and cleaning them on the corner of her zebra print wrap dress.

I waited, grinding my teeth and seriously considering attempting to wrench off my acrylic nails while waiting for the verdict. "Um, yes?"

"Your answers indicate that you're experiencing severe anxiety," Dr Tsang said gently.

"Oh." I felt like my internal organs – and maybe my bones too – had just disappeared. Inside me, there was a great whoosh of emptiness. "I..." I blinked, trying to do an impression of a functional human. "Okay."

"My recommendation is that you try out some medication and that you see a clinical psychologist to work on strategies to reduce and manage your anxiety."

"Okay," I said, still feeling blank and empty. "I..."

"This is a bit of a shock, isn't it?" Dr Tsang was clearly being kind. "I see a lot of patients with anxiety. In fact, more than half of my work as a GP is in mental health. You're not alone, Tessa. Anxiety is one of the most common mental health disorders."

And yes, I understood that she was trying to be nice. To be reassuring. But my brain was stuck on the word "disorder". I was disordered. There was something wrong with me, just as I had always feared. Maybe there always had been. Maybe—

"Um, that's good to know." That seemed like an appropriate response.

"I can give you a referral for a psychologist," Dr Tsang went on, turning back to her computer. "And I'd like to start you on an SSRI. That stands for Selective Serotonin Reuptake Inhibitor. There's still a lot of debate in the medical community about how these medicines work on your brain chemistry, but there's strong evidence that they can help people experiencing anxiety to feel better."

"Right. Uh, I guess that sounds good."

"But you need to know, there are some side effects that can come with these medications," Dr Tsang said, handing me a printout. "Now, most of these improve over time, but some, like sexual dysfunction, are more persistent."

Like a schoolgirl, I blushed at the words 'sexual dysfunction'. Bloody hell, was I twelve? And besides, it wasn't like I had a sex life to be dysfunctional. I thought of how my body had responded in Dylan's arms, his muscular body pressed against mine, the feeling of his mouth on my own, the heat and weight of him, the thrum of possibility in my blood and...

"That isn't really a problem for me. I'm not dating at the moment."

"I see," Dr Tsang nodded. "You might not experience any side effects, but if you do have side effects that bother you, we can always change your medication and see if the symptoms improve."

"And I... Medication is my best option?"

"Medication and building a relationship with a psychologist," Dr Tsang corrected. "Studies show that together they're more effective than either one alone."

"Okay. Um, I guess I can try it."

"If you experience any of these severe side effects, you'll need to seek medical attention immediately," Dr Tsang pointed to the bottom of the paper where fun possibilities like 'vomiting blood' and 'hallucinations' were listed. "But other than that, you mustn't stop taking your medication suddenly under any circumstances. If you want to stop taking it, come back to see me first."

"Okay." I watched, dispassionately, as the paper shook in my hands.

"I'd like you to make a follow-up appointment in three weeks," Dr Tsang went on. "To see how you're getting on. Does that sound okay?"

"Sounds great," I said weakly. "Really great."

I sat there with a bundle of information, a prescription, and a referral in my hands and wondered how the hell I was going to process all this on my own.

It wasn't like I could tell Dylan.

10 Dylan

"Hey, dude!" The door opened before I could even knock, and Tad appeared with baby Benji under one arm and a foul smell wafting from either my oldest friend or his adorable offspring.

"What's that?" I wrinkled my nose. "Seriously mate, if this healthy diet is making you fart like that, you need to quit."

"It's the little guy! His mummy fed him chickpea curry last night, and he loved it. Unfortunately, chickpeas go through a baby's system like...well, you can imagine."

"I don't have to imagine. I can smell it."

"I'm going to take him to the shower and wash him off. You can come with me if you like, see how it's done."

"Why would I want to do that? I think watching you hose toxic waste off your son goes beyond godparent duties."

"And just for that, I hope he does a double blowout when you babysit," Tad said. "Fine, if you don't want to be involved, go and make some tea. Alice is having a nap, but I bet she'd like one ready when she wakes up."

"Now that I can do. Regular tea? No coconut oil? No maca?"

Tad snorted. "Use the macadamia milk in the fridge, but regular teabags, okay?"

I saluted ironically and averted my eyes before Tad could let Benji – and his tsunami of shit – out of the duck-printed onesie and made my way into the kitchen. Flicking on the kettle, I examined the row of supplement bottles lined up in a little plastic tray. Memory Boost Gingko. Immunity Plus Blend. Vitality Vroom. Alice and Tad were certainly committed to being the healthiest parents possible for Benji. I had to give them full credit for that, even if some of the supplements smelled every bit as bad as Benji's blowout.

Ten minutes later, Tad emerged with a clean and fresh-smelling baby and the expression of one who has looked into the abyss.

"No more legumes until he's toilet trained," Tad said, handing Benji to me and taking a gulp of tea. "That was less of a nappy change and more of an exorcism."

I held Benji in my arms gingerly, afraid I might drop my infinitely precious and still not very familiar godson. "Hello," I said, looking down at him.

He gave me a gummy smile and fisted a plump hand into my t-shirt.

"Get your arm under him to take some of the weight," Tad advised, leaning on the counter and looking amused. "That's right."

Benji wasn't screaming, so I thought I was doing a decent job. I swayed back and forth, mostly because I had seen people do that with babies on TV. "You like legumes, huh?"

"I don't care if he likes them," Tad shuddered. "Never again, I'm telling you."

I looked down into Benji's face. "Your godfather will feed you lentils," I told him. "Lentils and beans. And then I'll give you back to your parents because that's what godparents do!"

Benji gurgled happily, taking another handful of my t-shirt and, unfortunately, some chest hair. I winced, and Tad laughed. "Serves you right," he said. "Anyway, how was that thing the other night? Surf n Sounds?"

"How do you know I was there?" I hadn't told Tad about my night out with Tessa, especially not about how it ended. I had been brooding solo over that particular embarrassment.

"Jess from school saw you and messaged Alice. She also said," he paused, "that you were there with a date. What's that about?"

"Why don't you ask Jess?" I was irritated. "She knows the whole story."

"Oh, don't be like that!" Tad said. "Why didn't you tell me you went on a date with Tessa? I need gossip like this! I'm the mostly work-from-home parent of a small baby; I need adult gossip!"

"It wasn't a date," I said, knowing that wasn't entirely true. "Well, it wasn't supposed to be. Tessa was going to Surf n Sounds with her sister, but then her sister got sick last minute, and she looked so disappointed, so I..."

"Went with her," Tad supplied when I trailed off. "How gallant of you."

"Hardly," I rolled my eyes. "I gallantly walked three blocks from my house and gave up my not very precious time that I would have otherwise spent doing absolutely nothing."

"Yeah, I suppose it's not very gallant to take a pretty girl on a date," Tad conceded. "So, what happened?"

"Nothing was supposed to happen," I shook my head and resumed my swaying for the benefit of Benji. "The music was pretty bad at first, so we got through a few of the signature cocktails. And then another band came on, someone her sister knew, and she asked me to dance, and..."

"And?" Tad demanded. "Come on, dude, what?"

"We ended up kissing," I admitted. "Well, I kissed her. But it continued. For quite a while."

Tad let out a sound of delight. "Yes!" He sounded genuinely thrilled. "We have lift off!"

"We do not," I said drily, "have lift off. It wasn't supposed to happen. As Tessa told me when she pulled away."

"Okay, less good. Then what happened?"

"Well, we kind of agreed it was alcohol induced, and we'd forget it, and then she said she was going home and kind of bolted."

"Oof."

"But I went after her because I wasn't going to let her walk home alone after she had been drinking."

"Now that is gallant."

"Not really," I frowned. "I'd be an arsehole not to."

"And then?" Tad demanded. "I swear, dude, you are the worst at telling stories."

"It's not my profession. And then...nothing. We got home and agreed that we'd forget about it and be friends."

"Well, that's boring." Tad took his mug of tea and sipped it.

"I told you I'm not looking to get involved with anyone. And especially not Tessa. She works for my dad!"

"And?" Tad shrugged. "I don't get why you think that's such a big deal. Besides, she's only got a bit longer on the contract with him, right?"

"Not the point," I said. "Anyway, now everything's awkward. I've been trying to give her space, but I don't know. Maybe that's just made it worse."

"When you say you're giving her space..." Tad watched me bounce his small son. "Do you mean you've been leaving the room every time she's there?"

"Um..." I twisted my mouth. "Maybe. How did you know?"

"Because you did exactly the same thing after you hooked up with Melanie Putcher at Timmo Davidson's sixteenth birthday party. And it didn't make sense then, either. But at least you had the excuse of being a dumb kid. Now you're a grown man, and you're still running away from the girl you like."

"I'm not running from her!" I insisted. "I still went and told her I hoped her appointment went well. That's not running."

"And how was her appointment?"

I swallowed. "I have no idea," I admitted. "I haven't talked to her since then."

"Because you're avoiding her."

"Giving her space," I corrected.

"Mate," Tad rolled his eyes and stood up to take Benji, who was starting to fuss. "You can't avoid her. If you really want to put it behind you and be friends, then you actually need to do that. I mean, you live in the same house!"

"She's in the studio," I muttered, but I took his point. "I just didn't want her to feel pressured. I mean, we had talked about how neither of us was looking to date anyone, and then I went and kissed her. That was kind of a dick move."

"Sounds like she kissed you back, though."

The memory of Tessa's mouth on mine, her body pressed against me, hot and urgent, came flooding back, and it must have shown on my face.

"I thought so," Tad looked smug. "I still think you should admit you're keen on her and let whatever's going to happen unfold. You're both grown-ups. Act like it."

"Ouch," I said. "Point taken."

"You needed to hear it."

"Maybe."

"Anyway, when are you going to babysit? You've now proven you can hold my kid for a decent length of time without him freaking out, even if you did run from his avalanche of shit."

"Avalanche of shit," I repeated. "That sounds like my life right now."

• • • • • • • • • •

When I returned to my dad's house, I found Tessa sitting on the sofa, engrossed in her laptop while a true crime documentary played in the background.

"Hi." I sat down in the stiff armchair that Marcel usually occupied.

"Oh, hey," Tessa said, pausing the show on a particularly grisly scene, blood and gore filling the screen. "Your dad's taking a nap. He said his back was giving him trouble last night, and he didn't sleep well."

"Is he okay?"

"He's fine. Marcel's with him. If your dad was tossing and turning, I bet he didn't get much sleep either."

"Probably not," I agreed. "Uh, I wanted to apologise. For avoiding you. I was trying to give you space, but I probably made you feel like... I don't know, but not good."

"It's okay," Tessa shrugged. "I mean, I was worried about what to say to you after the Incident That Shall Not Be Named. So at least I didn't have to."

"Still," I said. "I'm sorry. I know you worry a lot, and I'd hate to cause you any more anxiety."

At that word, Tessa grimaced. "It's okay, really," she said. "I'm supposed to be tackling this anxiety thing anyway. It's good practice."

"So, how did it go with your doctor?"

Tessa closed her eyes and let out a soft sound. "Honestly?" She opened her eyes. "It was kind of horrible. I was expecting her to say that everyone worries and I was wasting her time. Except, you know, in a professional bedside manner kind of way. But she didn't."

"No?" I had suspected that would be the case.

"No," Tessa gave me a wry smile. "Apparently, I have severe anxiety."

I let out a breath. "That must have been tough to hear."

"It was," Tessa nodded. "I just thought... Well, I've always been a worrier; I didn't think it was an actual clinical disorder. But apparently, it is. She prescribed me medication and gave me a referral to a psychologist."

"Well, for what it's worth, that sounds like it could be a good idea," I said. "And thank you for telling me."

"You were the one who forced me to make the appointment," Tessa inclined her head. "And we're friends, right? I couldn't really keep it from you."

"We're definitely friends," I said, even though the tightness in my chest, the clench in my stomach when I looked at her, begged me to reconsider my position on the 'just friends' thing. "And it's not, you know, shameful or anything. Plenty of people take medication and see psychologists."

"That's what Dr Tsang said," Tessa sighed. "But I feel like... Shouldn't I be able to sort this out myself? I'm reasonably smart, and my life is objectively good. Especially since I moved here. I thought moving to Brekkie Beach might change things, and I'd just...stop being like this."

"I don't think that's how this works," I said. "But I can understand why you'd feel like that. It's a lot, hearing that kind of diagnosis."

"Don't say diagnosis," Tessa wrinkled her nose. "I mean, I know that's what it is, but it sounds so serious and medical."

"Sorry," I said, looking away. "So, when are you seeing this psychologist?"

"I haven't made the appointment yet," Tessa admitted. "I will, I just..."

"I can call them for you if you want," I offered. "Sometimes making that kind of call can be tough."

"No!" Tessa shook her head. "I mean, that's very nice of you, but I can do this myself. I'm an adult."

"Well, how about I won't call so long as you do it by the end of tomorrow? Because I think you should."

"You're kind of bossy, you know."

"Well, I was the boss at my start-up. Maybe it's a hard habit to break, even now that I'm unemployed."

"Actually, that reminds me." Tessa bent to pick up a cardboard box from the floor. "I found this stuff when I was looking for an old magazine with a feature article about your dad. I thought you might want it." She put the box in my lap and looked expectant.

I looked down and huffed out a breath of surprise. "Oh man, I forgot about this thing." I picked up the outdated yet sturdy digital SLR that I had been delighted to receive for my sixteenth birthday. I flipped off the cap, testing the lens.

"And there's a tripod in the study too," Tessa looked pleased. "I thought it might inspire something. You said it was your hobby."

I looked up at her, that warm feeling in my chest once more. "That's very thoughtful of you."

"It's no big deal. I mean, it's your camera. I just found it. And charged it up. Just in case you did want to use it."

I flicked on the button, and sure enough, the camera came to life. "It still works!"

"Oh yeah, I checked," Tessa said. "I mean, it would be kind of crappy of me to drag it out and be all, 'here's your broken camera, enjoy!'"

"Thanks, Tessa," I took a test shot of the living room. A little image popped up on the screen, proving that, yes, the camera was in working order. "Maybe I should take this bad boy down to the beach. The light should be good."

"I have no idea how light works in photography," Tessa said with a small smile. "But if you think so, I'd say you're right."

"Do you want to come with me?" I cared more about her answer than I should.

"Only if you promise not to make out with me." Tessa bit her lip. "Crap, that was meant to be funny."

"It was," I lied, feeling my skin tighten. "We can joke about it, right?"

"That's what Abby said," Tessa said, her fingers clasping together in her lap.

"Well then," I cleared my throat, feeling like a much older and more pompous man.

"Just let me grab a hat."

"And some sunscreen?"

Tessa rolled her eyes, but she gave me a more genuine smile. "I won't forget that after last time."

• • • ● • ● • ● • •

I held up the camera, trying to find something to focus on. It was almost impossible to take a bad photo of Brekkie Beach, with its swaying palm trees, yellow sand, and glistening water. But I didn't want a typical tourist photo. And I had taken enough moody photos of footprints on the beach as a teenager.

Tessa had taken her sandals off and was scrunching her toes into the wet sand, a look of satisfaction on her face.

"You like the sand?" I asked, holding the camera up.

"Absolutely! Most beaches in England have pebbles. Pebbles, Dylan!"

I raised the camera again, snapping a few shots of her in quick succession.

"Are you ever going to warn me when you do that?" Tessa was pretending to be annoyed, but her smile was warm.

"Probably not. When people know they're having their photo taken, they get all stiff and fake."

"Better than me squinting with my mouth open," Tessa scrunched up her nose, and I took another shot. "Like that!"

"Sorry," I said. "But you were the one who wanted me to get inspired."

"I'm sure you can find something more exciting to take photos of than me," Tessa said, walking forward to let the ripples of water rush over her feet. Snap, snap, snap.

"Nope." And it was true. There was no one I'd rather take photos of.

"Hey, bro!" A yell came from behind me, and I turned to see one of the local surfers approaching, surfboard under one arm. "You, with the camera."

"Yes?"

"Do you, like, take photos and shit?"

"It's been known to happen." Over his shoulder, Tessa was dissolving into silent giggles.

"Can you take some shots of me catching that sick barrel?" The surfer pointed out at the waves. "Like, for my Insta?"

"I'm not a professional photographer," I told him. "But I think you'd need someone out there with you. With a waterproof camera."

"Oh, right." The surfer looked disappointed. "What if I put a Go Pro on my board? Would that work?"

"It might," I shrugged. "Like I said, not that kind of photographer."

"No worries, man." The surfer gave me a lazy grin. "Take it easy, okay?"

"No worries," I gave the standard reply, watching as he made his way back into the surf, ready to catch the apparently sick barrel.

"Not that kind of photographer, huh? So, what kind of photographer would you want to be? That kind?" She nodded to a spot further along the beach where a local influencer was kneeling in the waves in some pieces of neon string that were masquerading as a swimsuit. A long-suffering admirer was squatting behind her with an iPhone as she shouted directions, her bottom thrust prominently into the air.

"Definitely not. I like shooting people when they're doing things that matter to them. Or with people they care about. Ideally in natural light. What kind of photographer would that make me?"

"I have no idea," Tessa said. "But you're good. And you never look as contented as you do when you're taking photos. You should do it more often."

I looked at her again for a long moment. It sounded so easy. Just be a photographer, as though it was that simple. Pursue the very thing I had told myself I never would. And it seemed possible, too, at that moment. Maybe it was the smell of salt and sand. Perhaps it was the perfect natural light. Maybe – probably – it was because Tessa was smiling at me.

When Tessa smiled at me like that, almost anything felt possible.

Almost anything.

11 Tessa

"Fucking ow!" I swore, sucking my finger into my mouth. I had to fight to stay upright, the room swimming. The sight of blood didn't bother me, but I was pretty sure I was experiencing the third side effect listed on my Zoloft information sheet; dizziness.

"Did you damage the canvas?" Alan wheeled himself over to assess to the destruction.

"No," I said, examining my finger. "I just gouged my finger with the tape gun. The blood only got on the packing tape."

"Oh, that's good."

"It's not good." Dylan stood up from where he was covering a smaller canvas in bubble wrap. "Are you alright, Tessa? Dad shouldn't have asked you to do this."

I felt a little surge of warmth in my chest at the glare he gave his father, even though I shouldn't have. "I don't mind," I insisted. "I'm just going to put a band-aid on it. So I don't get blood on anything else."

"Yes, very wise," Alan said from his chair. "Dylan, don't be so rough with the corners."

"You know, Dad, there are professionals who do this. Maybe they'd meet your standards," I heard Dylan say as I went into the kitchen in search of a band-aid. When I opened the cupboard, I saw the bottle of aloe vera gel, and I felt another surge of warmth as I remembered how Dylan had rubbed it over my back, his hands warm and confident on my tortured skin.

I shook myself. I did not need to be fantasising about Dylan's hands right now. How they may or may not have felt on my body was irrelevant to the current situation. Equally irrelevant were my many detailed fantasies about how those hands would feel on my skin in contexts involving less aloe vera, acute sunburn, and clothing.

Ripping the packet with my teeth, I secured the band-aid on my finger and returned to the living room.

"I'm all sorted." I held up my finger for Alan's approval.

"Good, you can get started packing that big one there and then—"

"Absolutely not," Dylan cut him off. "I'll do it. Tessa, take a break. You shouldn't have to do this."

"I don't mind."

"She doesn't mind," Alan repeated.

"But I do," Dylan's voice was firm. "Seriously, Dad, this job is for your unemployed offspring. Not Tessa."

"I suppose you need the activity more than she does," my father looked thoughtful. "Take a break, Tessa. But stay close in case I need you for anything else."

Behind his father, Dylan rolled his eyes, and I suppressed a giggle.

"Can do," I said, settling into a chair and picking up my laptop.

"Marcel!" Alan called, rolling out of the living room. "Have you packed my teal suede brogues? I want them for the drinks reception!"

"He's a tyrant."

"It must be hard for him, not being able to do things for himself the way he used to."

But Dylan just scoffed. "Oh, he was like this before. Always had quite the aversion to manual labour, my dad."

"I guess his mind's always been busy with greater things." I watched Dylan carefully cover the canvas in bubble wrap, taping it neatly and managing not to slice his finger open. When he bent down, his shirt rode up to show his muscular lower back, and I definitely wasn't complaining about the view.

"That's what he'd tell you," Dylan said, moving on to the next canvas. "Are you sure you're okay? Zoloft can make you dizzy, right?"

"How did you know that?"

"I know about the side effects," Dylan sounded surprised that I thought he might not. "I looked it all up when you told me what the doctor prescribed. So I can watch out for you, especially with the nastier stuff that can happen."

I could only look up at him, open-mouthed. "I..." I swallowed hard. "That's incredibly thoughtful of you. Thank you."

"I thought it was the least I could do. After all, I made you go to the doctor. I should be supportive, right?"

"I think that goes further than being supportive. And I'm grateful. Really grateful."

"It's no big deal." Dylan looked down at the tape in his hands as though he didn't want to be thanked. "How's your writing going, anyway?"

"We've finished corrections on the first six chapters, and your dad's happy—"

"No, I meant your writing," Dylan corrected, breaking off a piece of packing tape with his teeth. And why was that sexy? It seemed to set off some sort of horny cavewoman reaction, like I was watching him tear open an animal carcass to feed my growing brood of grubby neolithic children.

"Um, it's okay." I held my laptop tightly as though Dylan could somehow see through it to my current work in progress. "I'm working on something new, which is...fun."

"What's it about?" Dylan sounded genuinely interested. And I was sure he would be if he knew my new character was based on him. Not that I was going to tell him. That would definitely make him think I was a massive creep and detonate the friendship we had managed to rebuild since the Incident That We Did Not Talk About.

"Well, it's for eight- to twelve-year-olds, so nothing very exciting," I faltered. "A boy struggling with school, hobbies, that sort of thing. Plus, there's a sassy talking cat because, you know, kids' book."

"Sounds awesome," he said encouragingly. "One of these days, you're going to have to let me read your stuff. I've read all the chapters you've done for Dad, and they're great."

"Your dad has had a fascinating life," I brushed away his compliment. "It's easy to make his story interesting. I'd be a useless ghostwriter if I couldn't."

"I don't mean the content," Dylan said, now expertly taping thick brown paper over the bubble wrap. "I mean the way you write. You're very talented."

My cheeks flushed because that was what every ghostwriter wanted to hear. "Well, I did think about sending one of my kids' books to an agent," I swallowed. "When you said I should, before. But I haven't done it."

"Why not?"

"You know why not." I looked down at my laptop. "I mean, tons of people want to write kids' books. People think it's easy because they're short, and you have to keep the language relatively simple. Actually, I think that makes it more of a challenge because you still want the story to be engaging. But it's so competitive, so I..."

"Maybe. But I don't know why you don't think you'll be successful, just because it's competitive. You're already a professional writer, and you understand publishing. And you're good."

"Thanks," I said, still staring at my laptop. I needed to clean the screen. I bet Abby had one thousand-and-one tips on keeping your laptop screen streak-free.

"You're not very good at receiving compliments, are you?" Dylan was looking at me again. "Maybe the psychologist can help with that."

"I don't know if psychologists cover that," I said. "Lots of women are uncomfortable with compliments. All your life, you're told not to seem arrogant or conceited, so when someone says something nice about you, it's natural to try and deflect it."

"Ah, the socialisation argument. I was thinking that maybe it makes you uncomfortable because you don't think you deserve to be complimented, even when it's true. And that's definitely psychologist territory, right?"

"Probably," I sighed. "You know, there should be a book that covers this stuff. How to accept a compliment. How to make a phone call for an appointment. How to have a difficult conversation with a loved one. What to do when someone's being passive-aggressive. Things that no one ever teaches you, but it would be really handy to know."

"Adulting for Dummies?" Dylan suggested. "I like it. Maybe it could cover how to graciously tell your friends you don't know how to hold their baby? Although I think I've managed to work that one out. We should include a chapter on living with your parents as an adult. Because I'm sure as shit not managing that one."

"You're doing pretty well. I mean, you haven't slammed your door or told your dad it's not a phase; it's just how you are."

"Doesn't count if I want to, though," Dylan smirked. "You can write the book, and I'll do the photos. Deal?"

"Deal. Except we'd need to find someone to give me the content because I don't have a clue how to do those things. We need a real adult."

"You're a real adult."

"An adultier adult. Like Abby. She'd know what to do. And if she didn't, she'd act like she did."

"She's a true adult, then." Dylan stretched the tape across the paper-covered canvas, sealing it up. "Just twelve more to go."

"I'll help you," I said, setting my laptop aside and jumping up. I reached for the roll of bubble wrap, but a hand, strong and confident, settled on mine. I looked up at Dylan, my mouth suddenly dry and my body reacting in all sorts of exciting ways.

"Not a chance. Packing this stuff is above and beyond your job description. I'm not going to let you do it."

"Not going to let me, huh?" I asked, trying to joke. "Is that a challenge?" I was horribly aware of how warm his fingers were on mine and my heart thudding in my chest. I was sure Dylan could hear it. Hell, Marcel and Alan could probably hear it, like the bass of a souped-up car with a teenage driver roaring down a suburban street.

"It could be." A smile was playing on Dylan's lips, teasing. But then he tugged the bubble wrap from my hands. "No more packing. Come on, you're a writer. We can't risk you damaging your fingers."

"I risk them every night making dinner," I protested. Still, I returned to my position on the couch. I was nowhere near brave enough to push it with Dylan. I didn't know what might happen if I did.

"Are you not finished?" Alan rolled back into the room. "The courier will be here in a couple of hours!"

"They'll be done by then," Dylan told him. "When's your flight?"

"Four. We need to get going; I do hate being late."

"And it's just the three nights, right?" I asked, even though I knew the answer.

"Just three," Alan confirmed. "They wanted me to stay longer, of course, but I find travel so tiring these days."

"I can imagine." I nodded sympathetically. "And it's okay if Abby comes for dinner, right?"

"Yes, of course. You're perfectly responsible. It's him I worry about." Alan jabbed a finger at his son.

"Dad, I ran my own start-up for years." Dylan looked a little hurt. "I'm responsible."

"I haven't forgotten the time that Marcel and I went to Perth, and your friends trashed this place."

"I was seventeen! And they didn't trash the place," Dylan protested. "Okay, so Tad possibly threw up in the oven, but that was a long time ago."

"Actually, I was going to say you should invite Tad and Alice. And Benji, of course," I said. "When Abby comes for dinner. They're new parents; I bet they'd like some adult conversation."

"A dinner party? How very adult."

"If that's okay with you, Alan?"

"I suppose it is. I do have to remember you're all grown up now." He touched Dylan's arm for a moment, looking up at his tall and handsome son. "I do trust you."

"Thanks," Dylan said, and I could see that it meant more to him than he'd readily admit.

"Just don't let that baby vomit on anything important," Alan said and rolled out of the room.

∙ ∙ ∙ ● ∙ ● ∙ ∙ ∙

```
Abby: worst freaking client today.
she said she had seen my work on insta
and loved it. but when i get there,
she tells me she doesn't like labels
on stuff. says it's visual clutter!
who hires a professional organiser
and tells them not to label anything?
```

Tessa: <sad face emoji>

Michelle: ...what did you say to her?

```
Abby: i told her she'd be better
off finding someone else. she freaked
out, told me she'd complain to my
boss. bitch, i am my boss! and i'm
not going to put up with that shit
```

Tessa: good on you! i probably would have just acted like everything was okay and vented to you guys

Michelle: when are you seeing that psychologist? you need it

Tessa: ouch

Michelle: i mean it with love!

Tessa: next week

```
Abby: and how's the zoloft going?
```

Tessa: i feel a bit dizzy and my stomach was upset. but that could have been from the green tea and dragon fruit bliss ball that nikki said was delicious. it wasn't, but i couldn't be rude and not finish it

Michelle: who's nikki?

Abby: but do you feel any different yet?

Tessa: nikki and nick run the coffee shop by the beach. coffee's great, food is too trendy for me

Abby: DO YOU FEEL ANY DIFFERENT

Tessa: not yet

Abby: probably too soon to tell. can you still orgasm?

Michelle: do antidepressants affect that? yikes!

Tessa: i'm not answering that question

Abby: it's a yes then

Michelle: nothing wrong with a little self-love. <winky face emoji> did you think about dylan?

Tessa: not answering that one either

Abby: another yes. i can't wait to meet him tomorrow. i need to see if he's worthy of your fantasies

Tessa: if you say anything embarrassing, i will kill you. literal murder. i've listened to heaps of true crime. i won't get caught

Michelle: yes, you would, they'd subpoena this chat, and there's your prior intent

Tessa: it would be worth it

Abby: i'll play nice. i still think he's a bad idea for you though. has he made up his mind about what he's doing with his life?

Tessa: not exactly

Abby: that's a problem

Tessa: it doesn't matter! nothing is happening between me and dylan. we're friends. just friends. men and women can be friends.

Michelle: sure they can. so long as at least one of them is gay

Abby: i can't tell if that's sexist or homophobic

Michelle: <frowny face emoji>

Abby: men and women can be friends. but not when both of you obviously want more

Tessa: i don't want more! okay, so i like him. but he's not interested in dating anyone, and i don't think i'm an exception to that. and like you said, his life is unstable. bad for someone with "severe anxiety"

Michelle: <hug emoji>

Abby: of course you're an exception! you're exceptional. what matters is whether he's good enough for you

Tessa: he's a tech millionaire. i make soup for his dad. i don't think him being good enough is the issue

Michelle: you're a professional writer!

Abby: who cares about money!? as if your worth is determined by how much $$$ you have. what a bourgeois cliche

Michelle: karl marx has entered the conversation

Tessa: and now i'm taking medication and seeing a psychologist. pretty sure that's not on anyone's ideal girlfriend wish list

Abby: oh hell no. you're actively managing your mental health which is mature and impressive. that's a good thing! it doesn't make you any less valuable or desirable

Michelle: ^^ what she said

Tessa: we're just friends. probably better i don't date anyone while i'm sorting this anxiety stuff out anyway

Michelle: i'd agree but only if it's because you don't want to. not because you think there's something wrong with you

Abby: exactly

Tessa: i should go. i want to work on my book tonight

Michelle: the girl who stands up to the bullies?

Tessa: no, this one's new. about a boy who loves soccer, but never wants to play because his dad's a professional

TESSA FINCH ISN'T GOOD ENOUGH 213

soccer player. he doesn't want to be compared to his famous dad

Abby: so exactly like dylan. have you told him about it?

Tessa: kind of. obviously i didn't tell him it's based on him. don't want him to think i'm a creep

Michelle: he'd be flattered!

Tessa: i doubt it

Tessa: it's not even really about him, anyway. but there's a talking cat that's totally based on abby

Abby: i'm flattered! <cat emoji>

Abby: if dylan's inspiring you, maybe you should try writing erotica. i bet you'd be good at that too

Tessa: i'll stick to middle-grade fiction

Michelle: did you know you can get erotica audiobooks? <flame emoji> <fireworks emoji>

Tessa: TMI!!!

Abby: no such thing as TMI with your sisters

Tessa: i disagree. gtg. writing calls

Michelle: hope dinner goes well. sad i can't be there <sad face emoji>

Tessa: we'll miss you

Abby: i'll take notes on dylan for you. and tell you if there's chemistry

Tessa: ...please don't

Michelle: maybe something will happen while his dad's away!

Tessa: absolutely zero chance of that happening

12 Dylan

"So, dinner party. Guess that means we have to feed them, right?"

"Generally speaking, yes. I'm doing a Beef Wellington. I haven't made it in years, not since my Nana..." Tessa trailed off. "There's no point making it unless you've got enough people."

"That sounds amazing." Everything Tessa made was amazing. "So, what needs to happen?"

"Well, I need to cook. But I was hoping you might help me set up."

"I can do more than that; I'm not completely useless. And I've got all the time in the world."

"You're not useless at all."

"So, you want me to cook then?"

"I was thinking more of a kitchen hand situation. You know, stirring pots, cleaning up."

"Chef's slave, I see," I sighed dramatically. "Well, I suppose I can manage it."

"I don't know if you can take orders," Tessa looked up at me. "With you so used to being your own boss. Abby sure can't. She'll tell you."

"I'm looking forward to meeting her," I said, entirely truthfully. I had heard a lot about Tessa's sisters and her beloved Nana. Much less about her parents, but from what I understood, they had been largely absent from her life. She didn't seem especially traumatised by it, but I wondered if it bothered her sometimes. "Even if she does sound a little terrifying."

"Oh, she is." Tessa opened the fridge and poked at what I assumed must be the pastry. "But she's great. I'm looking forward to seeing Tad and Benji again and meeting Alice."

"Tad's going to tell you all sorts of embarrassing stories about me," I groaned. "Like when I went through this phase in high school of wearing a peacoat and writing poetry in a leather-bound notebook."

"I don't need Tad to tell me embarrassing things about you. You do it all by yourself."

"I guess I feel comfortable with you, then," I said, and that was true. At least, mostly true. Sometimes, I felt like I could tell Tessa absolutely anything. Other times, she made me nervous as hell, and I wanted to show her only my very best, most highly edited self. But that was a losing battle. After all, she knew I had moved back in with my parents and was unemployed. Tessa knew almost everything about me, and she still seemed to like me. I guessed that made me lucky.

"Well, you already know that I'm halfway to crazy and look like a lobster if I get a touch of sun, so I guess we're past being embarrassed, huh?"

"You're not at all crazy," I said. "Anxiety isn't something you have to be ashamed of. And you're addressing it. That's a good thing. Lots of successful, interesting, awesome people have anxiety and take medication. And you're one of them."

"Thanks." I could see she didn't entirely believe me. "I mean, I know that logically, but..."

"Maybe your psychologist can help with that, too. Provided she's more useful than Julius was."

"I don't see how she could be less helpful without losing her board registration," Tessa said, her smile turning to a grin. I could see that little gap between her teeth, the corners of her eyes crinkling slightly. I wished I could take a photo of her right now. Not because the light was especially fabulous, but because I wanted to capture that smile as much as possible. Hell, I'd settle for a grainy flip phone camera and harsh flash, so long as I could get that smile.

"I think you're right about that."

"I meant to ask you, any dietary restrictions for Tad and Alice? Please don't tell me they're vegetarian. I've got so much beef ready." Tessa closed the fridge, leaning against it.

"Well, they're both trying to live to one hundred and fifty. Tad's taking a ton of weird supplements. Pretty sure at least one of them was banned in the European Union for making you grow webbed toes," I said, pleased when Tessa laughed. "But nothing apart from that."

"Well, I don't think Beef Wellington is known for its life-extending powers. But I was planning on honey-roasted carrots and baby beets with it. Vegetables are good for living longer, right?"

"That sounds incredible."

"Well, when it was going to be just Abby and me, I probably would have done pasta," Tessa admitted. "But now we've got a proper dinner party."

"Almost like we're real adults."

"I feel like I'm playing house while my parents are away," Tessa confessed. "I sat in the formal lounge last night and it felt like I was doing something forbidden."

"So long as you're not casting me in the role of your brother, I can live with that."

Tessa grimaced. "I definitely don't think of you as my brother."

"Good," I said. "Because that would be..."

There was an awkward silence as we were both clearly thinking about the Incident We Did Not Discuss.

"Um, do you think you could go down to the bottle shop and get drinks for tonight?" Tessa broke the silence. "I think your dad would run me over with his chair if I raided his wine fridge."

"No problem." I was glad to break the uncomfortable moment, as much as I wanted to spend more time with Tessa. "What are chef's slaves for?"

• • • ● • ● • ● • •

"Something smells amazing, and I know this guy had nothing to do with it," Tad jabbed a thumb at me.

"Hey, I helped!" I said, pretending to be offended. "I, uh..."

"Made me a gin and tonic when I was swearing at the pastry," Tessa finished. "Without that, I would have thrown the whole bloody thing out the window. It was a team effort."

"Well, I'd like a gin and tonic, even if I'm not about to throw anything out of the window," Tad said, taking Benji from the carrier strapped to his front and carefully placing him in the pop-up highchair that Alice had set up. "How about you, babe?"

"I've been ready since this morning," Alice said, letting out a sigh and sitting down heavily. Alice was tattooed, blonde, and always sported immaculate winged eyeliner, despite the dark circles under her eyes. "Teething is not okay."

"He looks happy now," I said cautiously, bending down to my godson's level. "Show me your chompers, Benji." Benji, however, reached for my nose, his adorable chubby fingers pinching me and surprisingly sharp baby nails cutting in. "Ow!" I stood up. "I'm going to make those drinks. Safer than trying to bond with my godson."

"Are you okay?" Tessa looked up at me with concern.

"I think I can just about cope with being manhandled by a baby," I said, even though my nose was stinging. "And even if I couldn't, I'd have to pretend I was for the sake of my masculine ego."

"Ah, masculinity so fragile," Alice sighed.

"You'll have to talk to my sister Abby about that. Her second favourite hobby is puncturing over-inflated male egos. She's very good at it."

"What's her favourite hobby?"

"Giving me and Michelle advice whether we ask for it or not. It's a big sister thing, I guess."

"I get that," Alice said thoughtfully. "I've got a little sister. I just can't help myself when it comes to the unsolicited life advice."

"This is where I'm glad I'm an only child," I said, looking up from the pieces of cucumber and lime I was cutting, according to the drinker's preference. "Okay, here we go. Mother's ruin. Sorry, Alice."

"Mother is ready to be ruined tonight." Alice picked up her glass and took a greedy gulp. "Oh, sweet baby Jesus that tastes good. I still haven't recovered from when I was pregnant, and Tad thought it would be a good idea to visit a craft brewery. I couldn't even taste anything and had to drive his drunk arse home."

"That was not my finest hour," Tad admitted, rubbing his face with his hands. "Lucky you're a kind, forgiving wife and didn't punish me harshly for it. Except in the way I like." He winked at his wife, who mimed lashing him with an invisible whip. I could see Tessa hiding her own grin behind her hand. Our eyes met, and she began to laugh again.

We were saved from having to comment on Tad and Alice's bedroom dynamics by the sound of the doorbell.

"That will be Abby." Tessa made for the door.

When she disappeared, Tad looked at me with raised eyebrows. "You two seem to be getting on well."

Alice scoffed. "Getting on well? They're like a married couple, finishing each other sentences."

"Why is it you two have so much difficulty with the concept of friendship?" I took a sip of my own gin and tonic and gave Benji a spare piece of cucumber to gnaw with his stumpy teeth.

"We don't," Alice said. "Friendship is great. It's just that this isn't one. You two are obviously dead keen to bone but too scared to make a move."

"Nothing to do with being scared. It's just a bad idea. Tessa works for my dad, and hitting on your dad's employee is the opposite of a classy move."

"She's a contractor, not an employee," Tad insisted. "Not the same thing."

"Very much the same thing," I disagreed, but before it could be debated further, Tessa came into the kitchen with her sister. Abby had the same dark hair and bright blue eyes as Tessa but was taller and had an olive complexion. Her eyes moved over me as though making a judgement. I just hoped I passed the test.

"Abby, this is Dylan. Dylan, my sister Abby. And this is Tad and Alice, and baby Benji, Dylan's godson."

"Hi!" Abby said, leaning up to give me a kiss on the cheek with supreme self-confidence. "Damn, you really are tall, huh?"

"Tessa told you about me?" I asked, joking but also really, really not joking.

"Nah, I've got cameras in your bedroom," Abby deadpanned, and Tad burst out laughing before the rest of us caught up.

"Are they live streaming my every move? Tell me, is my Only Fans doing well?" I played along. "Because if I've got a future as a Cam Boy, my whole career crisis might be solved."

"He's funny!" Abby pointed at me and nodded at Tessa. "Ooh, are we having gin and tonics? Make mine with lime."

"I'll get to it," I escaped to the safety of the kitchen. "Anyone for refills?"

"Yes!" Alice held up her glass expectantly.

"I'm on call with the little man tonight, so I'll pass."

"I'd better not," Tessa said. "If I let myself have one before dinner is on the table, it won't be."

"So responsible," Abby patted her on the arm. "Is this the kitchen you were telling me about? What did Alan say about putting pull-out drawers in the pantry?"

"I tried to tell him how space-saving it would be," Tessa shrugged as Abby inspected the pantry behind me. "But he wasn't very interested. Sorry, Abby."

"Well, some people can't be helped. I'm a professional organiser, if Tessa didn't tell you. So, I'm not going through your dad's cupboards because I'm nosy. I mean, I am, but I've got a professional interest too."

"They're my dad's cupboards, not mine. Feel free to look. And judge."

"Ooh, I do love judging." Abby pulled out a packet of dried basil. "This expired four years ago, Tessa. Your boss needs my help."

"Maybe he's saving it. As an artwork. On the nature of our disposable consumerist society."

"You joke, but don't give him any ideas," I said darkly.

"Wait up, let's get back to you being a professional organiser," Tad interjected, looking at Abby. "Do you ever organise baby gear? Because our house has been taken over."

"Completely invaded," Alice agreed. "We used to have this cute vintage boho vibe going on, and now it's just an explosion of infant."

"Oh, I'm all about organising with kids!" Abby abandoned the pantry and sat down between Tad and Alice. "Check this out," she pulled out her phone. "This client had triplets—"

Alice made a gagging sound like she was being throttled. "The worst!"

"And this is the before and after," Abby said triumphantly, and I could see that Tad and Alice were appropriately awed.

"Our people seem to be getting on." Tessa nudged me gently.

"They are," I said, looking down at her and trying not to notice just how close she was, how easy it would be to—

"We're doing a great job at throwing an adult dinner party, then, if our guests are getting on. Go team us." She held up her fist for me to bump, and I did, still smiling.

Team us. I could almost imagine that tonight was my real life. That the house was my home, that Tessa was not my dad's employee. That she and I were a real couple, putting on fabulous parties for our friends, and when they all went home, we'd...

"What are you thinking about?"

"I think I heard the oven beep," I lied. "Is the timer on? Do you need to check on our friend Wellington?"

"I should. I'll cry if I burn him."

"I won't let that happen." If only I could ensure Tessa never had to cry over anything.

• • • ● ● • ● • • •

"Okay, Judge Benji," Tessa's voice was solemn. "This is it. The chef has slaved over this dish for hours, but your judgement could send her home if it's not up to your standards."

Benji, for his part, was looking at the piece of beef and pastry with interest, and the whole table was watching him with bated breath. I raised the old SLR. Click. Click. Click. I captured him grabbing it in one chubby fist and the moment he mashed it against his mouth.

"Come on, Benji," Alice encouraged. "What do you think?"

Benji's face was solemn as he sucked the morsel in his mouth. Click, click. Then, slowly but surely, he pushed the rest of the piece into his mouth with a gummy smile. Click, click.

"And that's approval from the toughest judge on the panel! I won't have to cry into my pillow tonight!" Tessa clapped her hands, and I captured her as well, pink-cheeked and laughing, kneeling beside the highchair.

"Good decision, mate," Tad said, patting his infant son on the head. "If you didn't like this, I might have had to push for a paternity test."

"He's got your exact face!" Alice protested. "But if my kid couldn't appreciate the deliciousness of beef and pastry, there's a good chance he was swapped at the hospital."

Benji, overwhelmed by all the attention, began to whimper and Tessa jumped away. "Spoke too soon!" she said, returning to her seat. "Maybe I was applying undue pressure to his majesty there."

"I think he's just getting tired." Tad picked up his son. "I'll chuck him in the pram, see if he drops off."

"Thanks, babe," Alice said. "I'd do it, but—"

"But I want you to finish a hot dinner tonight, at least." Tad kissed his wife on the cheek as he moved away with Benji.

"I know I shouldn't praise him for simply being a decent dad," Abby began. "But he's definitely doing this right."

"I know," Alice said with a sigh. "My mother's group keeps telling me how lucky I am to have a partner who does half the work, but shouldn't that be standard?"

"It should be," Tessa said, frowning. "But it isn't."

"Whenever I'm out for a walk with Tad and Benji," I ventured, "we get people coming up to us, saying how great he is for babysitting and giving Mum a break."

"That's disgusting," Abby stabbed her fork viciously into a piece of beef that probably didn't deserve her anger. "Babysitting his own kid!"

"I know!" Alice agreed, nodding vehemently. "My dad was like that; he thought he was doing my mum a favour if he took us to get chips for an hour so she could do the housework in peace. I swore I'd never procreate with a man like him."

"You'll be pleased to know that Tad took my hand and told her that we were both the dads."

Alice choked, pastry flakes splattering onto her plate. "Sorry," she apologised, wiping her mouth. "That's why I'm lucky I married Tad. Not only is he a truly decent guy, but he makes me laugh every day."

"You definitely found a good one," Abby said approvingly. "What about you, then?" She turned her steely gaze on me.

"What about me?" I helped myself to another spoonful of honey-roasted carrots. Goddamn, they were good.

"When you have kids with someone," I noticed that Abby's eyes slid over her sister as she said it, and a rush of heat went through me. "Are you going to be a decent human being like Tad and do your fair share and not expect a parade and adulation for it?"

"Uh—"

"Of course he would," Tessa said loudly, looking at her sister and then at me. "After all," she said, her voice softening. "He wouldn't let Tad outdo him at anything."

"You've got me there," I said, wishing I could tell Tessa how much it meant that she had come to my defence at her sister's very awkward question. "But I'm not exactly thinking about kids any time soon. Being single and unemployed."

"Taking a break," Tessa corrected, her eyes fixed on mine. "Which you're allowed to do."

"The little connoisseur is asleep!" Tad announced, coming back into the kitchen. "What did I miss?"

"Quite an interesting discussion on how society praises fathers for doing the bare minimum, and Abby questioning Dylan on his own fatherhood potential," Alice said.

"Dylan would be a great dad," Tad said cheerfully, sitting down and returning to his Beef Wellington with relish. "If he ever manages to snag a decent woman. It's hard for him, of course. He can't rely on his looks like me." He winked at me, and I choked on a piece of carrot.

"Good thing he's got plenty of other qualities," Tessa said from beside me. Just for a moment, her knee pressed against mine under the table. It could have been a coincidence – an accident. But I didn't think it was. When I looked at Tessa, she was looking up at me, her lips slightly parted to show the little gap between her teeth. That gap was becoming very dear to me.

I shook myself slightly and raised the camera again, taking a few shots of Alice and Tad, their arms around each other, and their faces tired but happy. A couple of Abby, wine glass in one hand, finger pointing with the other. And about a million of Tessa. She seemed to draw my lens even when she was doing nothing more exciting than spearing beetroot with her fork.

"I should start cleaning up," Tessa said finally, pushing back from the table and reaching out to take my plate.

"Absolutely not," I put a hand on her wrist, and her skin was warm and soft beneath my touch, sending hot sparks shooting under my flesh and making the room feel suddenly as hot and stuffy as my dad's study. "You cooked. You don't clean up."

"You helped cook," Tessa objected, biting that full lower lip. Did she know she drove me more than halfway to crazy when she did that? If she did, was that why she kept doing it? Did I want her to stop?

"Barely." I stood up and took the plate from her. "Besides, I'm unemployed, remember? Let me make myself useful tonight, at least."

"Let him, Tessa," Abby insisted as she got to her feet. "I'll help him clean up. I want to see what kind of screwed-up system your boss has going on with the crockery, anyway. You don't lift a finger for the rest of the night."

Tessa held up her hands. "When the two of you gang up on me, I'm powerless to resist," she said, ostensibly to her sister, but she was still looking at me. "What am I supposed to do now?"

"Sit and talk to us. You can tell us how beautiful our son is and how well we're doing as parents," Tad grinned.

"Well, both of those things are true. So, I'm pretty sure I can handle this conversation."

I stood there, hovering by the empty dishwasher with my stack of plates, watching as Tessa chatted animatedly with Tad and Alice. I might have watched her all night if Abby hadn't nudged me. "Enjoying the view?"

"I was just—" I began, busying myself with the plates.

"I know," Abby said, and for once, she wasn't teasing or challenging. "I get it. My sister is amazing, isn't she?"

I let out a breath, unwilling to admit too much because I knew anything I said to one sister would be repeated to the other. But I could only agree. "She is."

Abby gave me a knowing look before taking the plates from my hands and explaining why everything I thought I knew about stacking a dishwasher was totally wrong.

• • • ● • ● • • •

"Are you sure I can't call you an Uber?" Tessa asked as Abby picked up her handbag, a little unsteady on her feet.

"No Uber is going to drive me three blocks, Tess. I'm fine; stop fussing!"

"You'd never let me go home alone like this. You've had quite a few."

"I have not," Abby held herself up very straight, "had quite a few."

"Ooh, I think we did," Alice giggled. "That second bottle of wine, remember?"

"Oh yeah!" Abby swayed slightly. "But it doesn't matter, I'm fine!"

"I can walk you home," I offered, but Abby put a hand to my chest as though pushing me back.

"No, no, no," she shook her head. "You stay here. With Tessa." Her wink was the opposite of subtle.

"Where do you live, Abby?" Tad jiggled the pram full of an apparently still sleeping Benji.

"End of Betty Street."

"Oh, that's near us," Alice said brightly. "Well, that's settled. We'll all walk together."

"I would have been fine by myself," Abby objected. "Brekkie Beach has one of the lowest crime rates in this country."

"That was before you moved here," Tessa teased her sister.

"Thank you for a beautiful dinner and delightful evening, my lovely sister," Abby kissed her loudly on both cheeks and wrapped her in a tight hug.

"Cheers, dude," Tad gave me a hug too. "We should do this again."

"Wish we could," I said. "But Dad doesn't go away much."

"Oh yeah, I forgot. I kept thinking this was your place." He shrugged, clapping me on the arm. "And it's going to take me a week of high-intensity interval training to burn off that pudding, Tess, but I don't regret it."

"Not for a minute," Alice agreed. "We'll see you soon, okay?"

"See you!"

There were at least four more rounds of hugs, kisses, goodbyes, reminders to send recipes, insistence on sending photos, and doubling back to retrieve a forgotten baby bib before the house was finally empty.

Well, sort of empty.

Tessa was very much still with me.

"Well, that was a success," she said, dropping down onto the sofa and dislodging Cyndi, who had avoided the entire party. Cyndi yowled but appeared to be mollified by a gentle stroke from Tessa. "I'm exhausted, though. Entertaining like a real adult is tiring."

"I should let you get to bed, then." I couldn't hide my disappointment. I didn't want to let this evening with Tessa end. There was an almost magical quality in the air, like this night could be our real lives if we only believed hard enough. And I knew enough about magic to be sure the feeling would be gone by the morning.

"No," Tessa shook her head. "My body's tired, but my brain is wide awake. I wouldn't be able to sleep if I did go to bed."

"I know that feeling," I said, sitting beside her. "Thank you for suggesting this. I don't know if I would have thought to invite Tad and Alice over like that if you hadn't suggested it. But they seemed to have a good time."

"I think they did," Tessa was looking at me. "But did you?"

"Couldn't you tell?" The question came out more like a challenge than I meant it to.

"Well, at first, I was too busy worrying about what might go wrong to be sure," Tessa said with a self-deprecating grimace. "But then..."

"Then what?" I was very aware of how close she was to me. How much I wanted to keep this moment, this magic alive between us. One wrong move and the spell would break.

"Then I could see how happy you were," Tessa said, her lips breaking into that smile that made me simultaneously want to kiss her and grab my camera to capture her forever. "It was a perfect night."

"I am happy," I said quietly, my voice coming out like a rasp. "And I..." I swallowed. "You make me happy." That wasn't what I had meant to say at all. It was too raw, too honest, and too sentimental all at the same time. But it was true, and I couldn't deny it.

"Dylan," the way she said my name was almost musical, but there was a note of warning in her voice. "Don't say things like that to me. Or we're going to end up with another Incident That We Don't Talk About."

"Maybe we should talk about it." I couldn't take my eyes off her face. "Or not talk about it. I know what I said about not wanting to get involved with anyone because I don't know what I'm doing with my life. But you know all about that. You know all about me, and if you..." I breathed out slowly. "If that doesn't bother you, then—"

I didn't have to finish my sentence. Which was for the best because I had no idea where I was going with it. Somewhere between asking and begging, I guess. Telling Tessa that if there was any possibility that she wanted to take a chance on a guy with no job living in his dad's house, then

I would be eternally grateful. But I didn't have to say any of that.

Because those full lips I couldn't stop thinking about were pressed against mine; warm, soft, and insistent. I pulled her close, trying to say, without words, everything that was inside of me. How I couldn't stop thinking about her. How much I cared. How incredible she was. I tried to put all of that into the kiss as I held her close on my dad's sofa in the soft light of a lamp that may or may not technically have been a sculpture.

When Tessa pulled back, her lips were wet and her eyes wide. "That's what you meant, right? I mean, you want this. With me?"

"Yes," I didn't let her go, holding her against me, feeling the way she was trembling. And maybe I would have liked to think that my kissing prowess was responsible for the trembling, but I hadn't forgotten that Tessa was managing serious anxiety. And I didn't want to make that any worse. I figured it was best to make myself absolutely clear. "I didn't think I should let myself get involved with anyone. Not while I'm... But I want to. Because it's you. And being with you makes me happy, makes me feel like, actually, I do have it all figured out. Or maybe it's just that it doesn't seem so important when I'm with you."

"You really are charming," Tessa said softly, her fingers brushing my cheek. "And, I want this too," she said, with a little nod. "Just in case that wasn't clear."

"I kind of guessed from the kissing, but I appreciate your clarification." I rubbed my thumb over her lower lip, letting out a groan when she sucked the tip into her mouth, tongue swirling over my skin.

"Clear enough?" She looked up at me with huge eyes.

"I don't know," I teased, pretending to think about it. "Maybe you could—"

But her lips captured mine again, cutting off any attempt at wit or banter and possibly severing the connection between my brain and body. I couldn't think, at least not in any way that was sensible. All I could do was feel. Feel how very much I wanted the woman in my arms, how much I didn't want to let her go.

"I'd say we should take this upstairs," I murmured in a break between kisses when my shirt had found its way to the floor and Tessa's dress was around her waist. "But I feel like my teenage bedroom is a definite turn-off."

"The studio, then?"

"Very good idea."

13 Tessa

My head was spinning as Dylan steered me down the hall. Somehow, entwined in each other's arms like the world's most clumsy ballroom dancers, we made our way to the studio, knocking into furniture, tipping over piles of paperwork, losing shoes, belts, and socks as we went.

When he pressed me down onto the bed, my skin was blistering hot, the need to be touched urgent and insistent. I gasped as Dylan pulled my dress over my head, sending it sailing through the air in a graceful arc.

"God, Tessa," Dylan breathed as he looked down at me. "You're so beautiful. It's been making me crazy, I can't stop thinking about everything I want to do to you."

"Really?" I bit my lip, finding it hard to believe that, even now.

"Absolutely," Dylan was dusting featherlight kisses over my collarbone, my skin prickling and hot waves of desire rushing through me. "I've been thinking about seeing you come for me. It's the hottest thing I can imagine."

And shit, I knew that might be a problem. A flicker of panic in my stomach, cutting through the dizzying heat. "Um—" I began, unsure of how to say what I needed to and feeling unbelievably embarrassed that I had to say it at all.

Dylan pulled back, looking at me with a tiny frown. "Are you okay?" He sat up, taking my hand in his. "If this is too fast, or you're not sure you want—"

"I'm really sure I want to!" I said quickly. "Believe me, I've been thinking about it too. A lot. But I," I looked down at my own bare legs, because I couldn't bring myself to look into those eyes as I said this. "Sometimes, I find it hard to..." I swallowed. "To finish. During sex, I mean." And of course I meant during sex, what else could I have meant? "And apparently, the medication I'm taking might make that worse, so I don't—" I swallowed again. "I still really want this, but I just don't want you to be disappointed."

"Tessa," Dylan's voice was low as he squeezed my hand. "I'm glad you told me. But you've got to know, there's no way I could ever find you disappointing."

"I hope not."

"I'm here with you." His mouth was once again trailing over my neck. "There's nothing more I could want."

And that was incredibly nice of him to say, even if I didn't completely believe it. But as his jeans joined my dress on the floor, and his body covered mine, hard lines of muscle, his skin warm against my own, I stopped caring.

In the soft light of the studio, Dylan's hands, his mouth, moved over my body. It was like he wanted to learn exactly which caresses produced a little gasp, a high-pitched keen of want, or a low moan of need. I had never been with a man so completely focused on what I liked, what I wanted. My last boyfriend had been much more interested in what I could do for him. But when I reached down to wrap my fingers around the hard length of him, Dylan just caught my wrist.

"You don't want me to?"

"I do," Dylan told me, his voice a low rumble. "But not yet. Right now, it's all about you. And trust me when I say I don't want anything else."

"But I could—"

I was completely unable to finish that sentence, because Dylan's fingers found the exact spot that made me arch off the bed, crying out his name like I didn't care if the neighbours – or their neighbours – heard. And I didn't, not when he was touching me like *that*.

"So hot, Tessa," Dylan groaned, pushing a lock of hair back from my face and looking at me like I was the fulfilment of every fantasy he had ever dreamed up. I hoped I could be.

My body was spasming, arching, almost levitating off the bed as he touched me, keeping up that perfect pressure, that precise rhythm inside my body. "Dylan!"

"Yeah?"

"I want you," I whispered. "Right now. Please."

"Are you sure?" Dylan's breath was hot by my ear, sending a fresh rush through me. "I could just keep doing this." Teeth grazed over my earlobe, and I let out a cry. "Because you seem to be enjoying it."

"Don't make me beg." My lips were so close to his that it was almost a kiss.

"You don't have to." He licked over the curve of my throat. He moved away then, and I couldn't help letting out a sound of disappointment, even though he was doing the responsible thing by scrabbling in his jeans for a condom. I didn't even have to ask him to wear one, and I knew that was a rare thing, based on Michelle and Abby's stories.

Biting my lip, I watched as Dylan carefully slipped the sheath over himself. It was a good thing he had brought his own, because the condoms Abby had given me as a 'Welcome to your new life in Brekkie Beach' present were standard size, and definitely would have struggled to accommodate him.

"Are you ready?" Those eyes were fixed on me, intense and dark with desire, as he drew my body close to his, wrapping my legs around his back like he didn't want me to ever let him go.

"Yes." I was completely certain and utterly sure that if he wasn't inside me in the next three seconds, I might actually implode. My body was tense, waiting for him, craving him, needing him.

When he pushed inside me, steady and careful, there were no more words between us, just moans, grunts, and cries as sweat-slick skin moved against sweat-slick skin. The curves of my body against the firm muscles of his in the soft light, the burning intensity between us growing, ready to erupt.

I didn't need to climax to enjoy every second of this, but then Dylan did something that no man ever had. Sliding his hand down my body, his fingers once again found that nub of pure pleasure. I gasped out his name, squeezing tight around him, as his touch urged my body closer and closer to the edge.

"Don't stop!" I gasped out, my hands tangled in his sweat-damp hair. "Please, don't stop! I'm going to—"

"Do it, Tessa," Dylan's voice was almost a command, and he didn't stop. Didn't stop the way he was touching me, didn't stop that perfect rhythm inside me until my pleasure bubbled over, erupting, as I squeezed tight around him.

At that moment, I forgot everything. My clinically-diagnosed severe anxiety. The fact that he was my boss's son, and we really shouldn't be doing this. I might have even forgotten my own name if he hadn't been groaning, growling it against my skin as he let go, losing himself inside me.

And as we collapsed against each other, gasping and breathless, I knew that whatever this was between us, whatever it might become, it was the real deal. This was me, Tessa Finch, falling for Dylan Huxley.

• • • ● • ● • • •

When I blinked to consciousness, I was suddenly aware of two things:
1. I really had to pee
2. I was not alone in my tasteful white linen sheets

Not even remotely alone, in fact. There was a strong arm draped over my bare body and warm breath on the back of my neck.

Holy shit. So last night really had happened, then. I turned carefully, and yep, there he was. Dylan Huxley, peacefully asleep. And very much naked. Which made sense, given the exciting and varied range of last night's activities. Still, it didn't fully prepare me for the reality of my boss's son naked in my bed the morning after, even though cause and effect would indicate that's where he would end up.

Ever so gingerly, I extricated myself from that strong arm. I didn't want to, but I figured that peeing in the bed would be the opposite of an aphrodisiac. I padded silently on bare feet to the bathroom, unable to stop myself from performing a little dance of glee once I had closed the door firmly behind me.

"It actually happened," I whispered to myself as I relieved my bladder. "In real life." I had certainly imagined waking up to Dylan in my bed – and the circumstances that would lead to such an occurrence – plenty of times. But I had never thought it would really happen. Despite the looks he sometimes gave me, the way he seemed to take my photo far more than was necessary for even a keen photographer, the way he stood up for me to his dad, and even the Incident We Didn't Talk About. All those things had made me wonder – and worry – about what might or might not happen between us, but I had never truly believed it could lead to this.

And what was this, exactly? I examined my reflection in the bathroom mirror. My mascara was a little smudged, and my hair definitely looked like sex hair, but other than that, I looked the same. What was I expecting? A tramp stamp with 'Official Girlfriend of Dylan Huxley' on my lower back to clarify the situation?

"He said he wanted to be with me," I told my reflection. "Well, kind of. Didn't he?" I tried to remember precisely what Dylan had said to me last night before we had moved on to activities requiring far fewer words. Definitely some kind of revision about the whole 'not getting involved with anyone' thing and me being the reason why. I bit my lip, feeling the familiar clench of anxiety in my stomach.

"I'm not going to worry about that right now. I'm going back to bed to do delightful things with that very handsome man."

My anxiety had never diminished at my request before, but maybe the presence of Dylan would help? I pushed open the door and found Dylan sitting up, blinking sleepily.

"There you are." He reached a hand out towards me. I then remembered I was still very much naked, and in the literal cold light of morning, I felt far more self-conscious than my actions last night would have predicted. "I thought you'd left or something."

"No," I said, getting back into bed beside him and pulling the sheet up. God, he was so warm. And firm. Don't forget firm.

"Good," Dylan's mouth was on my neck, trailing over my throat. "I'd be devastated if you left."

"Devastated, huh?" I managed to gasp as sparks of desire flared and burned under my skin. God, I wanted him so much.

"Devastated," he repeated, big hands moving over my body, drawing me closer. "Because I am so not done with you."

And as his mouth claimed mine, I discovered that maybe, just maybe, Dylan's presence under these particular circumstances could force my anxiety to remain at bay. Especially when he was mouthing over my body like he couldn't wait to taste every part of me. It was like he had woken up today with just one thing on his mind. Me.

When that head of dark tousled hair disappeared between my thighs, Dylan's eyes meeting mine for just a moment, I didn't have another coherent thought, anxious or otherwise, for a long time.

• • • • ● • ● • • •

"Good choice on the breakfast," I said, swallowing down a huge mouthful of a buttery, still-warm croissant.

"Ideally, I would have taken you somewhere nice for brunch," Dylan said, shrugging apologetically. "But the only place that does brunch is Nick & Nikki's, and their food is..."

"Experimental? But the coffee's good." I lifted my half-empty cup to emphasise my point.

"Very good," Dylan agreed. "I guess that's the one problem with Brekkie Beach. Limited dining options. Unless, of course, you happen to have access to 31 Pine Street's award-winning in-house chef."

"You don't even need a reservation."

"But I thought it would be churlish to ask you to make brunch," Dylan said, his eyes crinkling as he looked at me. "After everything last night."

"Are you referring to the arduous process of making Beef Wellington or the equally exhausting stuff that came later?"

"Both, I guess."

"Maybe you could open a restaurant, then," I said, leaning my head against his shoulder as we looked out over the waves and sand. A few surfers were trying their luck, but the waves were meek and insipid. "You know, as your next thing."

"You don't think the fact that I can barely boil a pot of water might be a drawback? I'm starting to think you have too much faith in my abilities, Tessa."

"Well, I didn't mean as the chef," I conceded. "Maybe you could be the Executive Director. Owner."

Dylan looked thoughtful. "I think I'd hate it," he said after a moment. "All that people management. I think that's why I sold my app in the end. If it had gotten much bigger, I would have had to spend all my time managing people instead of doing the stuff I was good at."

"That's kind of how lots of jobs work, isn't it? If you get to the top, you just end up managing people. I guess writing's different, thankfully. I don't think I'd like managing people."

"You'd be good at it," Dylan said, like it was a statement of fact.

"I don't think so," I disagreed. "Last thing anyone needs is a boss with an anxiety disorder." I laughed, but Dylan didn't join in. Instead, he took my hand and squeezed it.

"You need to stop saying that like it means there's something wrong with you." His voice was serious. "Because there isn't. Your brain is just an arsehole sometimes. And you're working on managing it."

"It sounds so simple when you put it like that." I liked the way he described it; my severe anxiety wasn't an indictment on my character but simply the result of an arsehole brain.

"And last night, what you told me about struggling to finish, especially with the medication..." Dylan coughed slightly and looked down at me. "It didn't seem to be a problem."

My ears turned pink, and I looked down at my coffee cup as though the recycling symbol moulded into the plastic was deeply fascinating. "No, that wasn't a problem. Not at all. You were...very attentive. And considerate. So, I..." I swallowed hard. "Thank you."

Dylan looked down at me with a soft smile. "You don't have to thank me, Tessa. I loved every second of it." He leaned down to close the gap between us.

I wanted to keep kissing him in the soft sunshine, the taste of coffee and croissants between us, and the smell of salt in the air. But the niggle – more than a niggle – in my stomach that threatened to turn into twisting snakes demanded that I use my mouth for something less pleasant.

"Um, so this..." I waved a hand, indicating the two of us. "This is happening. I think."

"Well, I thought so too. I hope you're not about to tell me it isn't."

"No!" I said firmly, squeezing his hand again. "It definitely is, and I'm super pleased about that. But I don't think your dad should find out. Or Marcel."

Dylan let out a breath, crumpling the paper bag that had held the croissants. "He warned me off you, you know," he said after a moment. "Told me not to 'interfere' with you. It makes a man feel grubby, knowing his dad thinks he might 'interfere' with someone."

"Well, there's a reason your dad's famous for his paintings, not his words," I said, swallowing down the lump in my throat. Alan had told Dylan not to get involved with me? That was either overprotective or quite insulting. I wasn't sure which, but it made me sure Alan wouldn't like this. "He said the same to me. Well, kind of. He said you were very charming, but..."

"But what?"

"Um, well, he said that while you were sorting out your life, it was best that you didn't get involved with anyone, so—"

"I bet that's not what he said. Were the words 'in no fit state' part of his little speech?"

I winced. "They might have been."

"I knew it. Good to know the old man thinks so highly of me."

"But he does!" I didn't want Dylan to think otherwise. "Do you know how much he brags about you? His handsome, successful, charming son? He even made me look at your old school reports."

Dylan managed a small chuckle at that. "He's proud of who I've been. He's not proud of the unemployed guy who doesn't know what to do with himself."

"I don't think that's true. I think he's worried about you and doesn't know how to tell you that, so he comes across as disapproving."

"Well, you probably know my dad almost as well as I do, writing his autobiography," Dylan said, looking out over the horizon. "But I wouldn't be so sure about that. Alan Huxley has very high standards. For himself and for his family. Me taking this unexpected sabbatical must bother him a lot."

"He loves you," I said earnestly, looking up at him.

"Oh, he does. But he doesn't always like me. And he definitely doesn't always approve of me." Dylan shook his head. "You're right; it's best he doesn't find out."

"And my contract's only another few weeks," I said. "After that, we can..." I trailed off, realising that I was making a massive assumption. Was whatever was happening between us still going to be happening in a few weeks? Maybe that wasn't in Dylan's plans. What if I was the only one thinking this was a serious thing? Our relationship, if it even was one, was less than twenty-four hours old, and here I was with greater expectations than bloody Charles Dickens.

This was precisely why I had told myself I couldn't get involved with anyone. How could I cope with the uncertainty of any new relationship while trying to tame my anxiety? An image came into my head of myself dressed as a lion tamer, complete with a top hat. My whip was raised, but the metaphorical anxiety lion had my head firmly wedged in its jaws. Apparently, I couldn't even control my anxiety in my own damn head.

I swallowed hard, clenching my fists and trying to take deep breaths. I was not going to let myself start panicking. Not while I was on a lovely beach date with Dylan.

"Well, that's not very long to wait," Dylan kissed the top of my head. "Shall we head back? Enjoy the empty house before you've got to go to your appointment?"

And that wasn't exactly a confirmation, but it was enough for now.

Wasn't it?

• • • • ● • ● • • • •

Dylan had offered to come with me to the psychologist's office that afternoon, and I had been very tempted to let him. If he had come with me, I couldn't run away at the last minute and take up a new life in Darwin as a crocodile farmer to avoid talking to this unknown woman about my feelings.

Still, I had told him no. I needed to do this alone, and I left him on the jetty after a kiss and a very tight hug. When he had whispered in my ear that he was proud of me, it had stopped me from feeling I wanted to throw up my writhing guts for almost a minute and a half.

But I was here now, sitting in the waiting room on the fifteenth floor of a city building. Waiting. The room was painted in a mint green that I imagined was supposed to be soothing. Instead of plastic chairs, there were two long, comfortable sofas. An assortment of magazines was available on the coffee table, and I even could have poured myself a cup of peppermint tea if the mood had taken me. Or if I didn't feel like I would immediately projectile vomit anything I tried to introduce to my stomach.

"Tessa Finch?" A middle-aged woman with a severe but trendy haircut, a brightly patterned smock dress, and a pair of red leather ankle boots appeared, looking around the waiting room expectantly.

"Um, that's me," I said, getting to my feet. My legs felt like they might collapse underneath me, and my heart was thumping like I had just taken up high-intensity interval training, but I was going to do this.

"Lovely," she smiled at me. "I'm Jillian Black. We'll just be in here today." She pushed the door of her office open a little wider. I could see another sofa, a desk and squashy swivel chair, and a wall of books. The sofa gave me pause. Was I supposed to lie down? Surely that was just a TV thing, right? Jillian Black didn't seem like the kind of woman who'd appreciate people's feet on her furniture.

I must have paused too long because Jillian spoke again. "If you'd like to take a seat just there and get comfortable, we can get started."

I sat right in the middle of the sofa, my hands in my lap. I looked down at my fingers. Glossy red polish, no chips or cracks, but I'd need an infill appointment soon, I thought. Would Dylan notice if my acrylics needed infills? Did he like acrylic nails? Did he even have a strong preference on the matter? Was he one of those guys who insisted women be 'completely natural' so long as 'natural' was hair free below the neck, smooth-skinned, and immaculately groomed?

I shook my head slightly, trying to gather myself. I wanted to sit on my hands so I wouldn't look at them, but I decided that would be too weird, and I didn't want to be diagnosed with anything else right now.

"The letter from your doctor explained that you're struggling with anxiety," Jillian said, sitting down opposite me. On her lap was an iPad and one of those pens that converted your handwriting to neatly typed text. Did they really work, I wondered? Maybe Jillian had very neat handwriting.

"Uh, yeah," I said, cursing myself for being so inarticulate. Jillian was going to think I was lying about being a writer. "I guess I've always been a worrier. But my sisters think it's been worse since... For a while, anyway. And a friend told me I should see the doctor about it, and I didn't think it was a big deal, but..."

"I see," Jillian made eye contact with me and nodded in a way I was sure was supposed to make me feel at ease. I appreciated the effort, but it wasn't helping. "Why don't we start off by you telling me about yourself. Your family, your background, what you do for work. Any events that might have made your anxiety become more of a problem. Then we can start talking about strategies to manage it."

"Right." I nodded again. "Sounds good."

It didn't sound good. Explaining my family background to people was never much fun. Everyone seemed to assume I must be deeply traumatised by my mum and dad being on the absent end of the parenting spectrum. But I didn't think I was; I had always had my sisters and my Nana. That had been more than enough.

"So," Jillian said, her pen poised above the glowing screen. "Let's start with your family."

I took a deep breath. "So, I've got two sisters..."

After I had been talking for so long that my mouth was unpleasantly dry, Jillian looked up at me. "Well, I think that's everything I need on your background." She flicked at something on the iPad. "Now, I'd like to talk about your experience of anxiety."

"Right," I forced a smile. "I guess I just worry a lot. That's all."

"An anxiety disorder is more than worrying a lot," Jillian's voice was gentle. "Anxiety isn't a bad thing, in moderation. Feeling worried or nervous about an exam might motivate a student to study harder to prepare. But anxiety becomes a problem when it actually impairs us. Like if that same student was so overwhelmed by anxiety that they couldn't study effectively. They might even drop out of their course to avoid the exam. Do you see the difference?"

I nodded, thinking about the Master's in Creative Writing I had dropped out of before our first assignment was due because I was utterly convinced I couldn't produce something good enough.

"Have you had experiences where your anxiety has caused problems in your life? Stopped you from doing something you wanted to do? Or distracted you so much that you haven't been able to focus on something important?"

"I guess," I said, looking down at my hands again. The red of my nails really was too bright, I thought. Maybe something more subtle would be better.

"The problem with avoiding things that make us anxious is that while it can make us feel better at the time, it ultimately limits your life. We learn that when we feel anxiety, we have to avoid whatever's making us feel that way. We can't confront it; it's too big, too strong, too scary. And that's a hard pattern to break."

"Mm," I made a noise of polite agreement. But inside, I was running through all the other things I had missed out on. Learning to drive. Backpacking around Europe. Smiling at a handsome stranger. Hell, even trying on a dress I wasn't sure would suit me. Things I hadn't done because my brain was an arsehole.

"You mentioned that you think your anxiety became worse two years ago. When your grandmother died. You were her carer, so that would have had a big impact on you."

"I..." I shook my head. "I mean, I was her carer, but it wasn't just me looking after her. I did the household stuff, but it wasn't like she was helpless and didn't do anything for me. She always... She talked me through things. Whenever I was worried about something, I'd talk to her, and she'd help me through it. And when she wasn't there anymore, I..." I swallowed hard, and a fat tear rolled down my cheek. "I just miss her."

"It sounds like losing her could have played a role in turning your worrying into serious anxiety. That's not uncommon. A traumatic event can ramp up anxiety until it becomes too much to handle alone."

"So what am I supposed to do? I mean, I started taking the Zoloft, but I don't know if it's helping yet."

"Medication can be helpful," Jillian said, tapping her pen on the iPad. "But what we can do together is work on strategies to manage your anxious thoughts and feelings." She swivelled in her leather chair and handed me a piece of paper from her desk. "Have you heard of Acceptance and Commitment Therapy?"

"No. But, um, I've read a bit about mindfulness." I didn't want her to think I hadn't bothered to do any homework at all.

"Excellent," Jillian nodded approvingly, and I felt relieved that I had at least gotten something right. "Acceptance and Commitment Therapy, or ACT, is about accepting our feelings, even the scary, difficult ones, rather than struggling, avoiding, or denying them. We also focus on moving forward by taking valued actions. It's not about getting rid of our negative feelings necessarily, but about not letting those feelings control us. Does that sound like something you'd like to learn more about?"

"Um, I guess so," I frowned. "I just thought...I thought this would be more, like teaching me breathing techniques or focusing on things I'm grateful for so that I stop feeling like this."

"Well, that's the bad news," Jillian gave me a rueful half-smile. "No psychologist on earth can make your distressing thoughts and feelings disappear entirely. Not with meditation, not with positive thinking, not with talking about your childhood."

"Oh." That was disappointing. But that would be rude to say, right?

"I know that's disappointing," Jillian continued. "But what I can offer you is strategies to stop these difficult thoughts and feelings from distressing you so much and preventing you from doing what you really want to in life. Like sharing your children's books with an agent. Is that something you want?"

I took a deep breath. "Yeah." I raised my chin. "Yes, it is."

And hadn't Dylan told me I should do that, too? Okay, so it wasn't like he had clearly stated that he wanted an actual relationship with me. But the fact that he had tried to convince me that my children's books were good enough to share with an agent must mean he cared about me at least a little.

Right?

14 Dylan

"So, what happened after we went home?" Tad asked, nudging me. Even Benji looked like he was smirking, in a toothless, chubby-cheeked sort of way. "You and Tessa, you seemed... Well, like something was going to happen."

"I guess it did," I said, looking down at the ground as we strolled towards the park by the beach. I was waiting for Tessa to return from her appointment, and Tad, being a good husband, had offered to take Benji out for a walk so Alice could sleep off her over-indulgence with Abby the night before.

"And?" Tad demanded.

"And it was...amazing." There was a flare of warmth in my stomach. My night – and morning – with Tessa had been amazing. No doubt about that. I had felt closer to her than I had to anyone for years. Maybe ever. But it was too soon to be thinking things like that, wasn't it? "And I'm not giving you more details than synonyms for amazing. Fantastic. Delightful. Perfection."

"Oh, you really like her!" Tad rubbed his hands together. "If you're not telling me, then it's serious."

"I don't know about that," I said as Tad disengaged Benji from the carrier to let him down onto the grass. "I mean, yes, I like her. I really do. But I don't know if it's serious."

"Well, it must be pretty serious," Tad said, watching as Benji cautiously reached out with one chubby hand. "Because you said you weren't going to get involved with anyone. You must feel pretty strongly about Tessa to change your mind."

"She is special. But it's not like I went into this with a plan. It just sort of happened. And I'm glad it did. But I don't know exactly what's happening between us. I mean, I don't know what she thinks, either."

"Have you asked her?"

"It's been, like, twelve hours!" I complained. "No, I haven't asked her to have a serious discussion about the nature of our relationship or if it even is one. She's got enough to think about without that too. We agreed we'd keep it quiet so Dad doesn't find out. He'd have kittens."

"I didn't know he was into performance art." Tad jogged after Benji, who, having decided the grass was no threat, was crawling away at a surprising speed.

"Anyway, I just—"

"Dylan? Dylan and Tad! No way!" An unfamiliar voice came from somewhere to my left, and I turned to see the grown-up version of a freckled face I hadn't seen in years. A face that I currently could not connect with a name. "It's been ages!"

"Hi," I said, looking frantically at Tad for help. He gave me the slightest of shrugs. Crap.

"How have you guys been?" The woman smiled brightly as she approached.

"Good," Tad said, giving her a wave. "This is my son, Benji. He's just hanging out with his godfather." He nudged me, and I forced a smile.

"I can't believe you're a dad now!" The woman got down to all fours to look at Benji, who immediately burst into loud, noisy sobs at the sight of an unfamiliar adult on his level. "Oh, poor little guy! Don't be scared! It's just Shelley!"

Shelley. That was it. Shelley had been at school with Tad and me, but we had never exactly been friends. From memory, she was good at netball, had been Deputy Head Prefect, and own a lot of brightly coloured scrunchies.

"Good to see you, Shelley," I said as Tad rocked the sobbing Benji. "How have you been?"

"Oh, you know," she shrugged. "I work in the city, but my dad's broken his leg, so I'm staying with my parents to help out for a few weeks. Just came out for a breather to enjoy the beach. What are you up to?"

"Uh..." I began. "I was working in America." That was safe and actually true. "And now I'm staying with my parents for a bit."

"Oh, I thought you were still local," Shelly looked up at me keenly. "I saw you this morning with a woman. I thought she must be your wife."

Tad let out a laugh that quickly turned into a cough and then into a crooning lullaby.

"Ah, no. Not my wife."

"Girlfriend, then?" Shelley sounded a little too eager for my answer.

"Uh, something like that," I said helplessly, looking again to Tad for help. But he just focused on his baby, the selfish bastard. "Anyway, we'd better get going. Get this guy down for a nap." I patted my godson on his back as though it might in some way comfort him. I wasn't above using Benji as an excuse.

"Oh, right," Shelley looked disappointed, "Well, it was nice to see you. We should catch up properly. Maybe we should plan a school reunion!"

Tad let out another cough-laugh, and I was forced to smile again. "Uh, yeah," I said. "Maybe."

As we made our way down the footpath back towards Tad and Alice's house, a still screaming Benji in Tad's arms, I nudged him. Hard.

"Ow!" Tad gave me a look. "What was that for?"

"For leaving me to deal with Shelley back there."

"Oh, come on," Tad rolled his eyes. "You're capable of talking to a high school acquaintance for a few minutes. You didn't need me to rescue you."

"I did," I muttered. "When you're unemployed and living with your parents, you definitely need rescuing when someone asks what you're doing with yourself."

"Why didn't you say Tessa was your girlfriend, anyway?"

"Because she isn't. I mean, we haven't had that discussion."

"Seriously?" Tad looked pained. "After everything that's happened between you two, you finally get together, and you can't even tell Shelley Jenkins that she's your girlfriend?"

"I..." I closed my eyes briefly, running my hands through my hair. But the truth was, I hadn't known what to say. Because I didn't know if Tessa was my girlfriend. And as much as I liked her – really, really liked her – I didn't know if she should be. "It's all very new."

I knew that was a bullshit answer, and so did Tad. But once again, my godson saved me. I owed him a large and shiny present. Something with batteries that made a horrible noise. Even my limited acquaintance with babies had taught me that the more a toy tormented the parents, the more the baby in question adored it.

"Look, I actually do have to get this guy home," Tad shifted Benji on his hip. "I'll call you later, okay?"

"See you around," I said and planted a kiss on the top of Benji's head. He stopped bellowing for a moment and reached up to grab my chin with his sharp little nails. "See you soon, little dude."

I turned and began the walk back to the jetty. I knew Tessa's ferry wasn't due for a while, but what else did I have to do with my time? I didn't know if what was happening between Tessa and I was a good idea, but I did know that it felt good – very good – to be with her. When I was with her, I wasn't thinking about what I was going to do with my life. I was happy just to be by her side.

At this time of day, the jetty was empty. And I was glad of that as I flopped down on the weather-beaten, salt-worn bench and looked out at the sparkling water.

"What the fuck am I going to do?" I asked out loud. Maybe I thought the water would inspire me to come up with an answer.

It didn't.

All I could do was sit, stew, and wait for the woman whose presence made me stop worrying about it.

• • • • • • • • • •

"I hope this counts as taking you somewhere nice," I said, looking at Tessa across the little table. "After this morning."

"This morning was great!" Tessa insisted. "But this is lovely," she gestured around her. I had chosen a Thai restaurant in one of the larger suburbs south of Brekkie Beach. It was small, with a minimalist interior of black and chrome, and delicious smells wafting from the kitchen. "You didn't have to take me out, you know. We could have had leftovers on the couch, and I would have been happy."

"But then I wouldn't have seen you in that dress."

Tessa ran a hand down her front self-consciously. The dress in question was made from lace and silk, and while the neckline was as high as a nun's, the patches of sheer lace offered tantalising glimpses of her soft skin beneath. "It's a bit much for tonight, really. But I haven't had a chance to wear it after Abby made me buy it. So, I thought..."

"I'm delighted you did," I reached across the table to take her hand in mine, long fingers interlacing with my own, soft and warm. "Because you look incredible. Like, seriously incredible. You always do, even in jeans and a hoodie, but..." I let my eyes rake over her.

"Thanks," she ducked her head, blushing. "I guess it makes sense to go out while we can, huh? Before Alan and Marcel get back."

I let out a groan. "I had almost forgotten." That wasn't true. I definitely hadn't forgotten that my dad would be back tomorrow, and the fantasy that I lived alone – or perhaps with Tessa – would be shattered. Tomorrow, I'd be back to living in my dad's house in my childhood bedroom with no idea what I was doing with my life.

"I was always disappointed when my parents came back from holidays," Tessa confessed. "I knew I was supposed to be happy to have them home, so I never said anything. But I was happier when it was just Nana and my sisters and me."

I squeezed her hand. "That makes a lot of sense. Your Nana was the one who really raised you."

"She was. But I still felt guilty as a kid."

"I felt the same whenever my mother came to visit," I confided. "She'd show up, looking glamorous as all hell – her family has a lot of money – with a load of presents for me. She'd take me to lunch, to the movies... And it wasn't like she was awful or anything. She's pretty good company. But she was a visitor, not part of my life."

"That must have been hard." Tessa was looking up at me, her blue eyes fond and caring. I wasn't sure I deserved that look.

"Not really," I said quickly. "She's my mother, but not my parent. Dad and Marcel have always been my parents. I mean, Marcel came along when I was ten, but you get the point."

"I do," Tessa nodded again. "So, is your mother an artist too?"

"She's got a gallery," I explained. "She's a curator. Prides herself on being able to pick up and coming artists before anyone else can. It's what she always wanted to do, so I guess she's living the dream."

"I wonder how many people end up doing what they always wanted to do," Tessa looked thoughtful. "You know, living their childhood dreams. And I wonder how many of them are happy."

"Well, my dad, Marcel, and my mum definitely are," I said, taking a sip of my wine. It was cool, refreshing, and tasted like I could easily drink too much of it if I wasn't careful. "They've always been so sure of what they want and so successful. Not like me."

"You've been incredibly successful," Tessa frowned. "I mean, you started your own company and sold it. Most people would give at least one limb to be that successful."

"I guess so." I took another, longer, sip of wine. "Doesn't help me now, though, does it? I still have no idea what to do with myself."

"You're still not considering making a go of it with photography?"

I let out a sound that wasn't very attractive. "Of course not," I said quickly. "That's just a hobby. Hardly a career." I swallowed. "Actually, I got an email from an old friend down in Melbourne. He's setting up a software development consultancy and wondered if I'd be interested."

"Are you considering it?" Tessa looked down at her wine. "Moving to Melbourne?"

"I mean, I wouldn't necessarily have to move there." I hadn't even thought about that part. "I haven't decided. But it's not like I don't have options. For an actual career."

"Plenty of people make photography their career," Tessa said carefully. "But if it's not for you, then that's fine. I just thought...you seem to enjoy it so much."

"It's just a hobby." I played with the end of an elaborately folded napkin. "If I tried to be a professional photographer, people would fall over themselves to book me. Because I'm Alan Huxley's son. I don't want that. I never did."

"That's...possibly true." Tessa scrunched up her face. "Is that why you wanted to go into tech in the first place? Do something completely unlike your dad, so no one could say your success had anything to do with him?"

And that was true. I knew it was true. But I didn't want to hear it.

"One session with this psychologist, and you're already analysing me?" The words slipped out, harsher than I intended, and Tessa shrank back, her hand slipping away from mine.

"I didn't mean—"

"No, I'm sorry," I said, wanting to kick myself in the shins. Or maybe the balls. "You're not wrong. It's just..." I didn't know how to explain it.

But I didn't have to because, at that moment, a young man with sweeping black bangs and an enormous diamond stud in one ear approached our table, iPad in hand.

"Are you ready to order, or do you need some more time?"

And I decided that, yes, I was ready to order. I hadn't even glanced at the menu, but ordering might distract Tessa from me having been a complete dick for no good reason.

• • • ● • ● ● • • •

"What are you thinking about?" Tessa's voice was gentle, her warm breath close to my ear. Her body was pressed into mine, her head resting on my shoulder and one slender hand on my chest. It felt almost proprietorial, and I liked it.

"Nothing," I said, even though it wasn't entirely true. "Honestly, I'm just happy being here with you. Right now."

"That's a perfect answer."

"What are you thinking about?" I asked, tilting my head to look at her. I liked how her mouth was open in a soft smile, so I could see that little gap between her teeth.

"About a million things, as usual," she said, grimacing. "But being here with you definitely turns down the volume a bit on my brain's constant replays of the 'Things You Should Be Worrying About' podcast. I don't recommend it, by the way. It's a terrible podcast."

I laughed softly and drew her closer. "I wish I could switch it off."

"Mm, so do I. But I'll settle for fuzzy background noise, huh? Between you, the Zoloft, and my psychologist, this anxiety thing has no chance. Right?"

"You're incredible, Tessa," I leaned in to kiss her gently, just a brush of lips. She sighed in satisfaction, resting her head on my chest once more.

Tessa might be dealing with severe anxiety, but at that moment, I envied her. Which was a ridiculous thought and absolutely not one I would share. Yes, Tessa's brain taunted her about all the ways in which things could go wrong, past failures both real and imagined, and future problems, but at least she was working on it. At least she had a plan. She was taking steps to address her issues, and I didn't doubt she'd succeed. Tessa was so freaking diligent; of course she would.

But me? I didn't have a plan. I had been back home in Brekkie Beach for a month, but I was no closer to working out what to do with myself than the day I had arrived. Seeing Tessa waving a penis-shaped potato at my father and sleeping in my childhood bed hadn't given me some magical insight and certainty about what I should do next.

But, I thought, there was one thing about returning to Brekkie Beach that had been worthwhile. Something delightful and unexpected. Tessa.

I just wished that I knew what I was going to do next. Because it wasn't fair on a woman like Tessa – a brave, clever, funny, beautiful woman like Tessa – to be stuck with some shmuck who couldn't work out what to do with his life.

I just hoped I could work it all out before she realised that.

15 Tessa

"That hat is giving me life," Abby tweaked the brim of my sunhat as she hugged me in greeting. "Even if it might take someone's eye out."

I touched it self-consciously. "Well, I didn't want to get burnt again." The hat was made from white straw and had a broad, floppy brim with a jaunty polka dot scarf tied around the band. It was far more attention-grabbing than anything I usually wore. "But is it too much? Too big?"

"It's fabulous, like I said," Abby insisted, patting me on the shoulder. "Come on, I know you're anxious, but you don't need to devote mental energy to worrying about the hat. It's flawless. Just like you, but I think you'll have an easier time believing it about the hat."

"Maybe," I agreed, managing a smile. "Smoothie time?" I pointed at the shop.

"God, yes. I need a Magic Mango Moment in my life."

The shop was empty, but the teenager behind the counter had her phone propped up and was filming herself doing a dance routine while holding a blender jug in each hand. When she saw us approach, her cheeks flushed. "Sorry," she said, straightening her visor. "I was just making a TikTok."

"Hey, we've all done stuff for TikTok," Abby said cheerfully. "You're a way better dancer than me."

The girl looked astonished that a 'real adult' like Abby was a TikTok user and gave her a look of unflattering disbelief. "Wow," she said, her eyes wide. "I didn't know, like, your generation used TikTok."

"This one doesn't even know what TikTok is," Abby prodded me.

"I know what it is!" I said, unsure why I felt the need to defend myself. "I just don't get it."

"Never change, Tess," Abby wrapped an arm around me. "Could I get a Magic Mango Moment?"

"Actually, make that two, please."

"No worries!" The girl sprang into action, busying herself with the blenders once more.

"So, you've nearly finished that book for Alan, right?" Abby was leaning against the counter.

"We're doing revisions; I have no idea how long that will take," I had to raise my voice over the crush of the blender.

"Yeah, but once you're finished, what are you going to do next?"

I scratched my nose and considered chewing on my acrylics. "Well, it all depends. My publisher back home was okay with me taking time off to do this as an independent project. They said they'd put in a good word for me with the Australian branch, but I don't know if that will work out," I said. "I can always go back to Birmingham if they don't, but I'd like to stay here."

"I'd like you to stay here too," Abby nodded emphatically. "I mean, you've got the beach, the sunshine, your fabulous sister..."

"And Dylan. I'm not exactly in a hurry to leave Sydney while that's...happening."

"Except you have no idea what he's planning to do next, right?"

I chewed my lip. "It's complicated. He won't even consider pursuing photography—"

"Why?" Abby interrupted. "I've seen the photos he took of you; they're great! Besides, his dad's a famous artist; he'd help him with contacts and stuff."

"And that's why it's complicated," I said. "He doesn't want to do anything where his dad's reputation will help him. He's got a whole thing about it. I think that's why he did the whole tech thing and moved to San Fran, to be honest. But it's obviously a sensitive subject; I'm not going there with him."

"Oh, the fragile male ego."

"I don't think it's a male thing." That felt unfair. "He just doesn't want to be successful just because of who his dad is, not his own talent or hard work. It's kind of admirable, in a way. Lots of people would love to get a career boost from having a famous parent."

"Okay, I get that. But if he wants to be a photographer, it's pretty stupid to just sit around doing nothing instead of doing that just because his dad's famous."

"You tell him that," I said, rolling my eyes. "I'm not going there again. Anyway, maybe there's something else he'd be happy doing. He just hasn't figured it out yet. And maybe it would mean he moves to Singapore. Or Prague. And this whole thing between us has a use-by date that I don't even know about. But if I ask, do I sound like I'm expecting too much? Being too needy?"

"Woah, slow down," Abby held up a hand. "I don't think it's unreasonable to ask the guy you're seeing if he's about to leave the country. But I also don't think you should make your plans around a man. Especially one who hasn't given you any kind of commitment."

"But it's only been a few days. It's too soon to expect any kind of commitment."

Abby opened her mouth, but a young voice interrupted us. "Two Magic Mango Moments!" the girl said breathlessly. "And, um, my TikTok is divyalovesit276. If you want to follow me."

"Will do!" Abby held up her phone as she picked up her smoothie. "Come on, Tess. Let's enjoy how picturesque the scenery is while we work out what to do about your boy problems."

• • • ● ● • ● ● • • •

"And I think that's all for today," Alan let out a loud yawn. "I'm still rather tired from my travels." Alan made it sound like he had been on a months-long outback journey in a run-down Jeep rather than a few days in Melbourne.

"No worries." The iconic Australian phrase was a complete lie whenever I used it. "I'll get those changes done and we can finish the next section."

"Yes, yes," Alan said, rising from his seat with the help of his cane. "I think I'll go and have a lie-down."

I didn't say it, but I thought a nap sounded pretty great. As usual, I had been tortured by my thoughts and had slept fitfully. My smartwatch had informed me, cheerfully, that my sleep quality had been poor and advised me to cut down on caffeine. I had responded by chucking it across the room before immediately running to check I hadn't damaged it.

But before I could nap, I did want to get started on some of Alan's corrections. Just a chapter, so it wouldn't be hanging over me.

And I shouldn't have checked my email. Emails had a nasty way of interrupting your workflow. But I did, and when I saw there was response from the agent about my middle-grade fiction, there was no way I could resist opening it.

I should have resisted.

I'm sure there's a mature, adult way of reacting to a professional rejection. A frown, a sigh, or maybe a murmured 'oh well, I'll just have to try again in the future'. Perhaps a chat with your professional mentor about where you went wrong. Going for an extra-long run, maybe, would be acceptable.

I did none of those things. Instead, I curled into a ball in Alan's stuffy, cluttered study and burst into tears. Ugly tears, the kind that gave you a red nose and the eyes of a heavy weed smoker.

The rejection, while polite, convinced me of several things:

1. I was a creative imbecile, and my only value as a writer was to tell other people's stories because mine were clearly terrible

2. It was only a matter of time before my publisher realised that I was in fact, a terrible ghostwriter as well, and I lost my job and ended up living on Abby's sofa

3. Dylan would soon realise I was a talentless hack and decide he had had enough of me already

4. If the thought of doing something made you anxious,

maybe there was a good reason for that. Leaving your comfort zone was seriously overrated

Each of those thoughts swirled around me in a dizzying eddy, like those little birds that appeared when someone banged their head in a cartoon. Except my birds were the kind dreamed up by Alfred Hitchcock; larger, considerably more vicious, and without the cutesy sound effect. My chest was tight, my heart was racing, and I felt like I couldn't move. I wanted to be in bed with the covers pulled over me, but the distance to my bed, while short, seemed insurmountable. So, I sat there on the floor and cried some more. Maybe crying was cathartic for some people, but it didn't seem to be helping me right now.

"Tessa?" A low voice. "Shit, Tessa, what's wrong?"

Strong arms wrapped around me, the smell of coffee and cologne, and Dylan's face appeared through my haze of hair and tears, looking handsomely concerned. "I won't ask if you're okay because you're obviously not."

I swallowed back another sob. "I'm fine."

"Well, that's a lie. Unless this is some new literary meaning of 'fine' that plebians like me are unaware of."

At the word 'literary', I let out a groan. "I'm just being silly. I'm fine, really. Just leave me to it."

"Nope," Dylan said, and he sat next to me on the floor, wrapping one arm around me and tucking my head into his chest so that my snotty tears were sure to end up on his fresh-smelling t-shirt. "I'd be a serious arsehole if I just left you here to cry like this. And I do try not to be. You don't have to tell me what's wrong, but I'm not going anywhere."

And that? That just made a fresh sob erupt from me. Because he was being so damn kind. Didn't he realise that I was unworthy of such kindness? I was the worst writer who had ever put fingers to laptop. There was erotic *My Little Pony* fanfiction with more literary merit than anything I could produce. And sooner or later, he was going to realise that I was crappy at writing, crappy at my job, crappy at life in general, and he wouldn't want to be with me. Which was perfectly reasonable, really. But it still made me cry even harder.

Through all my tears and mumblings that I was fine, Dylan just sat beside me, rubbing circles on my back and holding me close to him. It was like I was a child throwing a tantrum, and he, the stoic parent, was offering comfort. But I couldn't help myself from clinging on to him like a mollusc to a rock. That made me gasp out a half-laugh. He was a lobster, and I was a mollusc.

"Do you feel like you can tell me what's going on?" Dylan asked when I managed to swallow back my tears and my breathing returned to something vaguely resembling healthy for a human.

"It's so silly. Nothing to cry about."

"Tell me," Dylan's voice was tender but insistent. He wasn't going to let me avoid the subject.

"I..." I shook my head. "You know how I sent my book to that agent? Well, I got a response. And apparently, my work is not something the market would be interested in." I let out a breath. "See? I told you it was silly."

"I don't think it's silly," Dylan said quietly. "I mean, you were so nervous about putting your work out there. And I know I pressured you to do it, and your sisters did too. So, it must feel pretty shitty for it not to work out after all that."

I looked up at him, my mouth slightly open. "Well, yeah," I admitted. "That's pretty much it. I just feel like maybe the reason I was so anxious about sharing my work was because I knew, deep down, it sucked, and so I shouldn't have done it. This proves it."

"No," Dylan disagreed. "The reason you were so nervous is that sharing your creative work with the world to be judged is terrifying for most people. And you're dealing with serious anxiety too. It's no reflection on your books."

"You don't know that. You haven't read them."

"Would it make a difference if I read them and told you they were great?"

"Probably not," I admitted. "I'd think you were just being nice."

"I'm not that nice."

"You are to me."

"You must deserve it then," Dylan said, pressing a kiss to the top of my head. And that made me melt like a dropped ice cream on a hot summer's day. I was molten gooey sweetness, a total mess. All because Dylan was being so very kind to me. I was still sure I didn't deserve it, but right then, I didn't care. "There are other agents, Tessa. I'm sure you don't need to be reminded how many famous authors were rejected before they got that first chance."

I wrinkled my nose. "I absolutely do not want to think about other agents right now."

"And I fully understand and support you on that," Dylan said, taking my hand in his and kissing it. And yep, there we went again with the melting. I was like a particularly fine piece of gouda, turning to liquid in a fondue set. "So, let's talk about something else."

"Abby was asking me what I'm going to do once your dad's book is finished," I ventured. "I told her I wasn't sure. Hopefully, the Sydney branch of my publisher will have work for me, or maybe I can get a remote gig."

Dylan was silent for a moment. "Your job's based in England."

"This move was never supposed to be forever. But..." I bit my lip. "I do like it here. Even if the sun does have it out for me."

"I hope Australia can keep you, then."

And that wasn't exactly like he was telling me he wanted me to stay, was it? I closed my eyes and forced myself to ask the question I desperately wanted answered but feared asking. "Do you want me to stay?"

There was silence. And I felt the exact moment it became too long. I looked down at my hands, examining my newly pale pink fingernails. "Sorry," I said quickly. "That was a bit much, wasn't it? I mean, this whole thing is just—"

"I'd like you to stay," Dylan interrupted. "Of course I would. I just don't want you to make plans based on me."

I stared at my hands, wondering what the hell he meant by that. Those two statements seemed contradictory if you thought about it. If he wanted me to stay, surely that meant he wanted whatever was happening between us to keep happening. But if he didn't want me to make plans based on him, that sounded like he didn't think what was happening was serious.

"Right," I said, my voice sounding oddly loud in the stuffy room. "Right, of course."

"Because I don't know what I'm going to do next. With my career. It could...I mean, I could end up needing to be somewhere else and—"

"No, I totally get it."

"I just wouldn't want you to make a decision that you regretted. Because of me."

It sounded like he was saying he'd feel guilty if I made plans to stay in Sydney, and he took off. Which he might do. At any time.

"Well, Abby's here." My voice was still too loud. "It's nice being near my sister again."

"Yes, of course," Dylan nodded. "That makes sense."

"And Birmingham is... Well, it's not exactly the most desirable city in the world. Unless your only priorities are shopping and great Indian food."

"I do love a good curry," Dylan tried to chuckle again, but it sounded hollow and forced. I hated that I had made him defensive. It was so obvious he was trying not to upset me, not when I had just been crying, but didn't want to give me any false ideas about just what was going on here, either.

"Can you get a decent curry in San Fran?"

"You know, I never tried," Dylan was looking down at his feet, and his arm around me had become oddly stiff. "But I bet you could help me find some if you ever came to visit."

"You're thinking of moving back?" I regretted the shrill tone of my words as soon as they escaped my lips. That would definitely be on the highlights reel of the 'Things I've Fucked Up Lately' screening in my brain tonight.

"Well, I don't have any firm plans," Dylan said, retracting his arm. "I still don't..." He shook his head. "I just don't know what I'm doing, Tessa." The look he gave me then was so sad that I wanted to hug him. But given that he had just removed his arm from around me, I decided against it.

"You'll work it out," I said, partly to be encouraging and partly because I believed it. Dylan was too smart just to sit idle forever. Even if that did mean he might move on and out of my life.

"I hope so," he said, seeming to address the pile of papers stacked on the floor. "I really hope so."

• • • • • • • • • • •

"You," I addressed the pill held between my fingers, "are supposed to be making me feel better. Why aren't you working yet?"

The pale blue pill between my fingers didn't answer. If it had, I'd need a lot more medication.

"I know it's only been two weeks," I said, popping it into my mouth and swallowing it with a sip of water. "But any time you want to start working, I'd be grateful. I could really do with a little help right now."

I knew I was being ridiculous. Dr Tsang had told me it would likely take a month for any noticeable effect, but I couldn't help being disappointed. Why couldn't I have been one of the rare patients who noticed an immediate benefit? Why couldn't the little blue pills in their neatly marked packaging instantly fix everything that was wrong with me and ensure that I never had to deal with painful feelings again?

"I know that's not how it works," I muttered, tying up my sneakers and making for the sliding door. It was early. Too early for Dylan to be meeting Tad at the gym, I thought. I hadn't slept well and decided a walk would be good for me. And a walk where I didn't run into my kind of boyfriend would be even better.

I started a podcast that promised to give me all the grisly and disturbing details of Australia's most notorious killers and let my feet set a quick pace. If I walked fast enough and turned up the volume high enough, maybe, just maybe, I wouldn't have to deal with the barrage of my thoughts for a little while.

Currently, my brain was rotating between;
1. Would I ever find work again, in Australia or otherwise, given I was obviously a terrible writer, as evidenced by the rejection of my book?
2. Was Dylan going to leave Sydney when he decided what he was going to do next with his life?
3. Was there any part of Dylan that was considering me in his future plans?
4. Did Dylan care about me at all?

When I reached the top of the hill, I pulled out my earphones mid-post-mortem and let out a half-shout, half-howl of frustration.

"I don't know if I can do this," I told the street sign that marked the entrance to Jackson Lane. "I don't know if I can just act like everything's okay while I wait for him to leave me."

I closed my eyes. That was pathetic. It wasn't like Dylan would be leaving me, exactly. It was worse. He wouldn't think about me at all when he made his decision. I knew what Abby would say – don't make plans based on a man. And I knew Michelle would tell me to enjoy the time I had with Dylan, and not worry about the future.

But not making plans and not worrying about the future was not part of the Tessa Finch Operating System.

"I don't know if I can do this," I said again, more softly, as I looked down at Brekkie Beach, sleepy in the early morning sunshine. "I just...don't know."

16 Dylan

"Do you have a minute, Dylan?" My dad's voice came from the living room as I stood in the kitchen, attempting to make coffee. I was improving, but I could definitely rule out 'barista' from my list of future career options.

"Sure," I called back. "Just making some coffee. Want one?"

"I'll wait until Tessa gets back."

My coffee wasn't that bad. Although, compared to Tessa's, I suppose it was. When I finally had a cup of something drinkable, I made my way to the living room. I found Marcel and my dad seated on the sofa, looking at me expectantly.

"Is this an intervention?" I joked, sitting down and taking a sip of my okay-but-definitely-not-in-Tessa's-league coffee. To my horror, Marcel and my father exchanged a quick glance. I let out a breath. "Shit. Seriously?"

"Nothing so tacky!" With Cyndi on his lap, Alan looked like a knock-off Bond villain. "I've seen that program from America. Why do these people insist on publicising their private shame?"

I gritted my teeth and swallowed. "Fine. So, what is this about?"

"We just wanted to have a chat," Alan said carefully, "about your plans. What you're planning to do next."

"With your life," Marcel added, clearly thinking he was being helpful.

"It's been a month, Dylan. And it's wonderful having you here, it really is, but—"

"But it's been wonderful long enough?" I cut in. "I can move out. I've got money."

"This isn't about moving out." Alan ran a hand down Cyndi's back. "Or money. It's about you deciding what you're going to do with yourself. Are you going to just sit around here all day indefinitely?"

"I don't just sit around all day," I protested. "I mean, I've been spending a lot of time with Tad and Benji. And with you guys. Is that a waste of time, after living overseas so long?

"No, of course not. But it can't go on forever, you know."

"It won't go on forever," I insisted. "I'll work it out; I just..."

I didn't know what to say, how to explain it. That I was waiting. Not for a sign, I wasn't superstitious. I was waiting for something to become clear in my head. Some event, a chance comment, a moment of clarity. I was waiting for something to happen so that I would know, once and for all, with certainty, what it was that I wanted to do with my time on earth.

"Are you still seeing that careers advisor?" Marcel asked, fiddling with the sleeve of his turtleneck.

"No. He wasn't helpful."

"Perhaps it might be worth seeing someone else," Alan suggested, and I let out a shocked scoffing sound.

"You thought it was a bad idea that I saw anyone to begin with!"

"Well, that was before," he conceded. "But now, I think perhaps you could do with a little guidance."

"I'm not seeing any more careers advisors," I said firmly. "I worked my arse off for five years on my start-up. Is it really that unreasonable that I take a little time to work out what I want to do next?"

"No," my father said through pursed lips. "No, it isn't. Or it wouldn't be if I thought you had some idea of what you wanted to do. But you're not considering anything seriously, are you?"

"I talked to Alice about property investment," I said defensively. I neglected to mention that it had been over dinner and that my eyes had glazed over when she started talking about negative gearing and capital gains tax. "I'm considering that."

"Are you really?" My father looked disbelieving.

"I believe you said landlords were parasites clinging to the belly of society," Marcel frowned. I wished he didn't have such a bloody good memory.

"Maybe I was being too hasty," I lied, but it was useless. I couldn't pretend I was genuinely considering professional slumlord as my next big thing. "And I told you about that software consultancy gig with my friend in Melbourne. That's an option. Anyway, I don't see why I should rush into anything. It's not like I need the money."

"This isn't about money, Dylan!" My father's voice rose in anger, and Cyndi yowled loudly, jumping down from his lap and running from the room. I could have sworn she shot me a malevolent glare. "It's about you sitting around idle and refusing to have a real conversation about why you're wasting your life!"

"Wow, Dad. Tell me how you really feel."

"I'm your father, and it breaks my heart to see you wasting all of your talents, your brains, your creativity—"

"I'm not wasting anything!" I shot back. "This is about me never pursuing photography, isn't it? That's what you wanted for me. So that you could say that you inspired me. You're ashamed I went into tech!"

"This isn't about that!" Alan's voice rose. "Though I don't know why you decided that fiddling with mobile phones was the best use of your talents."

"I knew you never approved." I stood up, shaking my head. "You always told me I could do whatever I wanted, but that wasn't true, was it?"

"You can do whatever you want!" My father grabbed his cane as though wanting to stand, but then thought better of it. And then I felt like an arsehole. I was a grown man shouting at his disabled father. "I just didn't think you'd choose something like that."

"I'm going for a walk."

"Dylan, there is still much to discuss," Marcel began. "Perhaps with some coffee—"

"Marcel, I love you, and I'm grateful for everything you do for Dad, but right now, I need you to shut up."

I opened the front door. It was tempting to slam it hard enough to make the windows rattle, but I was an adult. The last thing I wanted was to play into my father's idea that I was a rebellious teenager, intent on spiting his old man. So, I carefully closed the door and took off down the hill.

And, of course, I bumped into Tessa.

"Dylan!" She pulled out her earphones and leaned up to kiss me. When I pulled back, she frowned at me. "Is everything okay?"

"Not really. Dad and Marcel sat me down for a talk about my future. Which was mostly just Dad listing all the ways that I'm a disappointment to him."

"Oh, I'm sure that's not true," Tessa faltered, a gentle hand on my arm.

"I'm making it up, am I?" I snapped, and her hand fell away.

"No, of course not. I just... The way your dad has always spoken about you to me, I know he's very proud of you. He brags about you, actually."

"Well, maybe that's what he wants outsiders to think," I said bitterly. "But I know what he really thinks of me. He's always hated that I went into tech; he thinks it's worthless. Because I'm not making art or doing anything creative. He probably thinks my soul is corrupted." I rolled my eyes, stuffing my hands in my pockets.

"You're not a Horcrux, Dylan. Your soul is just fine." Tessa gave me a tentative smile, that little gap between her teeth just visible. "But it must be shitty, feeling like your dad doesn't approve of you."

"Kind of shitty, yeah. I know he wishes I'd pursued photography. But I—" I stopped because I didn't have words to explain why I hadn't. Not ones that made sense, anyway.

"Well, it must be hard for him," Tessa ventured. "Because you're so talented, and you seem to enjoy it so much. I guess he doesn't understand why you don't want to do something that you enjoy. Especially now when you've got the financial stability to—"

"I don't want to be a fucking photographer!" The words came out too loud, too harsh.

"Fine." Tessa took a step back, her eyes narrowing. "Don't be a photographer if you don't want to be. Even if—"

"Even if what?" I knew what she was going to say.

"Even if it's because you've got issues about being compared to your dad or only being successful because of who he is," Tessa finished.

"You don't understand," I said, even though Tessa had just shown that she absolutely did. "I..." I shook my head. "Look, I need to clear my head. Don't say anything to my dad about me talking to you."

"Of course not," Tessa looked hurt. "I wouldn't do that."

And now I felt guilty because, of course, she wouldn't. She was a good person; I was the arsehole who went around shouting at disabled artists and beautiful ghostwriters. "I'll see you later."

"Okay." Tessa moved towards me and then pulled back like she had been about to kiss me and then decided it was a bad idea. She raised her hand in a half-wave. "I hope the walk helps."

I watched as she made her way towards the house, feeling waves of self-loathing roll over me like I was sitting in the waters of Brekkie Beach, neck deep and at risk of drowning.

The walk did not help.

• • • • ● • ● • • •

Tensely polite. The only words I could use to describe life at home after my blow-up with my dad and Marcel were 'tensely polite'. All three of us were walking on eggshells, unwilling to allude to what had happened but utterly incapable of acting like normal human beings around each other either.

Dinner was a silent meal, interrupted only by questions like 'would you be so kind as to pass me the rice?' Tessa kept shooting me sympathetic looks, but it didn't help. When she whispered that I should come to the studio after my dad and Marcel had gone to bed, I had shaken my head.

"Not tonight. I need to... I need to think, I guess."

"That's fine," Tessa had said, offering me a forced smile. "I understand."

Did she understand? If she did, she was a lot better off than me because I didn't have a clue what I was doing. I just knew I couldn't be around her, not with everything swirling around in my brain. I was a sailing ship about to be pulled into a whirlpool. A whirlpool inhabited by something with an alarming number of tentacles.

And I didn't want anyone else to be pulled under with me. Especially not Tessa.

• • • ● ● • ● • • •

After a sleepless night, I waited until Dad was taking his now-regular afternoon nap before I approached Tessa.

"Have you got a minute? I thought we could go for a walk."

"Sure," Tessa said, closing her laptop and standing up. "How are you feeling?"

"Terrific."

"I know this has all been really hard for you," she said quietly, one gentle hand on my arm. I wanted to shake it off, to tell her to stop being kind to me because she'd regret it after she heard what I had to say.

"It's..." I sighed. "It is what is. And it isn't what it isn't."

"Wise words," Tessa raised her eyebrows, following me from the house.

I figured it would be easier to do this while we were walking. If I just kept walking and focused on the familiar streets of my youth, I could do what I had to do. If we were walking, I wouldn't have to look directly into those wide, earnest blue eyes. Or see her lips curved into the soft smile, with that little gap between her teeth that had become so precious to me.

"I'm going to move out," I said abruptly. That wasn't how I had meant to start this conversation, but the words had slipped out and I supposed I was committed now.

Tessa just nodded. "I understand. After what happened, I get that you need your own space. And hey, it might make it easier to keep this whole thing—" She waved a hand between us. "Keep this whole thing quiet from your dad. I caught Marcel giving me a funny look last night. I think he suspects something."

"I..." I wished she hadn't jumped straight to that point. I had wanted to prime her first and explain my reasons. But now I just had to do it. "I don't think we should keep seeing each other."

Tessa stopped walking, frozen on the pavement, one hand still trailing through the ivy that curled over someone's picturesque picket fence. "Oh." She didn't look at me. Thank goodness she didn't look at me.

"I...I guess I wasn't expecting that." She swallowed, almost gulping. "Why? Is it because of my whole anxiety thing? I know it's a lot, but I'm working on managing it; I'm seeing the psychologist again on Thursday, and I—"

"It's not because of you," I said quickly, reaching out for her arm, but she shook me off. Tessa was looking at me now, but those blue eyes weren't soft and fond. Quite the opposite. "It's because of me. I'm...stuck. I don't know what I'm going to do with my life, and it's not fair on you to be involved with me while I work it out. I know it bothers you, not knowing if I'm going to move back to San Fran or—"

"I knew all of that before we got involved," Tessa pointed out. "I've never asked you to have everything figured out, to be with me."

"I know," I said, my head hanging. "I know. You've been kind and supportive and haven't pressured me, and I—" Why couldn't I get my words out? "You've been amazing. But this isn't right. This isn't fair to you. The way I am is... It's not good for you."

"So, you've decided that for me, have you? You're acting in my best interests without even asking me what I think?" Tessa rolled her eyes. "Thanks for that, much appreciated."

"I'm trying to do the right thing here," I said, my voice rising. "Look, I told you I didn't want to get involved with anyone while my life was so unstable, and I shouldn't have...with you. I let it happen because you're so..." My words failed again. "But I shouldn't have let it happen. I was being selfish."

"I wanted this, Dylan," Tessa looked up at me, her mouth a thin line. Well, as thin a line as was possible when the owner of the mouth happened to be blessed with plush and pillowy lips. "I'm not some innocent you seduced. We both wanted it to happen."

"I know." My words were coming out all wrong. "I know that, but I...I can't let this happen anymore. I need to...I need to work out what the hell I'm doing, and I'm not going to string you along and make you wait for me."

"So, you're dumping me for my own good," Tessa spat out the words, angry and hurt. "How noble of you." She paused. "Except that it's crap, isn't it? You're dressing this up like you're doing me a favour. Why don't you just admit that it's me you don't want? When you do decide what you want to do with yourself, you don't want to be burdened with the woman who makes soup for your dad and has severe anxiety."

My mouth fell open, and I couldn't form words for a few moments. "You can't think that's true," I sputtered. "Tessa, you're better than me. Better than anyone I've ever met."

"You're a tech millionaire on sabbatical," Tessa was blinking very rapidly, like she was forcing back tears. "I know what kind of women you must have been with before. And I know I'm nothing like them. Whatever you're planning for your future, I don't fit into it! I mean, I'm just a ghostwriter and I'll never be anything more because my real work is shit. As you know."

"Your work isn't shit," I addressed the least of what she had said. "And this isn't about you, Tessa. It's about me. I need to...I need to be by myself while I work out what I'm doing. God, Tessa, anyone would be lucky to have someone like you in their life. Beyond lucky. You're incredible; I've never felt like—" I cut myself off before words could come out that would make this situation even more painful. "You're amazing."

"Clearly not amazing enough," Tessa said, and when she looked at me now, the anger was gone, and there was only sadness. I could see the tears brimming in the corners of her eyes, and I hated that I was the one to cause them. I wanted to pull her close, hold her against me, and tell her that I hadn't meant it, that it didn't matter, and that she was the only thing I was sure of in my life. And it would have been true, too. Except that I knew I couldn't let this woman – this extraordinary woman – be a part of the mess that was Dylan Huxley. It wasn't right.

"Tessa, I'm so sorry," I said quietly. "You have no idea how much I want to... How much I wish things were different. That I could be the kind of man who's worthy of you."

But Tessa just shook her head. "Are we done?" she asked, biting her lip. "There's nothing more to say, is there?"

I didn't want it to be done. Because when this conversation was over, it really would be finished. And when she walked away, she'd be taking my goddamn heart with her. Ripped straight from my chest. And it was my fault, I knew, but that didn't make it hurt any less.

"I guess not. I...I'm sorry."

"Me too, Dylan."

"What the hell happened to you?" Tad opened the door, looking me up and down. "You look like shit!"

"I feel like shit," I said bluntly, dragging my suitcase behind me as I made my way into the house.

"You've got luggage," Tad raised his eyebrows. "You're coming into my house with luggage. You had a fight with your dad. Or Marcel? He doesn't seem like the kind of guy you could fight with, but—"

"My dad and Marcel had an intervention with me. About me not doing anything with my life. I had to leave," I said, sinking down onto the floor next to Benji, who was holding a toy mobile phone carved from wood in his chubby fingers and gnawing determinedly on the corner.

"Mate, you really can't crash here," Tad said awkwardly, sitting beside me. "I mean, I love you like a brother, but we don't have the space, with Benji's nursery and—"

"I know. I've booked an Air BnB, but I can't check in until tomorrow. I was just hoping I could crash on your couch for one night. I'll get up with Benji. I'll wash the dishes. I'll—"

"You can have my couch," Tad said quickly. "And I'll definitely let you wash dishes. But let's rewind a bit here. You had a fight with your dad. Well, I guess that was always going to happen, you're an adult living in your parents' house. What does Tessa think about all this?"

"I broke up with Tessa."

"Excuse me?" Tad looked shocked, and worried, in a way that he hadn't when I told him about arguing with my dad. "What do you mean? Why the hell did you break up with Tessa? How did that happen?"

"I don't want to talk about it. It's just a giant fucking mess." I paused. "Sorry, Benji. Hecking mess?"

"We agreed not to stop swearing in front of him until he starts talking. As a sanity preserver."

"Fucking mess, then."

"You really aren't going to tell me why you broke up with the girl you've been gaga over ever since you moved home? Seriously, dude, my kid and Tessa are the only things that seem to make you smile."

"I don't want to talk about it." I stretched out my hand to Benji, who decided that my finger was just as good to gnaw on as the toy phone. "Ow, dude. Those teeth are fierce."

"Yeah, Alice is glad she gave up breastfeeding before those came through. But mate, you're acting like a twat. Why won't you tell me what's going on?"

"I don't want to talk about it!" I raised my voice and looked up at Tad. "Please. Just...not yet."

"Mate, I don't even know what to say."

"Then don't," I said, scooping Benji into my arms. He smelled of organic baby wash, and though he was slightly sticky, his plump presence was oddly comforting. "How did you know?"

"How did I know what? That you're making a mess of things with Tessa? It's bloody obvious."

"No," I shook my head. "That you wanted to have a kid. Bring a whole human life into the world. I can't even decide what to do for a career."

"Well, I would never have done it on my own," Tad said, a small smile creeping over his face. "But with Alice, I felt like...like it was something we could do, together. I knew she'd be a great mum, and she made me feel like I could be a decent dad."

"Are you trying to make some kind of point?" I looked at him over the top of my godson's head as Benji fisted a small hand into my t-shirt.

"I wasn't," Tad huffed out a breath. "If I made you think about how it's possible to make life-changing decisions when you've got the right person by your side, that's on you."

I grunted and looked down at my godson. "At least you can't give me advice yet," I said, touching his soft cheek. "Or judge me."

"That's where you're wrong. He's got one hell of a judgemental glare. Just wait until the morning if you're late with his bottle."

"I'll take my chances."

"You okay, dude?"

I opened my eyes and looked back at my oldest friend. "Probably not."

"I didn't think so. We'll talk about Tessa when you're ready, yeah?"

"Yeah."

But I didn't know when I would be ready to talk about how I had ruined everything with Tessa.

17 Tessa

I DIDN'T CRY. As I wandered the back streets of Brekkie Beach, I kept thinking the tears would come, but I still didn't cry. Maybe the Zoloft was finally kicking in. And not a moment too soon, because Dylan had gone and done just what I'd been so afraid of. Dumped me because he realised that I'd have no place in his new life – once he figured out what that was. Whatever Dylan ended up doing, I wasn't going to fit in. That wasn't what he had said, but I knew it was true just the same. It almost felt like vindication. My anxiety had been right all along. About my children's book, and now about Dylan.

"Maybe I should be listening to it," I muttered as I climbed the hill back to Alan's house. "Not trying to accept my feelings and take goddamn stupid valued actions."

I closed my eyes for a long moment. I'd have to keep it together; I knew that. I couldn't let Alan and Marcel suspect anything had happened. The last thing I wanted was for Alan to find out that yes, I had gone and gotten involved with his too-charming son, and it had ended just as badly as he had predicted.

Making my way into the kitchen, I decided that now was a great time to make my own stock. I had always thought it was too much bother, but now? Now I needed the distraction.

"It is early to be making dinner," Marcel's voice interrupted me as I poked at the chicken carcass bubbling away on the stove with a wooden spoon. "And we will have one less. Dylan has moved out."

"I'm just making stock," I didn't turn around. "It will be useful. And wow, Dylan moved out? He did say he had a...discussion with Alan." That, I thought, was safe to admit. Marcel knew that Dylan and I were supposed to be friends. I couldn't play completely dumb.

"It was not a productive discussion," Marcel said quietly. "I do not think they want to understand each other."

And that was surprisingly insightful. "I guess not," I said, blinking against the rising steam. "Is Alan okay?" After all, Alan was my boss. He was supposed to be my primary focus. Not Dylan. Not Dylan at all.

"He is..." Marcel sighed. "Troubled. I believe he finds it hard to show how he cares."

"I get that." I wondered if something Alan had said had triggered Dylan's decision to break up with me. Or maybe he had just reminded Dylan that his life here in Brekkie Beach was only temporary. "I know how much Alan loves him," I went on, trying my best to ensure my voice didn't shake. But it did anyway, like a hapless beginner at an advanced yoga class valiantly struggling to balance on one leg. "And I know how proud he is of him. I mean, he's always bragged about Dylan to me."

"It is difficult, I think, for Alan to say these things to his son," Marcel mused, one hand to his chin. In his black turtleneck, he looked like a stock image of 'thoughtful man'. He could have illustrated a feature article about choosing suitable stock options or a gift for one's mother-in-law. "And to tell him he is worried about him."

"When your parents tell you that they're worried about you, I guess it can feel like criticism," I said, chewing my lip and wondering what Marcel would do if I emptied the entire pot of stock onto the lawn. It didn't smell at all appealing. Maybe there was something wrong with the chicken carcass. Or with me. Probably with me.

Marcel nodded, and then he looked at me. "You are close to Dylan," he said, and my stomach clenched. Was he saying he knew what had been going on? I thought we had been discreet, but I wouldn't be surprised if Marcel had worked it out.

"We're friends." I looked down at the chicken carcass and wondering if it, or my increasingly anxious stomach, was making me want to vomit. "But I guess...I guess I don't know him that well."

"He has shared much with you. Perhaps you can help him."

I let out a surprised breath. "Me?" I looked at him, incredulous. "I don't think anything I could say would make any difference to Dylan. We're not..." I couldn't say anything more. Not without admitting what had really happened between us.

"I see," he said and then paused again. "Tessa?"

Another clench of my stomach, and I really did have to swallow back bile this time. He was going to say it, I knew. "Yes?"

"I think something's wrong with that chicken."

I let out a laugh that became a sob, doubling over, hysterical, as the tears that had been threatening finally fell. Through the tears, I could see that Marcel looked horrified.

"It's okay!" I gasped, even though it wasn't. Nothing was okay. "The chicken's off. I'll get rid of it."

"Are you feeling quite well?" Marcel was still staring at me as I gasp-laughed at my horrible chicken, at my horrible brain, at my horrible life.

"Fine," I choked, managing to turn the heat off from under the pot. "I'll be fine."

Marcel gave me one final look of utter bewilderment as he left the kitchen.

I sank to the ground, my face in my hands, the tiles cool on my bare legs. "I'm not fine," I whispered quietly to myself. "But I can do this. I'm not going to fall apart because of Dylan Huxley. I'm not."

• • • ● • ● • ● • •

"So, how have you been since we last saw each other?" Jillian's pen was poised above her iPad. She was wearing another bold, expensive-looking outfit. This time it was a black and white abstract printed shirt over red trousers, paired with ballet flats that were definitely authentic Ferragamo's, not knock-offs like the ones Michelle had sent Abby and me from her trip to Shanghai.

"Um, okay," I said automatically. Then I paused. "Well, except the guy I was seeing broke it off. And moved out. Because he's my boss's son. It's complicated."

"I see." Jillian began to make notes on the iPad, her face betraying nothing. "How long had you been involved with this man?"

"A week," I admitted. "So, it's not like it was serious, except—" I scrunched up my face. That was a giant lie. The way I felt about Dylan was absolutely serious, even if the amount of time I had been seeing him didn't seem sufficient.

"If the way you felt was serious, then it's something we can discuss. Regardless of how long you two were together."

"I guess we got close pretty fast," I faltered. "And Dylan told me he didn't want to get involved with anyone while he was working out what to do with his life – he came home after selling his start-up – but then..."

"You became involved," Jillian finished for me.

"I had told myself I didn't want to get into anything either," I said. "But then, I got all these feelings, and when it seemed like he felt the same, I just..." I shook my head. "I guess I went ahead and let myself fall really hard. And the whole time, I couldn't stop thinking about how I knew he'd end it sooner or later. And I was right." I looked up at Jillian. "I know I'm supposed to be ignoring my anxious thoughts, but it seems like they were right."

"Tessa, the goal isn't to teach you to ignore your anxious thoughts," Jillian said patiently. "It's to make room for them in your mind so they can exist without controlling what you choose to do."

I swallowed. "I don't really get how that's meant to work," I confessed, feeling like an idiot.

"It's a hard concept to grasp. It takes most people a while to get the hang of it. So don't be too hard on yourself."

"Since Dylan broke up with me, I've been trying to do everything I'd usually do. Working, keeping a smile up around Alan and Marcel, going for walks, no matter how shitty I feel," I said. "Isn't that what I'm supposed to do? Take valued actions? Not let how I feel control me?"

"Not precisely." Jillian paused. "I admire your diligence, but you need to make space for your feelings. We can't just block our feelings out. Not forever, in any case."

"So, what am I supposed to do? I feel like I'm drowning in all these thoughts. That Dylan dumped me because I'm a shitty person. That I'll never have a proper relationship again. That I'll be stuck ghostwriting forever because I suck at everything else. I'll have to move back to England, and it will be like I never even tried to change my life, and I'll be alone and stuck and—"

I took a gasping breath. "What am I meant to do if I'm not acting like I don't have these thoughts or crying in bed all day with a bottle of wine?"

"There are more than two options, Tessa," Jillian said with a small smile. "Have you spoken to anyone close to you about your breakup? Have you considered writing about how you feel, perhaps a letter to Dylan? You don't need to send it. You could give yourself permission to spend a day in bed crying – perhaps without the wine – and let those feelings work through you. There are actions you could take that don't ignore your feelings but aren't self-destructive either."

When she said it like that, it seemed reasonable. Those were ways that emotionally healthy people dealt with painful feelings. No wonder I hadn't even considered them. "I guess I could talk to my sisters," I said finally. "And write about how I'm feeling. It doesn't matter if I'm a terrible writer if no one's going to read it."

"Tessa, I don't know much about writing," Jillian tilted her head. "But I do think you might benefit from challenging that thought. You've had a steady job as a ghostwriter for six years, correct?"

"Yes."

"And do you think it's likely that your publisher would keep offering you new contracts if you were a terrible writer?"

"No, but—" I swallowed. "Maybe I can do other people's stories, but my own stuff is terrible."

"Still, it doesn't seem true that you're a terrible writer."

"No," I admitted. "I guess not completely."

"I'd like you to work on making room for that thought when it comes into your head. Accept that you're having that thought, without necessarily believing it or challenging it."

"How do I do that?"

"That's what we're going to work on next."

• • • • • ● • ● • • • •

"Hey, you!" Michelle's face flashed on my screen and was quickly joined by Abby's.

"What's up?" Abby was at her kitchen table, frowning in concentration as her Cricut stencilled its way around what I assumed were labels. "Don't mind the Cricut; I'm just making pantry labels for this new client I've got. This influencer lady down in Mosman wants her pantry to be Insta-worthy."

"Um, I need to tell you something," I took a quick breath and rushed on. "Dylan broke up with me."

"That bastard!" Abby banged a fist on the table, making her Cricut pause for an ominous second before whirring back to life.

"When?" Michelle looked aghast. "Are you okay?"

"Three days ago, when—"

"Three days ago?" Both of my sisters spoke in unison.

"What do you mean three days ago?" Abby demanded. "Why didn't you tell us? I sent you that meme with the walrus, and you just sent back laughing emojis! You lied through emoji!"

"The walrus *was* funny." I hung my head.

"Why didn't you tell us, babe?" Michelle looked hurt.

"I thought that if I just ignored how I was feeling and acted like it wasn't happening, it would be easier," I admitted. "I thought that was what I was meant to be doing, with my whole anxiety thing. But I saw my psychologist today, and I kind of had that wrong."

"Damn right you did!" Abby was still furious. "How could you think it would be a bad idea to tell us?"

"Because my feelings felt so big and horrible that I felt like if I admitted anything, if I let them in, then I wouldn't be able to handle it! Jillian says that's quite common, actually."

"Oh, Tess," Michelle was sympathetic. "Well, you're telling us now. That's good."

"What happened?" Abby demanded. "I can't believe he did this! Is it because he's moving away? I told you he was too unstable for you!"

"Not exactly," I sighed. "He said that it wasn't fair to me, waiting for him to decide what he was going to do with himself. That he didn't want to do that to me, so he needs to be alone."

"Well, that sounds like a bunch of bullshit."

"It sounds like he's trying to be all noble and self-sacrificing," Michelle wrinkled her nose. "And usually I'm totally into that, but it's kind of patronising, him deciding you couldn't cope with the uncertainty."

"I don't think that was the real reason, anyway," I said, feeling emotion well up inside me. I tried to tell myself this was a safe place to let it out, that I was safe, here in the studio, talking to my sisters. My heart was still pounding, and my stomach still unpleasantly twisted, but it hadn't gotten worse. That was progress, right? "I think he realised that when he does decide what he wants to do, he wants someone better by his side. I mean, I'm just a ghostwriter with anxiety, and he's—"

"An unemployed adult living with his parents!" Abby cut in. "Tessa, you can't think you're not good enough for him."

"He moved out, actually, so now he's an unemployed tech millionaire living somewhere else," I said, even though that wasn't the point. "He had a fight with his dad the day before we broke up, so—"

"Wait, he had a fight with his dad?" Michelle interrupted. "That's probably what did this. It's probably not really about you at all."

"Thanks. That makes me feel a lot better." I didn't bother to keep the sarcasm from my voice.

"But she's right," Abby agreed. "It sounds like this is all his weird dude angst. Come on, Tess, it's not about you not being good enough. It's about his issues with his career and his dad, and he's not grown up enough to deal with that while being in a functional adult relationship. Men!"

"I hate men," Michelle nodded vehemently.

"Since when do you hate men?" Michelle was the one who read romance novels and fantasised about being swept off her feet by a tall, dark, and handsome stranger.

"Since the quarterly meeting today, when Hugo – that new hire – acted like he thought my ideas sucked, and then ten minutes later, repeated them like they were his own, and suddenly everyone was marvelling at how bloody brilliant he was!" Michelle looked ready to punch through her computer screen. "I thought the whole glass ceiling thing was over, but it's still a man's world. In the corporate sphere, anyway."

"Bloody patriarchy," Abby looked mutinous. "When I went to meet my new client today, her husband was there. I said I had a meeting with his wife, and he was all, 'ooh, I'll leave you girls to gossip'. What a condescending arsehole! It was a business meeting, and she's a paying client."

"It's settled then. Men are the worst."

"Yep," Abby nodded. "The absolute worst."

"So how harshly will you judge me if I tell you that I can't stop thinking about how much I miss Dylan? I just wish I could find out if he's okay, and I wish that I could be enough to make him—"

"Oh, Tess," Michelle said sadly. "I'm not going to judge you at all. I just feel sad for you. It seemed like he was one of the good ones."

"He sure had me fooled," Abby admitted ruefully. "I mean, it seemed like you two were actually being honest with each other, not just putting up a front. And when I saw him with you, it was obvious he thinks the sun shines out of your beautiful bottom."

"I thought he really liked me," I confessed. "He actually knew me and still liked me. And I always thought he'd realise his mistake, but when he actually did, it still..." I wiped my eyes pre-emptively.

"I don't think you should let yourself believe he doesn't like you," Michelle said soothingly. "Or that he doesn't care. He's too caught up in his own issues to be sensible."

"I think she's right. You didn't do anything wrong. Hell, maybe he likes you so much that it scared him off. Commitment-phobia, maybe."

"Or maybe it's me," I said glumly, thinking about sneaking into the main house to pilfer the bottle of wine Alan had deemed too cheap to drink and put in the pantry for cooking. It was definitely good enough for me to drink.

"No!" Abby insisted. "I know you're not going to believe us, at least not tonight, but it's not you, babe."

"It's definitely him. Because all men suck. Except for Ryan Reynolds. And unless Blake Lively has an unfortunate accident, he's taken."

I managed a weak smile. "I'm sure he's only with her because he hasn't met you yet, Michelle."

"Obviously," Michelle flicked her hair. "Are you going to be okay, Tess? I'm just about ready to tell work to fuck off and fly over there to look after you."

"I'm okay," I said, blinking back my tears.

"You're not," Abby said. "Clearly."

"No," I agreed. "I'm not okay. But I've got you two, Jillian the psychologist, and these—" I held up my blister pack of Zoloft. "So, I will be."

"You forgot the most important thing," Michelle said.

"What's that?"

"You, idiot! You're strong as hell. You can totally deal with heartbreak. We believe in you. Right, Abby?"

"Yeah, Tess. We do."

I felt the tiniest bit better. For about three minutes, anyway.

18 Dylan

In my defence, there hadn't been a huge number of Air BnB properties available in Brekkie Beach at short notice. And I had been in a reasonably distraught state when I booked the 'She Sells Seashells Cottage'.

So, there were extenuating circumstances as to why I was currently residing in a house where a wooden sign with 'Wash Your Worries Away!' spelled out in seashells decorated the bathroom. I scowled at it as I staggered to the shower. I needed to wash away my sweat and the dregs of an abysmal night of sleep, but unless the hot water system was infused with an hallucinogenic, I wouldn't be washing my worries away any time soon.

As I turned on the tap, I noticed more seashells were glued to the handle. Well, that was just unhygienic, I thought, twisting it and waiting for the hopefully scalding water. If I had been expecting the shower to wash away my sins or perhaps awaken some new clarity inside me, I was seriously disappointed.

Wrapping a towel (yes, printed with seashells) around my waist, I made my way back to the bedroom to get dressed. But instead, I sat on the bed with my face in my hands, damp, inert, and utterly incapable of action.

"What the fuck am I going to do?" I asked out loud, rubbing my fists into my eyes until I could see flashes of light and was probably doing long-term damage to my retinas. When I finally blinked my eyes open, the first thing I saw was a framed poster on the wall, reading 'Good Vibes Only'. Well, that was rude. Apparently, I was unwelcome in the bedroom I was paying far too much for.

Because if there was one thing I was lacking right now, it was good vibes.

Long after lunchtime, I was finally dressed and munching on a cold slice of the not-very-good pizza I had ordered the night before. My laptop was propped in front of me like it was daring me to do something productive.

I swallowed the last of my bad pizza (soggy base and insufficient cheese) and let my greasy fingers hover over the keys. Quickly, before I could think too hard about it, I typed in 'photography course Sydney' and hit enter. As soon as the results page appeared, I slammed the laptop shut, annoyed with myself.

"Stupid," I muttered. "I can't..." I shook my head and opened the pizza box again to discover it was empty. Probably for the best.

I was saved by a knock at the door, and if I had believed in any kind of god, I'd be thanking him right now. Or her. Her seemed more likely, all things considered.

"Hey dude," Tad was in the doorway, Benji strapped to his front and straining to get out, his tiny arms flailing.

"Hi," I said, stepping aside to let father and son in.

"Nice place." Tad was smirking. "Really suits you." He pointed to an enormous sign made from driftwood which bore the words 'If you're not barefoot, you're overdressed!' "I bet you'd like to keep that one when you move out."

"Don't start with me," I grunted. "Can I get you anything?"

"Do you have anything?" Tad raised his eyebrows, following me into the kitchen. The cupboards were whitewashed and adorned with pastel starfish, and there was a feeling of gritty sand underfoot.

I opened the fridge. "Beer?"

"I'll take a beer," Tad helped himself, twisting off the cap. "Aren't you having one?"

"I had enough last night," I admitted, helping to unstrap Benji from the carrier. I held my godson to me for just a moment, inhaling the smell of his soft hair before Benji made it abundantly clear he wanted to explore. "Okay, little mate," I said, carefully putting him on the ground. "I don't think there's too much you can get into here."

Benji immediately made for an artificial fiddle leaf fig, his chubby hands intent on pulling off the leaves. Tad laughed and redirected him back towards me. "If there's anything on floor level he can destroy, he will," Tad told me. "I've been crawling around at home, trying to figure out what to baby proof."

"You're really selling parenthood to me," I said, sinking onto the couch. It was white linen, which I supposed fit the theme, but the number of stains proved it was a poor choice for an Air BnB.

"I didn't realise I was supposed to be. Given you just broke up with your girl."

I closed my eyes and let out a grunt. "I don't want to talk about that."

"Well, it's either that, or we talk about what you're going to do for a career. Your choice, dude."

"Can't you just tell me very detailed stories about the various substances my godson has ejected from his body lately? With pictures?"

"Nope," Tad said. "Come on, I gave you time to process. But you've got to tell me now. Why the hell did you break up with Tessa? I mean, you two weren't exactly together very long. What, did the passion fade?"

"The passion," I said, "did not fade."

"Then what?" Tad demanded. "Because you seemed like you were really keen on her. You were so relaxed with each other. And she already knows all your family bullshit and that you're unemployed, so it's not like you had any bombshells to drop. What, did she drop something on you? Does she have a husband back in England? Is she a Russian asset intent on the destruction of decadent Western Imperialism? If she is, you should get back with her because she might kill you if you don't."

"None of the above. Look, I told you she's dealing with anxiety, right?"

"Right," Tad repeated. "Is that what put you off? That she's seeing a psychologist? Dude, heaps of people have anxiety! My sister is on anti-depressants, and she's a fancy lawyer – as my parents always remind me. And Alice started seeing a psychologist after having Benji! It's not a big deal."

"I know that!" I interrupted. "Do you seriously think I'd break things off for that? I was the one who encouraged her to get help with the whole thing. Tessa's amazing, the way she's handled it all alone for so long, and she's so brave to finally get the help she deserves, and I..."

"Then what?" Tad moved to stop Benji from pulling the TV cord out from the wall. "What the hell happened?"

"I still don't know what the fuck I'm going to do with myself. I thought I'd have figured it out by now. If I came home, gave myself some space, explored options... But I don't know! I still don't know. I've tried! What if I decide I should move back to San Fran, get back into tech?"

"You told me you'd rather move to hell than back to San Fran," Tad said, letting his son tug on his shoelaces with small but surprisingly agile fingers.

"But what if I decide that's the right thing to do? Or what if I need to move to Chicago? Tessa deserves better than waiting for me to make a decision that could hurt her like that. The only right thing to do was to break it off."

"Mate, you're talking like you have no agency in making this decision," Tad said, taking off his shoe to allow Benji full reign over the laces. "Like this decision about what you're going to do is just going to drop into your head, and you'll have to go with it. But you're the one deciding. If you really care about Tessa, and you don't want to hurt her by moving to Chicago, then don't!"

"But I don't know what I want to do. What if Chicago is the place I should be?"

"I doubt it. You don't even like deep-dish pizza."

"Not the point," I said, frustrated. "Look, the way I am right now? Sitting around, not knowing what to do with myself? I'm not good enough for her. I'm just going to make her more anxious. And if I need to leave Sydney, then I'd hurt her even more."

"But Tessa knew all about your career crisis when you got together!" Tad poked me. "She knew you were less One Direction and more No Direction, and she still wanted a piece of your sorry arse. Why don't you let her decide whether the uncertainty is too much?"

"That's what she said. She told me I was being patronising."

"She's absolutely right. And I like that she told you that."

"She didn't even believe me," I said, cringing at the memory. "She thought I ended things because there's something wrong with her, that she wasn't good enough for me. You know, because I've got money, and because she's got anxiety and works for my dad—"

"Tessa's about a million times too good for you, dude."

"That's what I told her. She didn't believe me. She thought I was trying to be nice. The whole 'it's not you, it's me' thing. I tried to tell her I'm not that nice."

"You're definitely not," Tad agreed, watching as his son inserted the end of his shoelace into his mouth appraisingly. "That tasty, buddy?"

Benji gurgled out a laugh, gnawing on the shoelace.

"Well, you know what I think?"

"I think you're going to tell me."

"I think you're a coward," Tad said, looking straight at me. "Who thinks he doesn't deserve to be happy until he's got everything figured out. You had one thing in your life that was great, and you threw it away because you decided that she couldn't cope. And I think you were wrong. And an idiot, with a pinch of arsehole. Actually, a whole side dish of arsehole."

"Thanks," I said, layering the sarcasm so thick even Benji would have picked up on it. "That's very helpful."

"Can't change the truth, dude. Now, what are you going to do about it?"

"I don't know," I said, covering my face with a cushion and then throwing it at him. "That's the whole problem. I don't bloody know."

Tad picked up the pillow. "Live, laugh, love," he read. "Well, you're doing none of those things. Look, you need to stop thinking that you're going to magically wake up one morning and realise what it is you want to do. If you want to make a decision, then bloody well make one!"

"Fine," I said, standing up. "I'm making the decision to have a beer and go back to bed."

"Just don't give up on Tessa, dude." Tad picked Benji up from the floor, where he had begun drooling on the horrible cushion. "Because she's awesome."

"I know she's awesome. But I'm not."

"No, you're not at all awesome right now," Tad agreed. "But you *can* be. And you will be again."

"I doubt it."

Tad just sighed. "Look, give your godson a cuddle, go and mope in bed, and I'll come back tomorrow. If you haven't made some kind of progress by the end of the week, I'm going to enlist you in the Navy."

"I don't want to join the Navy."

"Then you'd better work something out. Because this shit? It cannot go on."

And I knew he was right. This shit could not go on. I just wished I had some idea how to stop it.

• • • ● • ● • • •

Later that evening, I was standing in the kitchen and trying to decide whether I would endure horrible pizza again or call an Uber to go out and get something more palatable when a knock came.

For a moment, I wondered if it might be Tessa and then cursed myself for thinking it. Why would she come to see me? After what I had done, the most I could expect was that she might turn up to throw eggs at my car. Except she'd never disrespect perfectly good eggs that way. And I didn't have a car.

"Coming," I called out. Maybe it was a serial killer cruising for their next victim. Right now, that didn't sound like an entirely bad thing. If I was murdered this evening, I wouldn't have to work out what to do with my life.

When I opened the door, nothing could have prepared me for who was standing there.

"Dad?"

"Well, I'm hardly a stripper-gram." Alan was leaning heavily on his cane. "Are you going to let me in or keep me out here all night?"

"No, of course not," I said, moving aside. "Do you need any help with the step?"

"No," my father said firmly, the rubber tip of his cane making a dull thump against the stone as he made his way inside and past me into the living room. "What a ghastly place! Whoever decorated it should be tried for crimes against humanity!" He sat down in a low armchair with a grunt and pointed at a set of canvas prints of dolphins with his cane. "That," he said, "is the opposite of art."

"No arguments from me," I said, hovering awkwardly beside the sofa. "Um, can I get you anything? I've really only got beer."

"No, thank you." Alan rested his cane across his knees. "I came to talk to you."

I slid down onto the sofa. I suspected this was a conversation I'd better be sitting down for. "Right." I bowed my head. "I guess we haven't really talked since our argument."

"Our argument?" My dad scoffed. "That's not why I'm here!"

"Then why are you here?"

"I came to ask you what on earth you did to poor Tessa!" Alan rapped the table with his cane as he said it, making a bowl of decorative seashells jump.

A rush of guilt in my stomach, followed by a flare of embarrassment. I considered whether I should try to lie, but that had never worked well with my father.

"I'm sorry," I looked down at my bare feet, which apparently meant I was not overdressed for my horrible cottage. "I know you told me not to get involved with her, and I didn't mean for it to happen—"

"But you did anyway, and then you went and broke her heart!"

"Is that what she said?" I looked up at him. "Is she okay?" I wanted to know. I desperately wanted to know if Tessa was okay and had even taken to stalking her sister's Instagram in the hope of finding something. Unfortunately, all Abby seemed to post was neatly organised pantries and aesthetically arranged wardrobes.

"*Tessa*," my father emphasised her name, "didn't say anything. She didn't have to! It didn't take a genius to work out something was going on between the two of you. I saw the looks you were giving each other."

"I didn't plan it like this. I wasn't looking to get involved with anyone, but with her, I just..." I shook my head. "I couldn't help myself."

"Well, you should have!" Alan rapped his cane again. I suspected he rather enjoyed having it as a theatrical prop, even if he resented having to use it. "Why would you go and make that poor girl fall in love with you just to break her heart?"

I felt like I had just swallowed an ice cube. "Tessa's not in love with me." I couldn't let myself believe that.

Alan just scoffed. "Of course she is. You think I can't tell when someone is in love? And then you went and broke her heart! She's being very brave, of course. Never said a word to Marcel or to me. Keeps a smile on her face. But I can see it."

"I didn't mean to hurt her. I knew if we kept seeing each other it wouldn't be good for her. I was trying to do the right thing. Break it off before either of us got in too deep. I guess I messed that up."

"You surely did." Alan closed his eyes for a long moment. "Why do you think you weren't good for her? It's obvious that you care for her. More than care. And the only times you've seemed happy since you came home are when you've been with her."

"I know," I said, the words coming out hoarse. "I do care. I—" I couldn't say just how much, not now. "And she does make me happy. When I'm with her, I feel like...like the future doesn't matter so much. Like I don't need to know what I'm doing next, because it's so good just being with her. But it would have been selfish of me to keep things going just because she was good for me. Not when I was bad for her."

"But why, Dylan?" My dad was almost pleading, very unlike him. "Why do you think you were bad for her? I know I was a little harsh with you the other day, but you're an exceptional young man. Smart, successful, and you've got a good heart. Not to mention handsome, but that's a given. You're my son, after all."

"Because I don't know what to do with myself," I almost shouted. "I'm thirty-one years old, I sold my start-up, I could do anything I wanted, and I don't know what to do! It's pathetic, and I couldn't string Tessa along while I try to figure it out."

My dad was silent for a long moment. "I'm sorry," he said quietly, "if I made you feel like it was pathetic not to know what to do next. I've been worried about you – very worried – but I've always been proud of you. You're not pathetic in the slightest."

I raised my head. I wasn't sure I had ever heard my father apologise. I opened my mouth, but nothing came out.

"And I was never disappointed in you for choosing tech," Alan went on, his voice a little unsteady. "I was surprised, though. And I apologise if I made you feel like I was disappointed. I always assumed you'd pursue your photography. You were so talented! Remember when your work was chosen for that exhibition when you were still in high school?"

My chest clenched, and I let out a breath. "Dad," I said quietly. "You know why my work was chosen for that show. It was because of you."

"I don't think that's the case—"

"It was," I said, swallowing hard. "It was. At the opening night, I was so bloody proud of myself, getting into the exhibition. And then..."

"And then what, Dylan?"

"Then I heard people talking. About how they had let some high school kid into the show because of his famous dad. That it didn't matter that my photos were trash because of who you were."

"Why on earth didn't you ever tell me? Who were these people?"

"Just people." I shook my head. "But it was true. After that, I could never... I didn't want to be successful just because of you."

Alan let out a long breath. "I always thought you chose not to pursue photography because you didn't want to be anything like me. When you chose such a different path... Well, I suppose it felt like a rejection. And perhaps I was too proud to tell you that."

I opened my mouth again and swallowed. "Dad..." I blinked. "What's brought all this on?"

"Tessa, of course," Alan said, with a wry smile. "Not that she did it on purpose. But working on this book with her, reflecting on the course of my life... Well, perhaps I can see where I made mistakes. And I'm old enough and ugly enough to own them now. So, my son, I'm apologising, if I ever made you feel like I was ashamed of you for choosing a different path. And if what you truly want is to go back to tech, then I'll still be proud of you."

"Thanks," I said, my voice husky. "Tech was...I guess it was something where my success or failure would be on my own terms."

"And you were a success! I still don't fully understand what your app did, but I know you were a success."

"Tessa said you always bragged about me."

"Perhaps I'm partly to blame for her falling for you, eh? I talked you up."

"Maybe."

"But it worries me to see you like this now. Without a purpose, without a direction. If you were happy, it would be a different matter. But you're not, are you?"

"No," I admitted. "I feel like...like I've been waiting for the right decision to come to me. Like it will just drop out of the sky without me having to do anything. Don't worry; Tad's already told me how stupid that is."

"Smart boy, that Thaddeus."

"Don't call him that to his face."

"It's a fine name!"

"I guess I'm lucky I didn't end up with it then," I said, raising my eyebrows. "I'm not sure I could pull it off."

"Oh, I think you could," Alan said, placing his hands on his knees. He was silent for a moment. "You've proven you can be a success on your own terms, now, Dylan. No help from me. Are you still absolutely certain that you don't want to be a photographer?"

I let out a half-laugh, half-groan, and stood up. I retrieved my laptop from the table and opened it, placing it on my dad's lap.

"Fundamentals of Photography at the College of Modern Art. Oh no, you can't do that. I know the lecturer; he's a total hack!" But then he paused, looking up at me. "So, you do want to be a photographer. What's the problem? You can't still be thinking about what those bastards said at that show when you were seventeen, can you?"

"The problem," I said, taking the laptop from him. "The problem is that they were right. I've always felt like I'd be in your shadow. Either people would say I was nothing compared to you, or I'd get a whole lot of success I didn't deserve because I'm your son."

Alan let out a long breath. "I see," he said slowly. "Do you still feel that way? That you can't do it because you're my son?"

"I don't know," I said, and that was the truth. "I always said it was because photography was just a hobby. That I didn't want it as my career. But Tessa guessed the real reason."

"I bet she did. She's a smart girl."

"She told me it wasn't a good reason not to do what I loved," I said slowly. "Do you think she's right?"

"Tessa's a smart girl," Alan repeated. "A smart woman, I should say. One ought not to engage in casual misogyny, even unintentionally."

"No."

"So," Alan said, struggling to his feet with the aid of his cane. I got up to help him, and this time, he let me. "Thank you. So," he said again. "What are you going to do about all this, now?"

"I've got no idea. But I know a guy I might ask for advice. Legendary Australian artist. He's got an autobiography coming out, actually."

"You'll always have me, Dylan. And Marcel. And if you play your cards right, you might just get Tessa back too."

"I don't know if that's possible."

"You'd be surprised by what's possible," Alan said, "when you've got some help."

I could almost believe that was true.

19 Tessa

"AND WE CALL OUT to the universe, sisters!" The woman was shouting, her dreadlocks bouncing as she drummed furiously. "I love myself, completely and wholly!"

"I love myself, completely and wholly," I mouthed, giving Abby a look of the deepest disgust as she drummed next to me. It was because of Abby that I was here at the Healing Women's Circle led by Skye Hawkins, a local yoga instructor and self-described women's empowerment guru.

"Sorry," Abby mouthed, her eyebrows knitting together.

"And now a primal yell, sisters!" Skye urged. "Scream your truth to the heavens! I want to feel your spirits!"

Abby cringed and gave me another apologetic look. At least she didn't look like she was having any more fun than I was.

Twenty-six minutes, one admittedly glorious sunset, and more affirmations than I could count later, it was over.

"That was so empowering, sisters!" Skye crowed. "Now, if you'd like to stay for organic cacao and more drumming, you'd be most welcome."

I gave Abby a pleading look, and she spoke up. "We've got to head off," she said loudly, leading me away and waving to Skye. "Dinner reservation."

"But you haven't even—" Skye began, but Abby just waved again, leading me off the beach and across the street.

"I am *so* sorry." Abby let go of my arm. "Do you hate me? I thought it would be good to try something completely different. But it was awful, wasn't it?"

"The sunset was nice?"

"My ears are going to be ringing forever," she moaned, putting her hands up to them. "I swear I didn't know there would be drumming."

"The flyer definitely didn't mention drumming. And I know you wanted to help."

"Did it help at all?" Abby twisted her mouth. "Does your spirit feel empowered?"

"Absolutely not. But it did remind me I've got a big sister who cares about me."

"That you do," Abby gave me a one-armed squeeze. "Well, we've tried spiritual empowerment. What do you say to hitting the pub and shit-talking men?"

"Oh god, yes," I groaned. "I don't think I've ever wanted a drink as badly as I do right now."

"You and me both. Maybe the women's circle would have been better if we had pre-gamed."

"I don't think Skye would have liked that."

"Probably not," Abby shrugged. "Come on, let's grab an outdoor spot at the pub, and watch the rest of this sunset."

Ten minutes later, I was sitting on a weather-beaten but comfortable wooden bench, a glass of perfectly acceptable white wine in my hand, one sister by my side, and the other on Abby's iPad.

"Oh, so it's wine time, is it?" Michelle looked pained. "I'm still at work!"

"You're always at work."

"Technically true, but not the point," Michelle conceded. "Anyway, what's up with you two?"

"Abby took me to get my heart healed. There were bongo drums."

"Why did you think bongo drums would help our heartbroken sister?" Michelle demanded. "Bongo drums never help anything!"

"I didn't realise there would be bongo drums," Abby said defensively. "The advert said Women's Healing Circle. And okay, not my usual sort of thing, but Tessa here is a woman in need of healing."

"It's true," I admitted. "It could have been worse."

"How?" Michelle wrinkled her nose.

"Well, at least it's a nice day. It could have been cold and wet with bongo drums."

"Look at you, seeing the bright side!" Michelle nodded encouragingly. "Are you feeling better about things with Dylan?"

I took a gulp of wine. "Not really," I said. "I just keep thinking that I've never felt this way about someone before. Not even Todd and I was with him for two years! But with Dylan, it felt so right. He really got me, you know? But I guess once he got to know me, he just didn't like me enough."

"Oh, we're not getting into that again!" Abby scolded. "We agreed it wasn't you, it was him and his weird dude angst, remember?"

"Sorry," I said, taking another gulp of wine. "I guess...sometimes I believe that. That the situation he's in, not knowing what to do with his life, was why he felt like he couldn't be with me. And other times, I'm convinced it's because I'm terrible in every way. But only some of the time! That's an improvement!"

"Your psychologist must be helping, then."

"Maybe. Or my Zoloft is finally kicking in."

"I still think he's an arsehole with dude angst and commitment issues," Abby declared, waving her wineglass. "But I gotta admit, when I saw you two together, I kind of thought it was the real deal."

"Maybe it still can be," Michelle said brightly. "You know. When he gets over his dude angst."

"What, and she's supposed to sit around and wait for him to act like an adult? No way!"

"I don't think it's going to work out like that," I said, biting my lip. "As much as I wish it would." I closed my eyes for a moment. "On a happier note, I got confirmation from the publisher that I can start working with their Sydney office. So, I won't be moving back to Birmingham."

"That's amazing news!" Abby hugged me. "Why didn't you tell me before?"

"I was distracted. By the drumming," I said. "Now all we need is for you to move to Sydney, Michelle."

"Look, I put in a request. And another one. And then one more. All ignored."

"You should switch jobs."

"Yeah, like it's that easy," Michelle rolled her eyes. "I'm on the Partner track; I don't want to screw that up."

"I'm glad you're staying, anyway," Abby said to me. "I thought maybe you'd move back after the whole Dylan thing."

"What, and have to find a new psychologist?" I paused. "I like it here. And you were right; I was in a rut in Birmingham. I never tried anything new, never got help for my anxiety. I just let my world become smaller and smaller. I don't want to go back to that."

"Good for you," Michelle enthused. "That's all of us out of Birmingham now, huge achievement! We should take a holiday to celebrate."

"If you ever take time off work, we can," Abby said. "But you've cancelled our last three holidays."

"I know," Michelle winced. "I kind of suck at work-life balance, huh?"

"Maybe you need a psychologist too."

"I don't have time for one! Anyway, I gotta go. I want to finish this report. Then I need to put the fear of, well, me into some interns."

"Atta girl," Abby gave her a thumbs up as the call ended.

"So, drumming didn't work," Abby said conversationally. "But you need to do something to work through your feelings on this whole Dylan thing. Didn't your psychologist have any suggestions?"

"Well, I've done one of them," I said. "Reaching out to a trusted friend or family member. But she also said maybe I could try writing down how I feel. Like a letter or something."

"You should! I hope it makes him feel awful."

"I'm not going to send it! It's for me, not him."

"Maybe we could ritually burn it on the beach. I bet Skye could build a good bonfire."

"Do you really want to involve Skye in any of our plans?"

"On second thoughts, no," Abby said. "Come on, I'll get you another drink. Get you in the right head space for writing your Dear Dylan letter."

At least I had a supportive sister.

20 Dylan

It was stupid o'clock when I left the She Sells Seashells cottage with my old SLR and tripod. Like, still dark o'clock.

I felt vaguely nauseous as I walked towards the beach, an instant black coffee sloshing around in my stomach. I couldn't help but think of the coffee Tessa made. Gently foamed milk, freshly ground beans, and that gap-toothed smile as she handed it to me, her fingers brushing against mine. The memory made my chest clench, and I stumbled over a gap in the footpath.

"I just had to go and fall for her, didn't I?"

The beach was completely deserted when I arrived; setting up my tripod in the sand and asking myself what the hell I was doing. Technically, I was here to capture the sunrise. Maybe even a few surfers if the waves were sufficiently tempting. But why was I doing this? Was I trying to prove to myself, once and for all, that I'd never pursue photography?

Or just the opposite?

But as I peered through the lens, clicking as the first tendrils of sunlight filtered out over the water, I stopped thinking about the why. As I adjusted the focus and settings, my movements became fluid, almost automatic.

When a familiar trio of surfers began to slope down the beach toward the water, we exchanged the masculine nod of recognition. They were too intent on their destination to pay me much attention, and I was glad to have some human subjects. Sunrise was all well and good, but people? Capturing people was far more interesting.

The surfer with the curly hair came out of the water first, shaking his magnificent locks in the early morning sun, his surfboard slung under one arm. Click, click, click. I captured his grin, his thumbs up to his friends still in the waves, the way he shook like a dog, droplets of saltwater flying out onto the sand.

"Hey mate. Thought you weren't a real photographer." It wasn't a challenge; the words were spoken with lazy good humour.

"I'm not," I said. "But maybe I want to be."

"Sick as! Can I see your shots?"

I hated sharing my photos – after all, I was sure most of them were garbage – but it would have been rude to refuse.

"Sure."

The surfer stooped in front of the tripod and flicked the button. "Damn! Check out that sun."

"It put on a good show for me."

"Look at these!" He had reached the photos of himself and his friends out in the waves. "Mate, I need these! Could you send them to me?"

"Yeah, for sure. I'm not a professional or anything, but you're welcome to have them."

"It's me!" The surfer laughed as he reached the photos of himself coming out of the water. "Dude, look at my face!"

"I can delete those if you like," I said quickly. "I was just messing around."

"No way!" The surfer shook his head, showering me with saltwater drops. "They're dope! I look all soulful and shit in this one." He jabbed a finger at the screen. "I didn't know I could look like that. Don't get me wrong, the sunrise pics are sweet as, but these ones of me are, like, next level."

"You want me to send them to you?"

"Give us your phone, I'll put my number in."

I handed it over, bemused but more than a little gratified.

"My mates are gonna be filthy. I can't wait to chuck these on Insta. My DMs are gonna be chockers with thirsty chicks."

"Glad to be of service."

"Mate, I know you're not a real photographer, but I reckon you should be," the surfer said as he handed me back my phone. The screen informed me that "Hazza" was now a contact.

"Maybe," I said, shielding my eyes against the rising sun. It felt genuinely possible.

• • • ● • ● ● • • •

"Bloody hell, it's early for you," Tad opened the door, clad in a dressing gown and an expression of total exhaustion. "But you brought an offering, so you're forgiven." He took a coffee from the tray, taking a sip with an air of deep satisfaction.

"I was at the beach this morning."

Tad let me into the house. In the living room, an equally exhausted-looking Alice was sitting on the sofa, Benji greedily sucking on a bottle. "Look who I found," he said to his wife. "He brought coffee."

"You're a gentleman and a scholar." Alice took the coffee with her free hand. "Benji's teething. It's the worst."

"I can imagine," I said, even though I couldn't really. "Sore teeth, mate?" I ruffled his soft hair. "That's rough."

"Especially for us," Tad agreed, sitting beside his wife and taking Benji from her. "Anyway, I don't think you're just here as our personal caffeine fairy. What's up?"

I sat down and took a breath. "Look, if you've had a rough night, I don't want to come here and emote all over you."

"Oh, Dylan, we don't mind you emoting on us." Alice sipped her coffee. "It's a nice distraction from my screaming infant. Kind of like my own personal reality TV show."

"Thanks?"

"You know what we mean," Tad grinned from the sofa. "So, what's up? Some kind of revelation on the beach? Do you finally know your purpose in life?"

"Actually, that kind of is what happened." Trust Tad to guess and ruin my big reveal. "I think I want to be a photographer. For real."

"Oh, thank god for that!" Alice burst out and then covered her mouth. "I mean, that's great!"

"I may have vented my frustration to Alice that you wouldn't get over yourself and admit that's what you want. It's hard to see your favourite character making self-defeating decisions."

"I'm just glad I'm your favourite character."

"So, what brought all this on?" Tad pressed. "You went out to the beach to take photos and decided this was actually what you wanted after all? Is that all? Did you take a morning acid tab and feel the warm fingers of god stroking your cheek?"

"Honestly, I think I've known the whole time," I admitted, letting out a sigh. "I just didn't want to accept it. Because I always said I'd never do something like this because of Dad. But he came to see me the other day, and..." I let out a breath. "I think maybe I can do this after all."

"That's awesome, dude," Tad said. "I mean, you're a pain in the arse for taking so long to figure it out, but we still love you." He propped Benji up on his lap. "Except Benji. Today, he hates everyone and everything." In response, Benji let out a loud wail and shoved his fingers into his mouth.

"Let me take him." I reached out for my godson. "You two look like you need a nap."

"I'm going to die," Alice said, groaning softly. "I thought the newborn stage was the worst for sleep deprivation. But this is way worse. He lulled us into expecting a peaceful nine hours every night and then he turned into a goblin." Her face softened. "A very handsome goblin who I'd give my life for."

"But still a goblin." Tad stretched his shoulders and rubbed his face. "So, what are you going to do now?"

"I told you. Try and make the photography thing work."

"I meant about your other big fuck up. Tessa."

My stomach clenched unpleasantly. "I did fuck that up, didn't I?"

"Epically," Alice agreed, nodding. "Do you know how annoying it is when the couple you're rooting for finally gets together, and then one of them goes and ruins it?"

"Well, if it's anywhere near as bad for you as it's been for me, then I'm sorry." I hung my head. "She's...amazing. I've never felt like this about anyone. That I could just be myself, even my crappy, indecisive, living-with-my-parents self, and she still liked me. We just worked so well together, you know? And then I ruined it."

"Is it like, ruined as in ruined forever? Or do you think you could still fix this?"

I let out a slow breath even as my heart leapt in my chest at the thought that maybe I could. "I don't know." And that was the truth. "I mean, she thinks I broke up with her because she wasn't good enough—"

"As if."

"I know!" I said, exasperated. "I tried to tell her that wasn't true, but it was like she wanted to believe it."

"You said she struggles with anxiety, right?" Alice looked thoughtful. "She probably was thinking of all the ways it could go wrong the whole time, so when it did end, she just slotted in the worst-case scenario."

"Maybe. But if she thinks that, I've got no hope of fixing this."

"So defeatist!" Tad chided. "Remember when Alice and I broke up when I went on exchange that semester in uni?"

"Uh, yeah?"

"I thought I was doing the right thing. You know, not tying her down while I was away. And six months seemed like a lifetime back then."

"And I thought he just wanted to sleep with as many cute Canadian girls as possible. I was devastated and called him a man whore bastard. Which was both unfair and slut shaming. I'm sorry for that."

"Well, I can see why you said it," Tad inclined his head. "I mean, that's why most people break up when one of them goes on exchange. But I didn't want to break up at all. When I realised just how badly I had messed up, I had to do something big to show her I really meant it."

"He bought me a plane ticket to visit him," Alice explained, smiling tiredly at her husband. "And for a broke university student, that was practically a proposal. So, I forgave him. And now, here we are."

"See?" Tad said. "You and Tessa could be parenting an adorable goblin of your own in a few years if you apologise and make her see that you never thought she wasn't good enough. And show her you really want a future with her."

"She told me she had nothing else to say to me," I said, wincing at the memory.

"Oh, I told Tad that too. Didn't stop me from driving past his house every night."

"I knew it was you!" Tad crowed. "You denied it!"

"I was embarrassed!" Alice scrunched up her face. "But I hadn't given up on you. Even though I was super angry. And hurt."

"Well, I don't think Tessa's been driving past my house. How do I know if she's given up on me or not?"

"You don't, mate," Tad clapped me on the shoulder, where Benji was drooling crankily. "You have to put yourself out there and be ready for her to tell you to piss off. If she's worth it, you'll do it anyway."

"She's definitely worth it," I didn't have to think very hard about that. "She's...perfect. Okay, no one's perfect. But she's perfect for me. And I feel like if I get my shit together, get over myself and try to make photography work, then maybe I could be good for her too."

"Then we just need to come up with the right apology," Alice looked excited. "I've seen tons of rom-coms; I've got lots of ideas!"

"And besides, you're rich and handsome. Definitely helps with making the big gesture. All the movies would agree, huh, Alice?"

"Definitely," Alice said, nodding. "We're going to need some butcher's paper and markers!"

"I thought you guys were exhausted? I was going to watch Benji for a few hours while you get some rest."

Alice yawned hugely. "Sleep does sound good."

"Besides," I said. "I think I know what I need to do."

"Seriously?" Tad covered his own yawn. "You're ready to get your shit together and win back your girl?"

"I'm ready to try."

21 Tessa

"I don't see why it has to go to an editor," Alan tapped the pile of pages with the head of his cane. "It's perfect, just as it is. Just send it to print! After those last few changes, of course."

"Well, I'm glad you like it. It's been a pleasure working with you."

"Oh, don't flatter me! I know I've been a pain in the arse. And I know you're the one who's done all the hard work. All I've had to do is talk about myself." He dropped his voice. "And between you and me, I think we both know I don't find that very difficult at all."

I fought the urge to laugh out loud – or agree. "I've enjoyed it," I said again. "I mean, I knew nothing about art when I moved out here. Now I think I could go to a gallery opening without embarrassing myself too much."

"After being my house guest, I'm sure you know more than half the curators in Sydney!"

"Let's not get carried away."

"So, what's next for you? You're welcome to stay here as long as you like," Alan said. "I don't want you to feel you have to leave before you're ready just because my son is an idiot."

"What do you mean?" I felt my stomach clench unpleasantly, and my skin did that horrible itching, tightening thing. But I knew it was useless playing dumb. Alan knew. Of course he did.

"Tessa, give me some credit," Alan raised his eyebrows, which were so like his son's. "I'm an artist. I deal in passion and emotion. As soon as I saw you and Dylan together, I knew something would happen. It was pointless to warn you, but I did try. He's a good man, really, but he's behaved abominably towards you. I'm very sorry for that."

"I..." My mouth was dry like I had combined a night of heavy drinking with a chaser of desert sand. "You don't need to be sorry. What happened was nothing to do with you."

"I don't know if that's entirely true," Alan said, looking uncomfortable. "When I confronted my son about what he planned to do with his life, it didn't go well. You probably already know that. I handled it badly, I admit. And that, I think, made him believe he was in no fit state for a relationship. Especially one with a woman of your quality."

"I don't think that was the problem," I said quickly. "Maybe when Dylan really thought about his future, he just realised I wouldn't fit into it. I mean, I'm sure I'm nothing like the sort of women he must have dated in San Francisco."

"I wouldn't know," Alan quirked his mouth. "Because apparently, none of them was ever important enough to mention by name. With you, it was different. I've seen my son through crushes, girlfriends, and flings. It was always different with you. I just hope he sees sense."

"It didn't—" I began, trying to squash down the tendrils of hope that were escaping my treacherous heart like weedy vines intent on taking over my well-tended garden of realistic expectations. "Look, I'm not in the best place for a relationship either. I've been working through some things, and it's probably best I do that on my own. I wasn't lying when I told you I wasn't looking for anything."

"I know you weren't, my dear." Alan shifted in his chair. "But I don't think the circumstances matter when two people are right for each other. You know the story of how Marcel and I met almost as well as I do myself. I was barely functional. A step away from being an unfit father, so wrapped up in myself, my work, my growing fame. If I hadn't met Marcel when I did, I dread to think what might have happened."

"I'm glad it worked out for you two," I said, gripping my laptop tightly. "Because you're perfect together. And I know Dylan's glad, too."

"If two people are right for each other, it doesn't matter what you're going through," Alan said, leaning forward slightly as though he wanted me to truly hear his words. "Because you go through it together."

"Maybe one day, in the future, if we met again..." I shrugged. "But I don't think that's what he wants."

"Tessa, my son's been in denial about what he wants for months. Years, probably. If he gets his head screwed on straight, he'll be begging you for another chance. Mark my words." Alan nodded smartly, clearly feeling he had made his point.

"I appreciate that you think I'm good enough for your son. But I think it's probably over, for good," I said flatly.

"Oh, Tessa!" Alan let out a loud snort of laughter. "Good enough for my son? Of course you're not! You're far too good. But I hope," he added in a conspiratorial tone, "that you might still care for him anyway."

• • • • ● • ● • • •

"I think," I said, twisting my hands in my lap. "That I'm doing okay. All things considered. I mean, I still wish things had been different with Dylan, but—" I let out a breath. "I mean, I'm not crying into my pillow every night." I paused. "Well, I am, but not for as long as I was when it first happened. That's good, right?"

"Crying's nothing to be ashamed of, Tessa," Jillian said, making a note on her iPad. What did it say, I wondered. 'Still crying over fling', perhaps? 'Obsessed with man she barely dated'? "It can be extremely cathartic. A way of letting out our feelings and working through them."

"I don't know if I've worked through very much." I bit my lip. "But I'm still functioning. I kind of know what I'm doing next. I mean, I'm staying in Sydney. When I move out of Alan's studio, I'll be crashing with my sister for a while, and then I'll find a place, get started on my next ghostwriting project, and hope like hell Dylan moves away from Brekkie Beach so I don't run into him at the coffee shop." I let out a loud laugh, even though what I said wasn't at all funny. Jillian gave me a polite smile.

"Do you think you'd feel uncomfortable if you did see him again? That your feelings would be stronger than you believe you can handle?" Jillian's pen was poised. Today, she was wearing a sheath dress printed with palm fronds, paired with a cropped green leather blazer. When I was as grown up as Jillian – if I ever was – I hope I dressed as well.

"Probably," I admitted, fiddling with the hem of my sweatshirt. "I mean, I don't know what I'd do if I bumped into him somewhere. Especially if he was with someone else, and he tried to introduce me to her, and she was everything I'm not and—" I cut myself off, aware my voice was becoming unpleasantly high-pitched and panicky. In other words, shrill.

"Would you like to discuss some strategies for how you might handle seeing Dylan again?" Jillian asked. "Do you think you'd benefit from preparing for this? It seems to be causing you some distress."

I let out a breath. "I guess so," I said and sighed again. "I'm sorry, I just thought..." I twisted my hands in my lap. "I mean, I'm taking my medication. I've been doing the exercises you showed me. I've been seeing you every week. I just thought that if I did all that, I wouldn't still have these painful feelings. And I know that's stupid."

"Not stupid at all," Jillian said, her voice gentle. "But as we've discussed, there's nothing that can stop us from having feelings. Especially difficult, painful feelings in response to events that distress us. Our goal is to lessen the impact of your anxiety on your life. To make you feel that you can handle your difficult thoughts and feelings. And I think," she paused, "you've made considerable progress in that regard."

"Progress," I repeated, nodding. "So, I need to give up on the idea that one day I'll wake up and feel awesome all the time, forever?"

Jillian let out a rich, throaty laugh. "Yes, Tessa," she said. "I think you should give up on that one. But you're doing important work, and you're making real progress. You deserve to feel proud of yourself for how far you've come already."

I nodded again, taking in her words. Then I lifted my chin. "Okay," I said. "So, strategies for if I see Dylan again. Let's do it."

• • • • ● • ● • • •

Michelle: how did it go with the good doctor?

Tessa: she's a psychologist, not a doctor

Michelle: ...so how did it go with the good psychologist, then? <eye roll emoji>

Tessa: sorry. um, pretty good. we went over strategies for what i can do if i see dylan again. i just really hope he leaves brekkie beach

Abby: he better leave, if he values that handsome face of his

Tessa: please don't do anything to him. i still care way too much <sad face emoji>

Tessa: his dad told me that he thinks he'll realise he's made a huge mistake and fix things. but i don't believe it

Abby: he definitely made a huge mistake messing with my sister!

Michelle: if he did come and apologise, would you take him back?

Michelle: hello?

Tessa: sorry, i was thinking. i don't know. i still feel so much for him, but i don't know if i could trust him again. i'd have to be really sure he was serious

Michelle: like, down on one knee serious?

Abby: must everything be about marriage?

Michelle: no, but maybe this is

Tessa: i don't know what it would take. but it doesn't matter. i think the chance of dylan coming back and begging me for forgiveness is about the same as this agent liking my new book

Abby: so, an excellent chance then

Michelle: a one hundred per cent chance! make sure you're wearing nice underwear for when it happens

Tessa: remember what happened last time i tried to find an agent for my own work?

Abby: you got one rejection! one! that's nothing!

Tessa: ...please don't tell me how many times jk rowling got rejected

Abby: you're better than jk rowling!

Michelle: ^^ agreed! and way less controversial on twitter

Tessa: i don't even have twitter

Tessa: but i'm going to send the book now anyway. because i'm not letting anxiety stop me from taking valued actions

Michelle: \<gif of Michael Jackson eating popcorn\>

Abby: you know that's for when you're watching drama unfold, not when you're waiting for something, right?

Michelle: don't gif shame me!

Abby: you need a little gif shaming sometimes

Michelle: \<gif of monkey flinging faeces at another monkey\>

Abby: that one was perfect! you're improving!

Tessa: ...i sent it

Michelle: how do you feel!?

Tessa: kind of like i want to vomit. or get so drunk i don't even remember I sent it. but thanks to jillian i'm going to journal my feelings and go for a walk. just pray i don't bump into dylan

Abby: maybe i'll go for a walk and bump into him on purpose. with my van

Tessa: still not ready for acts of violence, but i appreciate it

Abby: \<thumbs up emoji\>

Michelle: i bet if you do bump into him, he begs you to come back

Tessa: i don't want to see him!

Michelle: fine. i hope you don't see him yet. and i hope abby doesn't either

Abby: i promise not to do any permanent damage if i do

Tessa: that's not very reassuring

Abby: that's my best offer

Tessa: i'll take it. i love you both so much <heart emoji>

Michelle: i love you both too! gif shaming and all!

Abby: <gif of hugging women> i love you both, even if you drive me nuts sometimes

Michelle: what are sisters for?

22 Dylan

"How much did you sell that bloody app for?" Tad's eyes widened as he paced around the living room, bright sunlight streaming through the windows. "You never gave me a number, but it must have been a hell of a lot if you can buy this place outright."

"It was enough," I said, unwilling to share the actual sum. "So, you think I should make an offer? It's got great bones, but the kitchen needs work, and the bathrooms are..."

"Pink?" Tad offered, sticking his head into the bathroom adjoining the living area. "I'd go so far as to say aggressively pink."

"Not even Barbie's Dream House had that much pink. But the views are amazing, it's a perfect location, and it's not like I can't manage a few contractors to get the kitchen and bathrooms redone."

"You say that now," Tad shook his head darkly. "Alice says getting our kitchen renovated was the most stressful thing she's ever done, and she gave birth to Benji. Huge head and all."

"Well, that's another cool thing about this place," I said. "I know Alice is still on maternity leave, but she made a few calls to get me in to see it and took me through herself. So, she'll get the commission if I buy it."

"In that case, the contractors will be no problem. Buy it. Buy it now."

"Do you think Tessa will like it?" I asked, my heart making an odd fluttering sensation, caught between utter despair and overly optimistic hope.

"Probably," Tad shrugged. "But I gotta be real with you. I don't think the house itself will be what makes her decide whether or not to forgive you."

"I know," I made a face. "But I want her to see I'm serious about settling down here. That I'm not going to just take off and break her heart. Again. And buying a house seems like a good way to do that."

"Lifestyles of the rich and not very famous, huh?"

"Well, I do have to live somewhere. And Sydney real estate with water views? Pretty solid investment."

"You're right there," Tad agreed. "And I, for one, am glad you're choosing to settle down five minutes' walk from your godson. And me. If Tessa tells you to go drown in the bay, at least we'll be nearby to comfort you."

"Thanks."

"So, you're definitely putting in an offer?"

"I'll call Alice now," I said, pulling out my phone.

"Good," Tad clapped me on the shoulder. "Let's go and get a beer to celebrate. Or lots of beers. I feel like this is a lots of beers kind of occasion."

"You won't feel like that when Benji wakes you up with a full nappy at four in the morning."

"No. But that's future Tad's problem. Right now, I just want to celebrate my best friend finally making a good decision."

"Well, with encouragement like that, how could I say no?"

• • • ●•●• • •

"Are you sure I should register the domain name now?" I asked, taking another gulp of my beer.

"Yes," Tad nodded enthusiastically. "Right now! Just make sure you've got the spelling right."

I squinted at my phone. 'dylanhuxleyphotography.com' seemed right, and I hadn't had that many beers. "I think I can spell my own name."

"I wouldn't be so sure. Remember that one time you got an award for the maths competition, but your handwriting was so bad the certificate had your name wrong?"

"How could I forget? Seeing as you called me Pylan for six months. And it doesn't exactly roll off the tongue."

"Pylan," Tad repeated. "Man, that was funny."

"I've definitely got it right this time," I said, looking down at my phone. "Okay, I'm going to do it." I clicked 'pay now' and was glad that my phone remembered my credit card details because I certainly couldn't.

"How do you feel?" Tad nudged me, making me spill my beer. "Good? Like you're doing the right thing?"

"I feel fucking terrified, to be honest," I confessed. "But yeah. Terrifying is the right thing, I reckon. Probably not as terrified as I will be seeing Tessa tomorrow, though."

"Do you think your dad and Marcel worked out your plan?"

"I think they've guessed something's up," I said. "I wanted to tell Dad about the house and registering the business, but I know he can't keep his mouth shut, and I want to tell Tessa first. But they're going into the city tomorrow for Dad's appointment with the specialist, so I thought that would be a good time to head over. Best if I don't have an audience for this whole thing."

"Shame," Tad scrunched his face. "Alice really wants to see you make your big speech. If you'd let her, she'd be there with popcorn and a folding chair."

"Grateful as I am to your wife for getting me the house and marrying you, I think that might be more than I can offer," I said, finishing my beer. "And Tessa deserves some privacy. You know, if she cries. Or slaps me."

"Or both."

"Or both," I had to agree. "But I have to take the chance, don't I? That she might tell me to fuck off and that she'll set her sister on me if I ever contact her again."

"Abby? She seemed nice!" Tad laughed. "But definitely protective. Alice's sister gave me a very thorough talking to when we got back together after the whole exchange program screw up."

"Guess it's what siblings do. Reckon Benji will be reading the riot act to a little sibling's boyfriend or girlfriend one day?"

"Are you seriously asking if we're having another kid?" Tad groaned. "Mate, we're in the trenches! Barely keeping our heads above water!"

"Why is there water in the trench?"

"Because it's raining, dickhead! I'll mix my metaphors if I want."

"Fair enough," I conceded. "Look, sorry if that was pushy. Just... You guys are good at this. Parenting, I mean. The world needs more good people, and I reckon you and Alice will raise good people."

"Well, shit, now I'm going to get teary," Tad said, turning his face away. But then he looked back with a grin. "I will say, there's a much better chance of us conceiving another little goblin if you volunteer for some overnight babysitting. Deal?"

"Deal," I said. "I'd better get going; I don't want to be hungover for tomorrow. Kind of hoping to make a good impression."

"You're probably right. I don't want to leave Alice alone with the little dude too long. Gotta be a responsible dad and all."

"You're a great dad. And a bloody great friend. You know I'm grateful, right?"

"I know," Tad clapped me on the shoulder. "I'm awesome. A joy. A blessing. You're lucky to have me."

"And you'll be around tomorrow if it all goes to shit, and I need to throw myself on your couch and tell you why life isn't worth living?"

"Absolutely. But I reckon," he went on, "that you won't be doing that at all. You're an idiot with what you did. But you're also a good bloke, and I know how much you care about Tessa. How serious you are. If you can get her to see that, it'll be fine."

"I'll keep my fingers crossed."

"Toes, too," Tad suggested. "You need all the luck you can get."

And that, I thought, was the truth.

• • • ● • ● • ● • • •

I had never been so nervous standing outside my own childhood home. Not even when I was fifteen, highly inebriated with vomit all down my t-shirt, and no keys. Back then, I had only had to fear my dad laughing at me, and Marcel giving helpful hints about not mixing alcoholic beverages. This time, I was putting my whole heart on the line for the woman I cared about more than I ever had about anyone and facing the very real possibility of a cutting rejection. And the worst part was that it was entirely my fault.

Swallowing, which was a bad idea as my mouth was as dry as the morning after that unfortunate teenage incident, I knocked on the door and waited. And then waited a bit longer. Was Tessa out for a walk? Should I wait and hang around, or would that be creepy? Was it less or more creepy, given that it was my dad's house? I definitely wouldn't let myself in, even though I still had a key.

As I debated whether it would be creepier to sit down to wait or pace back and forth, I heard footsteps. The door clicked and then opened.

Tessa. Tessa, her eyes as wide and blue and her lips as full as ever. She looked a little tired, perhaps, but otherwise, just as I remembered. Which wasn't exactly a surprise – it had only been a week since I had last seen her. It wasn't like she could have changed that much. Unless Abby had taken her for a post break up haircut, but that—

"Dylan," Tessa breathed out my name softly like she couldn't quite believe it. I had been standing, gawping and wondering, too long. Then her expression changed and became guarded. "Uh, your dad and Marcel aren't here. Appointment in the city. They should be back around—"

"I know they're out. I came to see you," I blurted out. That wasn't exactly how I had planned this, but the way I had rehearsed this in my head didn't seem to resemble the reality currently playing out in front of me. Now, I didn't want to have to use coherent words at all. I just wanted to reach out and touch her, hold her, wrap her up in my arms and never let go. But from her expression, I didn't think that was an entirely wise plan if I wanted to avoid a slap.

"Oh." Tessa wasn't giving me much to go on. But, I thought, she hadn't slammed the door yet. That was a promising sign, right?

"Uh, can I come in?" Mentally, I crossed my fingers.

Tessa paused. "Of course you can," she said eventually. "It's your dad's house."

That really wasn't the response I had been hoping for. "But is it okay with you? If you don't want to talk to me, I'll go."

Tessa looked at me again for a long moment, and finally, she nodded. "You can come in," she said. "It's okay with me."

And that was a relief. I was hoping I'd at least get to say what I came here to tell her before she chucked me out. I followed her into the formal lounge, and she sat in one of the stiff armchairs, arms and legs crossed over defensively. I winced, but I supposed I deserved that.

"Um, how have you been?" I asked, and damn, that sounded really stupid. Now was not the time for small talk.

"Fine," Tessa said, and then she let out a tiny laugh. "Well, not really fine. Kind of devastated, actually. But I'm coping." There was a defiance in her tone, and she raised her chin.

"Well, that's good," I said, pacing up and down and wondering when the right words would drop into my head. "You look well."

A pause. "Thanks?" Tessa made it sound like a question. "If you're feeling guilty about hurting me, and wanted to check that I'm okay, then don't worry," she said after a moment. "I mean, yeah, what you did hurt like hell. But I..." She swallowed. "I'm going to be okay. I've got my sisters, and I've still been seeing Jillian, and I...I'll be okay. Eventually."

"That wasn't why I came over," I said. "But I'm glad to hear you're okay. Not surprised, though, because you're strong as hell. Not that you should have to be strong, because I shouldn't have done what I did. And I'm here to say I'm sorry."

Tessa frowned, a tiny line between her eyebrows. "You're sorry that you hurt me, or you're sorry because you regret what you did?"

"Both," I answered. "Especially since..." I let out a breath. "It was a completely fucking stupid thing to do. The worst decision I've ever made. And I wish I could take it back, but I can't. All I can do is tell you how sorry I am. I should never have tried to assume that you couldn't deal with me being uncertain about my future. You're way stronger than that. I was...afraid, I guess. Of not being the man you deserve because I couldn't figure myself out. And it seemed better to break things off than wait around for you to work that out."

Tessa let out a sound somewhere between a gasp and a sigh. "I..." She stopped. "I don't get it. You think you made the wrong decision, breaking up with me? You were so sure. What changed?"

"A lot, actually," I said, pacing again. "I finally admitted to myself that I want to be a photographer for a start." I turned to look at her. "Just like you said. You were right, of course."

"You weren't pleased with me when I said it." Tessa's face was unreadable.

"I was working through a lot of stuff," I said. "I mean, with my dad being who he is, and... You were right about that, too. About why I didn't want to let myself try because I couldn't live up to him. Or because I might be successful, even if I didn't deserve it, because of who he is."

"So why did you change your mind?" Tessa at least looked like she was interested in my answer, so I took that as a promising sign.

"I'm still afraid of those things," I admitted. "And I tried to bully myself into wanting something else. Anything else. But I couldn't. I realised that not letting myself do the thing I really wanted was...incredibly stupid, really. And I'm trying to be less stupid."

A small smile. "Wise words," Tessa said quietly. "So, you're sure about this?"

"I'm really doing it," I said and took an envelope from my pocket, handing her the piece of paper within.

"This is..." Tessa scanned the paper. "A registration of your intent to run a business in Australia."

"Yep," I said. "And I reserved the domain name, too. Dylan Huxley Photography dot com. And there's more," I rushed on before she could tell me that it was great that I was pursuing my passion, but it had nothing to do with her.

"More?" Tessa looked up at me, her lips parting ever so slightly to show that tiny gap between her teeth.

"More," I repeated. "I bought a house. Right here in Brekkie Beach, it's about a ten-minute walk from here. You can see the water right from the deck. The kitchen and bathrooms are horrible, but I can get those fixed. The really cool thing about the house," I said, "is that there's a workshop next to the garage. Which I can set up as a dark room. You know, if I want to go old school and develop photos myself."

Tessa let out a soft breath. "You bought a house in Brekkie Beach? I guess that means you're sticking around."

"It really does," I said, and finally, I felt brave enough to sit down in the armchair next to hers. "I'm not going anywhere. I finally feel like I'm sure – completely sure – about what I want from life. And that's living in Brekkie Beach, doing photography and..." I took a breath. "Being with you." I paused. "Actually, I always knew I wanted to be with you. Even when I was a complete arsehole idiot dickhead and broke up with you. It wasn't because I didn't want to be with you. It was because I felt like you deserved better. But now." Another quick intake of breath. "Now I feel like I can at least try to be worthy of you. If you'll let me."

Tessa's face hadn't moved, but she was twisting her hands in her lap. "Dylan," she said quietly. "That's...that's a lot."

"I know," I said hurriedly. "And look, I'm not asking you to give me an answer today. You need time to think about all this. And maybe more time before you want to see me again, and even if you do, maybe you'd prefer we keep things casual at first, and I wouldn't expect you to make a big commitment—"

"Dylan," Tessa interrupted me. "I wrote you a letter, you know. After I saw Jillian and told her what happened."

"Did you?" I felt a wave of fear crash through me. Not a sick barrel like Hazza and the surfers liked to catch. Just a horrible, icy wave. "I didn't get it; I'm sorry. Did you send it to Tad and Alice's place? I've actually been at an Air BnB. It's pretty shit. Really awful beachy décor." I realised I was rambling and stopped.

"I didn't send it," Tessa explained, shaking her head slightly. "If I had been planning to send it, I wouldn't have been able to be so honest about how I was feeling. And that was what I needed to do. Be honest about everything I felt, so I could work through it, one day at a time."

"What did it say?" I asked. "Can I read it now?"

"Oh, no way. There's about three full pages of angry ranting about how you broke my heart and how you toyed with my feelings when you knew I had my issues, right from the beginning. I still thought you broke up with me because I wasn't good enough for you—"

"You have to know that's not true," I interrupted.

"Let me finish," Tessa admonished, but there was a touch of a smile on her full lips. Enough of a smile to give me hope, anyway. "But at the end, I wrote that if you really were telling the truth, that you felt like you couldn't be with me because you didn't know what you wanted to do..."

"That was the truth," I said. "Sorry, I know you told me not to interrupt. I'm shitty at following instructions. This is why I have to be my own boss."

Tessa shook her head, this time her smile showing her teeth. "If it was true, I wanted you to know I'd wait for you. Until you worked it out. Because you're worth it. I've never felt like this about anyone else because," Tessa looked down at her hands, fidgeted again, and seemed to make a decision. "Because I love you."

There was dead silence in the formal sitting room. I could have sworn that even the ever-chirping birds and the distant sound of the ocean had gone silent in reverence to those incredible, miraculous words that had just left Tessa's beautiful lips.

"Holy fucking shit," I burst out and immediately winced. "Fuck, I mean— That's not what I wanted to say, I—"

"Not quite the response I was hoping for," Tessa looked like she was trying to make a joke but was on the verge of crumbling into a million tiny pieces right there in the stiff armchair.

"I love you too," I said quickly, and a strange warmth filled my body. My stomach clenched, performed a series of energetic flips, and then stilled. It was true. It was real. I did love Tessa. And she loved me. This was actually happening. Even in my most wildly optimistic fantasies of how this conversation might go, I hadn't let myself imagine that she might say those words. That she might think I was worth those three words after just how badly I had messed up.

Tessa let out a sound somewhere between a sob and a laugh, and threw herself from her armchair into my lap, her arms wrapping around my neck. The chair creaked ominously, but I gave zero fucks about my father's expensive mid-century modern chairs as I held her close, breathing in the smell of her hair, glorying in the warmth of her body, the weight of her, real and here and with me again.

"So, I'm guessing this means you forgive me," I said after a moment. "Though, if you did want me to do some begging, I'd be down for it. Even pleading. For you, I'd do both."

"I don't think you've ever begged for anything in your life," Tessa said, pulling back to look at me, her eyes wet with unshed tears.

"I haven't. But I will, here and now, if you want me to."

"You don't need to beg. Of course I forgive you. Abby, on the other hand, you might need to beg. And plead. Even beseech. Do you think you could beseech?"

"I could definitely beseech," I said, tracing a finger over the shape of her cheekbones, down the tip of her nose, just around those full lips.

"That tickles!"

"Sorry," I murmured. "Maybe I'd better—"

I don't know who kissed who. All I knew was that finally – finally – those lips were on mine once more, and maybe, just maybe, everything was going to be okay. All that searching and wondering about what I should do with myself was finally answered. I should be right here, right now, with this woman.

When Tessa pulled back, her lips were once again curved into that bright smile I knew – and loved – so well. "So, we're really doing this, huh?"

"I sure as hell hope so," I said, hugging her close to me. "Otherwise, it's going to be very awkward at Nick and Nikki's."

Tessa let out a groan. "I spent all of my last session with Jillian coming up with strategies about what I'd do if I saw you again. Especially with someone else. Apparently, that was a total waste of time."

"There couldn't be someone else, Tessa," I said, tucking a strand of her dark hair behind one ear. "Not after meeting you."

"I bet Jillian will bitch to all the other psychologists about her time-wasting client."

"Let her," I said. "But I bet she'll be happy for you. Because you're awesome, and you deserve to be happy. Even if she probably thinks the worst of me right now."

"Actually, she just said it sounded like you had some issues of your own to work through."

"Well, she was right," I said, leaning my forehead against hers.

"So, do you think two people with serious issues can somehow have a healthy relationship?"

"I think," I said, "that we can do anything in the world. As long as we do it together."

"That's pretty much what your dad said, actually."

"He did?"

"He did," she confirmed. "He told me that he hoped you'd come to your senses and to forgive you if you did. I told him that wouldn't happen. But here we are."

I let out a groan. "Oh god, he was right again! He's going to be insufferable, you know."

"Probably," Tessa agreed. "But I'm too happy to care. He can roll around the house chanting 'I was right' for the next week, and I'd be totally cool with it."

"Marcel could back him up, with pom-poms."

"Now there's a disturbing thought," Tessa said. "But I was thinking..."

"Yes?"

"They won't be back for hours. They had a lunch reservation after the appointment. Somewhere very expensive with some industry people. So..."

"So?" I felt my heart speed up and other parts of my body respond to what I really hoped she was implying.

"So, I think we should make up for lost time," Tessa said firmly, pressing one hand under my t-shirt and making me groan at the touch of her warm fingers on my bare skin. I would have sworn I had never been touched until that very second. My skin was hot, my jeans suddenly and uncomfortably tight.

"I think," I said quietly, "that's a very, very good idea. Maybe I can make up for my stupidity some more. I've got some ideas that you might like."

Bright blue eyes were fixed on me. "You always have ideas I'll like. You're always so focused on making me feel good."

"Would you believe me if I told you it was because you deserve it?"

"I think it might take a few more months with the psychologist for that," Tessa stripped off my t-shirt, pressing her lips to my bare skin like a prayer.

"Fine. What if I told you it was completely selfish?" I slid one hand over her bare thigh, so close to where I knew she was hot and wet for me. "Because making you feel good is my biggest turn on?"

Tessa's hand trailed lower, pressing over where I was so ready for her.

"Now that," she whispered. "I think I could believe."

"Well, that's a start."

23 Tessa

"So, is Marcel cooking?" I whispered as Dylan rang the doorbell. "If it's eels, I need to prepare my face."

Dylan squeezed my hand. "If it's eels, I'll come up with a mysterious illness, and we'll make a quick getaway."

"We can't do that!" I whispered back in mock horror. "The whole gang will be here!"

Before Dylan could reply, the door opened to reveal Marcel, who I was delighted to see was not wearing an apron.

"You rang the doorbell," Marcel frowned at us. "Why?"

"Well, to let you know we're here." Dylan looked like he was suppressing a laugh.

"But you are family," Marcel objected. "It is not required."

"I'll remember that," Dylan grinned. "How are you going? Cooking up a storm?"

"No. My skills were not required this evening. Alan insisted on getting everything in from the Thai restaurant."

"Well, that saves you a fair bit of work," I said, placing a kiss on Marcel's cheek. "And I bet you're busy."

"It has been busy since you left," Marcel admitted as we followed him down the hall. "I do not think that Alan has forgiven Dylan for—"

"There you are!" Alan was seated at the head of the table, a glass of wine already in his hand. "Dylan, I'll never forgive you for stealing the best housekeeper we've ever had."

"High praise," I said, leaning down to give Alan a kiss.

"Tessa should never have been your housekeeper. Not when she's such a talented writer," Dylan told him.

"She was perfectly capable of doing both!" Alan retorted. "And now I'm here, all alone—"

"With Marcel," Dylan interrupted. "And that nice couple who come and clean and do the ironing twice a week."

"It's not the same. I hope you two are blissfully happy together. After leaving me."

Dylan took my hand in his then, and I looked up at him, unable to keep the cheek-straining smile from my face. "We're very happy."

"Sickeningly, disgustingly happy."

"Well, that I can believe," Alan said. "Come on, sit down. The others must be about to arrive."

At that moment, the doorbell rang again, and Marcel hurried away.

"Thanks for inviting the whole crew," Dylan said to his father in a low voice. "I know you find babies a little challenging."

"I raised you well enough, didn't I?" Alan nudged his son. "And I want everyone to be included. This is a special night for all of us."

"Hey, babe!" Abby's voice reached me before her hug, and I let myself enjoy the slightly suffocating squeeze. "And you must be Mr Huxley." She politely offered Alan her hand. "I've heard so much about you."

"Alan, please," Alan scoffed at her formality, although I suspected he liked it. "You're very welcome here."

"Hi guys!" Tad called out, holding his son at arm's length. "I gotta change this guy before I hug any of you; he's smuggling chemical warfare in his nappy!"

"Thank you for sharing that, Tad," Alan said tartly, "before we eat."

"Sorry, Alan," Tad shrugged. "But the smell will hit you soon enough anyway."

"I'll help." Dylan stood up. "Sounds like a two-man job."

"Good man," Abby said, thumping him on the back. "A few hundred more good deeds like that, and I might just forgive you."

"Abby," I said warningly.

"Sorry," she rolled her eyes. "Protective big sister reflex. Of course I forgive him. He sorted his shit out, and he's making you so happy. But it doesn't hurt to keep him on his toes."

"What are we talking about?" Alice asked, joining us at the table and helping herself to a glass of wine.

"Keeping men on their toes, apparently," Alan snorted. "There's something to be said for it."

"Agreed," Alice said, raising her glass to chink against Alan's. "And I have to hand it to you, Alan. You raised a great man, there. Dylan's a proper godfather. He does nappies, overnight babysitting, the works."

"I'm very proud of my son. For many reasons."

I reached out and squeezed Alan's arm. "I guess I should thank you too for raising such a good guy."

The heart-warming moment was immediately broken by Marcel popping the cork on a bottle of champagne so violently that it hit the ceiling and landed in front of Abby, narrowly missing her nose.

"I apologise," Marcel looked mortified. "The gas was too strong."

"I thought we weren't doing any more toilet humour?" Tad came in, followed by Dylan who was holding Benji. "Okay, let me get this portable highchair set up, and we can eat. I can smell Thai! The little guy loves a Pad See Ew. My mother's horrified he doesn't prefer Pho. She reckons he's denying his sacred Vietnamese heritage."

I watched as Dylan held Benji in front of him, making faces for his adoring godson and not showing the slightest reaction as tiny fingers hooked into his nose or pulled his lip. Dylan *was* a good guy. And better still, he was my guy. I wasn't sure how I had gotten so lucky, but I was going to try to appreciate every second of it.

"Well, as we're all here," Alan said, picking up his cane and standing up with a grunt. "I wanted to say a few words before we eat."

There was a general cheering, and Tad even thumped his hands on the table, emulating a drum roll.

"That's quite enough of that," Alan said drily. "As I was saying, I wanted to say a few words. I had been approached about an autobiography before, but always turned the publishers down. It seemed maudlin, somehow, to tell the story of my life while I was still living it. But," he went on, "eventually, I was persuaded. And what a wonderful experience it was to tell my story and see it all there in black and white. The fact that I actually enjoyed the process is, of course, because of Tessa here."

I blushed as the cheers began again, and Dylan leaned over to kiss me on the cheek, his eyes full of warmth.

"I was almost disappointed when we finished the book because I knew that we'd be losing Tessa, and she's become such a valued part of our little family," Alan said, and I felt my heart melt. "Luckily, I had an ace up my sleeve in the form of my very handsome and charming son."

Dylan laughed loudly, putting his arm around me.

"I did tell them to stay away from each other," Alan went on. "And you can all see how well they listened to me."

There was a general murmur of laughter, and Marcel interrupted. "But that was not what you truly wanted, was it?"

"Perhaps not," Alan conceded. "Though my son did almost ruin everything."

A low hiss from Abby.

"But I'm pleased to say, my son managed to rectify his mistake, and now I have the joy of my boy and his lovely girlfriend living right here in Brekkie Beach. Where they both belong."

More cheers erupted, and Alan smiled with satisfaction.

"So, without any more of this sentimentality, I'd like to share with you the very first print proof of *Story of an Artist*."

The clapping and wolf whistles were so loud that Benji's lip quivered. "Hey, little dude!" Dylan rubbed his back. "Don't worry! Everyone's just happy." The small and chubby face began to smile once more. Crisis averted.

Alan nodded to Marcel, and I saw that Marcel had one of those old-fashioned silver serving platters with a cover, like something from a banquet in a Disney movie. And maybe it was a little over the top, but I felt excitement – not anxiety – bubbling in my chest just the same.

Marcel whipped the top off the serving platter to reveal the book. I let out a gasp. I hadn't seen the final cover until now, and suddenly I understood why.

"You used my photo!" Dylan sounded astonished, taking the book and staring at it.

"I merely submitted it," Alan told him. "It was the publisher who insisted on using that one instead of any of the others. If I had my way, they would have chosen something from the nineties, when I still had all my hair. But this one, they said, was the best. It captured my spirit, apparently."

The photo in question had been taken down at the Brekkie Beach jetty, where ferries travelled to and from the city. Alan was seated on the weather-worn bench, the cloudy sky's filtered light illuminating him against the water. His gold-topped cane was across his knees, and he wore a soft, thoughtful expression on his face.

"It's a beautiful photo," I said, taking the book from Dylan to look more closely. "I bet the guy who took it is very talented. And handsome."

"I hear he's got this super-hot girlfriend too. Who's an amazing writer. Total power couple."

"If you two could keep the foreplay to a minimum," Abby rolled her eyes. "It looks great. Great photo, great story, great words. Have I complimented everyone?"

Alan let out a chuckle. "I think you have," he said. "Now remind me, Abby, what is it that you do? Some sort of tidying, was it?"

"I'm a professional organiser. And you really need to hire me. Your kitchen cabinets are terrifying."

Marcel coughed. "I think, perhaps," he said gravely. "We do need you."

"Well, there you go," I said. "You lose one Finch, you gain another, huh?"

"I'm nowhere near as polite as Tessa. But I'm good value."

"I'm sure you are," Alan said. "Now, Marcel, can we get this food on the table? It would be a shame if I died of starvation before the book launch."

An hour later, I was pleasantly full of Pad Thai and Massaman Beef when Dylan nudged me, a question in his eyes. I felt a slight thrill of fear, but I nodded back just the same. I wasn't going to let my anxiety dictate my actions anymore.

"While we've got you all here, we have some more news," Dylan began, and the table went oddly silent. Even Benji paused in mashing noodles into his hair.

"Tessa's pregnant?" Alice guessed, and her hands flew over her mouth.

"Dylan proposed?" Abby looked at me.

"Tessa proposed and Dylan's pregnant?" Tad suggested with a grin.

"Well, now this will seem like a letdown. Seriously guys, we've only been together a couple of months," Dylan shook his head.

"Yeah, well, you're meant to be." Tad waved a hand. "There's no timeline."

"So, if it's not that, what is the news?" Abby pressed, looking at me keenly.

"Well," Dylan said and smiled at me. "I think Tessa should tell you herself."

"Um, the agent who was interested in my book, *Soccer Shocker* – the new one I wrote while I've been in Australia – well, she called me today. Apparently, two different publishers want it. So, it looks like I'm going to be published. As myself."

"Oh my god, I'm so proud of you!" Abby leapt up from her chair to hug me, pressing a loud kiss to the top of my head. "I knew you'd get published, you're too talented not to be!"

"Well, it nearly didn't happen," I admitted. "I was ready to give up forever after I got that first rejection. I wasn't sure I could face putting myself out there again. But luckily, I had you, and Michelle, and Dylan, of course, to encourage me to try again."

"And Jillian," Dylan added. "Don't forget Jillian."

"I'd never forget Jillian."

"Tessa, this is wonderful news, but who on earth is Jillian?" Alan looked perplexed.

"My psychologist," I said, surprised by how easy it was to say, even in front of so many people. "I've been seeing her to help manage my anxiety."

"Anxiety?" Alan frowned. "But you don't seem in the least bit anxious! Are you sure about this?"

"Dad, you're an expert on a lot of things," Dylan said. "But not on this one. I'm very proud of Tessa for getting help and not suffering in silence. Just because she's good at hiding it, doesn't mean she didn't deserve to feel better."

I looked at Dylan then and squeezed his hand. I wanted to kiss him madly and possibly climb into his lap. But, given the company, I settled for squeezing his hand again.

"Oh, I meant no disrespect," Alan said mildly. "You're a very bright girl, Tessa. If you think this Jillian is helpful, I'm sure you're right."

"Dad, are you actually admitting you might be wrong?"

"No," Alan said, dabbing delicately at his mouth with a napkin. "Just that Tessa may be right."

And at that, both father and son began to laugh. I caught Abby's eye across the table, and she winked at me.

• • • • • • • • • •

"That was a good dinner party." I flopped down onto the sofa.

"It was," Dylan agreed, flopping beside me. Putting his feet up on the box that was currently serving as a coffee table, he let out a yawn. "I am so full of Thai food I might be sick. Or Tad's right, and I am pregnant."

"And here was me about to proposition you," I teased, grazing one hand over his stomach, which still felt both flat and muscular.

Dylan let out a groan of dismay. "Can you hold that thought for maybe an hour? I need to digest, but I definitely want to be propositioned."

"Sure," I said, snuggling into him. "After all, I need to keep testing whether the Zoloft is causing any unpleasant side effects."

"So far, so good?" Dylan asked, eyebrows raised.

"Based on our current performance, what do you think?"

"You gave every impression that you were both keen and satisfied this morning."

"I was both," I said, smiling at him. "But I do worry, sometimes, that it could affect things between us. In the bedroom. And I'd hate that."

"It could happen," Dylan said, taking my hand and bringing it to his lips. "And if it does, we'll work through it. I won't get weird and take it personally. We're in this together, you and me."

"You mean with my anxiety?"

"I mean with life," Dylan said quietly. "I know it's cheesy because my dad said it. But when you find the right person, it doesn't mean that you never have problems ever again. It just means you can work through them together. Us versus whatever life throws at us."

"Your dad is extremely wise sometimes," I said, leaning my head on his shoulder. "You know, I think his whole plan from the beginning was to get us together. That's why he warned us not to. Kind of a reverse psychology thing."

"And we fell for it."

"Oh, I don't know about that," I said. "You're pretty cute. I think I would have fallen for you no matter what he had said."

"Charmer." Dylan leaned down to kiss me. I let myself sink into his kiss, my body pleasantly warm, and I felt like I could just melt right into him, like a chocolate bar left on the seat of a hot car. Except slightly less messy.

"Have you digested yet, then?" I murmured, my mouth moving over his neck.

Another groan. "Working on it," he said. "Remind me not to go to town on Massaman Beef again. The potatoes stick in my gut like concrete."

"Now there's a mental image that gets me going." I pulled over a box to put my own feet on, sighing contentedly.

"I think we need more furniture."

"I have to agree," I said. "This place is gorgeous, but I feel like we're on the wrong side of minimalism. Abby said we could borrow her van, if you wanted to check out that vintage furniture place you mentioned."

"Abby's great," Dylan said. "Even if she still feels the need to warn me that if I break your heart again, I'm a dead man."

"I guess that's big sisters for you," I said. "You're not planning to break my heart again any time soon, are you?"

"Never," Dylan said firmly, squeezing my hand. "I love you, remember? And not just a little bit. A ridiculous amount. I've got love coming out of my ears. Nostrils, too. And any other orifices you can think of."

I couldn't help giggling at that. "And I love you too," I said softly, tracing one finger over the line of his jaw. "You know what I was thinking?"

"What?"

"We should get a cat," I said. "I kind of miss Cyndi. She was great company when I was writing."

"I've only just become free of that wrinkly hell beast!"

"So that's a definite no?" I asked, combing my fingers through his hair. "That's okay."

"But you want one. So I'm willing to consider it. As long as it's less tempestuous. And has fur. No fur is a dealbreaker for me."

"I definitely was thinking of a more traditional kind of cat. Like a tabby or something."

"Fat, lazy, and hates Mondays? Like Garfield?"

"We're not naming the cat Garfield," I shook my head. "Too derivative."

"Oh, so we've got to be original, then?" Dylan looked amused. "I suppose Whiskers and Tiger are out too, then?"

"Definitely. I think we should give it a human name. Like Adrian."

"We are not," Dylan said, "naming this cat Adrian. The other cats would make fun of him."

"Samson?"

"He'll lose his powers if we ever have to shave him," Dylan pointed out. "Leonard."

"No, he'll write depressing songs, and I don't need that in my life."

"Fair point. Being named after a depressing songwriter myself, I suppose I can't inflict that on my feline son," Dylan mused. "Dexter?"

"He'll kill us in our sleep!"

"True. What about Wilson? If it's a good enough name for a volleyball with a face, it's a good enough name for a cat."

"Wilson," I chewed it over in my mouth. "I could do Wilson."

"Wilson it is then," Dylan nodded. "Look how good we are at problem-solving! We can go to the shelter tomorrow if you like."

"Seriously?" I blinked. "I wasn't sure you were totally on board. You can think about it, you know. Take time to make a decision."

"You convinced me," Dylan pressed a kiss to my forehead. "I'd do much more than adopt a cat to make you happy, Tessa."

"Then I'm pretty much the luckiest woman alive," I said softly, tangling my fingers in his dark hair.

"You know," he murmured. "I think I've finished digesting."

"Oh, I love it when you talk dirty to me!" I straddled him, laughing. "So, you wouldn't object to me doing this?" I angled my hips against him, earning a hiss of arousal in response.

"No objection whatsoever."

After that, no more words – about cats or anything else – were necessary.

Epilogue: Dylan

Two Years Later

"I CAN'T BELIEVE IT took you so long to do this, Dylan!" My father broke the silence with a thump of his cane. "Such beautiful work! You've been depriving the world."

"It's just one wall at one little exhibition. I'm still mostly doing portraits and events work."

"Your portraits are works of art," Tessa said loyally, coming up behind me with two glasses of champagne in her hands. "Here, have one of these before it all disappears."

"A good idea. Some attend these events simply for the free wine." Marcel bowed his head. "My younger self was one such delinquent."

"Well, it worked out pretty well for you, didn't it? Found your passion and all that."

"Yes," Marcel said, looking at my father with the kind of love it was legitimately heart-warming to see after so many years. "I did."

If my dad could convince someone to love him for a lifetime, then maybe I could too. After all, I was forty per cent less demanding and at least thirty per cent less arrogant. I hoped so, anyway.

"Plenty of people have been looking at your work tonight," Tessa told me. "And I've been eavesdropping. You're getting rave reviews."

"And I had nothing to do with it," Alan added. "You don't need my help to be a success, Dylan."

"Thanks," I said. "But I do need your support. All of you, actually. All the support I can get. I have a fragile artistic ego now."

"Fragile isn't exactly the word I'd use to describe you." Tessa ran a hand over my bicep.

"Now, now, children," Alan said warningly. "None of that. Not when sensitive homosexuals are forced to hear it."

I couldn't help snorting, bubbles of the champagne fizzing through my nose in a most unprofessional way.

"Sorry, Alan. But can you really blame me? I mean, he's very handsome."

My father made a scoffing sound as he leaned on his cane. "I think we'll have to call it a night," he declared. "My legs won't put up with too much more of this."

"We should have brought your chair," Marcel frowned in concern.

"No," Alan insisted. "I want to walk when I can. While I can."

"I really appreciate you making the effort, Dad."

"Of course I did! This is my son's big night, after all. Do you two want to share the taxi with us? It will be a bloodbath finding one when this thing's over."

"Actually," I said. "I think we'll get the ferry back. The city at night is picturesque as hell."

"It is indeed," Marcel agreed. "I will see your father safely home, Dylan. And I congratulate you on your success tonight."

"Thanks, Marcel," I said, touching his arm for a moment. Our relationship had never extended to hugs, but I hoped he knew how much I valued him just the same.

We watched them leave, and then Tessa turned to me. "I didn't like to say it in front of Alan, but a few people have been saying your work shows some of your dad's spirit. I don't know how that works, given that he's a painter and you're a photographer, but I think it's a compliment. I hope you don't mind."

"I don't." It was perfectly true. "It would have bothered me once, but now...I guess I do take it as a compliment."

"Good," Tessa said, leaning up to kiss me. "I'm very proud of you, you know."

"Well, I had to do something pretty cool to be worthy of my best-selling children's author girlfriend. It wouldn't do for me to be a failure."

"You could never be a failure," Tessa wrinkled her nose like the very idea was ridiculous. "And I'm hardly a best-selling author. It was just for a couple of weeks. And only because of that interview on that morning show."

"That totally counts! And isn't that a mark of your success too, that you were asked to be on that morning show?"

"The presenter told me her son liked my books. It was random, really."

"I'm not going to let you explain away your success," I insisted, serious now. "You're hard-working, incredibly talented, and you deserve every bit of your success. I hope you know that."

"I know you believe it," Tessa told me, one gentle hand on my face. "And that means that sometimes, I know it too. I'm still a work in progress, you know."

"Aren't we all?"

"Mm, very deep. I supposed you have to be, now you're a celebrated artist."

"One wall at one small exhibition."

"Well, you're an artist, and I'm celebrating you," Tessa told me firmly, those full lips curved into a smile, the tiny gap in her teeth just visible. "So, take the compliment."

"For you? Anything." And I meant it.

• • • ● ● • ● • • •

"I really should have brought a jacket!" Tessa shivered, wrapping her arms around herself. "The lights are beautiful, but I think I'm going to go inside. I am never going to get used to Australia being cold. It's not right, you know. All those tourism commercials are false advertising!"

The lights of the city surrounded us as the ferry chugged its way through the dark water, making me feel like we were in a kind of fairyland, outside of space and time.

"Not yet," I said quickly, digging my hand into my pocket. "Do you mind staying out here just a moment longer?"

"If you're enjoying it, I guess I can cope," Tessa sighed and pressed her body against mine. "But you have to keep me warm."

"I can do that," I said, wrapping one arm around her tightly. That didn't put me in an ideal position for what I had planned, but I could hardly expect Tessa to freeze just because of what I wanted to do. It paid to be flexible, I had learned.

"Mm, you are warm," she snuggled into me. "Probably because you're always at Muscle Land with Tad. Your metabolism must be like some sort of combustion engine, and your body just pushes it all out as heat."

"That sounds very scientific." Then I paused, my stomach writhing like one of the eels Marcel so enjoyed, and I swallowed hard.

"So, I wanted to talk to you about something. Something important." Tessa's eyes widened in alarm, and I rushed on. "Good important! At least, I think it's good. Good for us."

"What is it?" I could see that her brain was still more than capable of coming up with a list of horrible possibilities, despite all her hard work with Jillian. But now, Tessa didn't lose herself in those thoughts. Not anymore.

"It's..." I took a deep breath. "The thing is..." The words had gone from my mouth. The speech I had prepared? Totally evaporated. Words had always been Tessa's thing, not mine, after all. Instead, I just reached into my pocket and pulled out the box. "It's this." I flicked open the lid, and I felt Tessa freeze against me mid-breath.

"Holy fucking shit!"

"Not quite the response I was hoping for."

Tessa bit her lip and just stared at me silently.

"I'm asking you to marry me. Because I love you, and I can't imagine my life without you. Well, I can, but it's pretty terrible. Whereas when I think of spending my life with you, that sounds better than anything I could have ever dreamed up. So... I'm asking. If you will." If the ring box shook slightly in my hand, I blamed the crashing waves beneath us.

Tessa let out a breath and looked at me, those blue eyes glistening with tears in the soft yellow light of the ferry. "And I'm saying yes," she whispered. "And apologising for the swearing. I totally get why you did the same thing back when we..." She shook her head. "I'm saying yes!"

I let out a delighted – though oddly hoarse – bark of laughter. My throat had gone dry, and it was a hell of a good thing we were sitting down. My legs – even though Tad would never let me skip leg day – felt like they might have buckled beneath me.

"Thank god for that," I said. "I didn't realise how nervous I was until..."

"You seriously thought there was any possibility I might say no?"

"Well, I didn't exactly think you'd say no," I conceded. "It was more that I really, really hoped you'd say yes."

"I'm definitely saying yes," she said, looking up at me with the smile I knew so well and never got tired of seeing. "One hundred per cent yes."

"Good," I breathed out a sigh. "Now we just have to decide whether to tell your sisters or my dad and Marcel first. Or Tad!"

"Sounds like we're going to need another dinner party," Tessa suggested. "Tell them all at the same time."

"Good idea. We can show off just how fabulously domestic we are with the new kitchen. I'll be on my best Kipfler-peeling duty."

"I guess that's where it all started, huh?" Tessa's eyes crinkled. "With Kipflers and penis jokes."

"It did," I agreed. "And look where it led."

Tessa snuggled into me, chuckling. "Won't that be a story for the grandchildren?"

About the Author

Rita Harte is a romantic comedy author who likes to write books with big laughs and big feelings. She firmly believes that characters struggling with mental health, family drama, and painful pasts deserve a fabulous happily ever after.

Living in sometimes sunny Sydney, Rita is powered by caffeine, loud music, and the loving support of her family.

Printed in Great Britain
by Amazon